The towers of Canary Wharf loomed ahead.

Greg released more ballast and spun the second wheel to put the airship into another climb. He leaned forwards. Something like a spirit level blipped. The creaking and groaning of the hull communicated itself to the cabin via an open hatchway. They soared but fast enough? On and on went the towers, up and up, with no sign of the top, just storey after storey, each one closer than the last. A man in a suit at a window raised his pale eyes in time with their ascent even as he sank as if in a lift.

Finally, sky, clouds, filled the sloping windshield.

Greg levelled out and, hinged on them, the horizon came back up.

The pointy tower of One Canada Square passed to the side.

Below, the Isle of Dogs merged with Lewisham, which merged with Tower Hamlets, which merged with Southwark, which merged with the City. All had been subsumed into one vast stretch of pewter punctuated, in patches, by buildings.

Occasionally running a hand through his drying hair, Greg stood steaming in his clothes as he followed the course of the river.

The Shard came up on their right. With its windows, decks, empty again, it stuck up above them with its familiar unfinished quality in the upper reaches before sliding by.

He leaned out over the slanting side windows and checked behind them. Except for a giant bomb-shaped shadow at water level, no airship followed them.

His eyes lingered on the Veniced streets, the islanded landmarks. The river ran on both sides of the London Eye. It surrounded the Houses of Parliament.

He thought of all the dead still going through the motions of their lives, underwater, and—somewhere down there—the piece of office equipment at the heart of it all.

GAME CHANGERS
OF THE
APOCALYPSE

BY MARK KIRKBRIDE

In memory of
Dorothy Porteous
5th June 1914 to 2nd February 2016

PART 1

CHAPTER 1

ACTS OF GOD

Someone else's dreams. Greg couldn't remember them now but that was what they'd been like—someone else's dreams.

A laser-thin shaft of sunlight poked through the curtains. Aerial dust that would never have been visible otherwise churned within it.

"What do you mean, you can't get excited about our wedding?" said Polly.

She'd put him on the spot before he'd even had a chance to engage whatever apparatus normally enabled him to circumvent his own feelings on the subject. Now something like the immobilization of muscles that occurs in sleep pinned him to the bed. "It's just… It's like it's not happening to me."

However much he'd tried to keep on top of preparations, she'd been five steps ahead, making him feel as if he wasn't doing his share. Until finally he wasn't. He hadn't organized transport, got the rings or booked the honeymoon.

He stared at the sunbeam slanting across the bed.

"Greg?" She rolled onto her side to face him.

He turned his head. "Yes?"

"You're saying you don't want to get married?"

On any other day, they'd have been doing a groggy *pas de deux* about the flat by now. Yet he couldn't keep the genie bottled up any longer. "I do, and I don't."

"Greg, it's a simple enough question."

"No…?"

The mattress rocked and sea-rolled. Creaky springs squeaked.

Off the bed, she spun round. Her arm shot in his direction, swung sideways. "Then you're free to go."

He jerked upright.

For a second, he had a million motes in his eye. Sunlight scoured his senses. *What?*

He shuffled to the edge of the bed. "Come again?"

She stood a few feet away, shaking violently. He'd never seen her like this. "If this is how it's going to be, it's better to get it over with. I wouldn't want to use up any more of your time. You can leave, now."

Eh? " Er, can we talk about this?"

"What's there left to talk about?" She flung an arm out. "Everything's obliterated."

*But I don't—*He raised his hands. "Polly, listen, I'm really sorry. You caught me off..."

"I'll give you five minutes."

She grabbed some underwear from a drawer, a lemon dress from a hanger and streaked from the room. The swooshing-shut door collided with its frame, causing different-sized perfume bottles and make-up jars to rattle on the dressing table. The pictures they'd chosen together shook on the wall.

She didn't mean it. Did she? Technically it was her flat.

What's wrong with me? His heart twanged like a plucked double bass string. *Why do I have to say what I think?*

Head buzzing, he stepped into his pants and tugged on some socks. Pulling his arms through the sleeves of his cotton shirt, he buttoned it up. *She's upset.* He stepped into his thin suit trousers and threw on his unlined suit jacket. *She'll have calmed down in a minute.*

He gathered up his keys and wallet, stuffed his tie in his jacket pocket and veered out of the bedroom.

Lemon dress on, Polly put a foot on the edge of the sofa, showing off first one long, sleek, tapering leg then the other as she did up the tiny clasps to the sides of her wedge sandals amid the lounge's creams and browns and oranges.

Her lips remained pursed and her thirty-year-old profile as sharply delineated as minted coinage.

She looked up. "Keys."

"What?"

"Your keys."

He handed them over. "Polly, it doesn't have to be like this." *This is silly. Why can't we just talk normally?*

"You've humiliated me!"

He held a hand up. "Baby, don't take it so personally."

"Don't take it personally? Don't take it personally! How can I not take it fucking personally?"

"Polly..." He moved his hand towards her.

"Don't..." His fingers paused, mid-air. "You'd better get going. She'll be waiting."

His hand dropped like a wounded bird. "What? Who?"

A flash of hazel eyes. "Nicola."

"Oh, Polly, for the billionth time, that was five years ago, before I even knew you existed. I can't help it if we still work at the same place."

"I always wondered why you stayed there. Now I know." She pushed him towards the door.

He hadn't even had a shower. Picking up his shoes from the shoe rack, he tried to put one on. Her chivvying hand at his back had him hopping along and he had to abandon the attempt.

She opened the front door, gave him an extra shove. "You can collect the rest of your stuff at the weekend."

"Polly, this..." The light hurt the back of his eyes. The doormat prickled his soles. He whirled around. "I..."

She thrust a large plastic bag into his chest. "Here."

"I'm..." He managed to hold the bag but dropped his shoes.

"Don't worry about it. I wouldn't go out with you if you were the last man alive."

The door slammed. He recoiled as if he'd taken the full force of the impact.

He put the bag down and stepped into his shoes. Stooping to tie them, he peered at the bag. Pink with red lettering that read "H&M", it had flat sides, sharp corners and didn't close. Inside, he could make out their photograph album containing every snap printed by or for them and the bulging scrapbook in which he'd lovingly archived everything they'd ever done together.

He reached for the handles and stood up.
My life in a bag.

A plane shrieked overhead. Still adjusting to the sun's glare, Greg stumbled along the pavement. He had to concentrate on each and every step and stop to swallow down sobs. An elderly woman walking three lamb-like poodles stepped off the pavement and took the long route, round a post box. He'd only made it a few more yards when a choke engulfed him. *What am I going to do?* He had to lean against a lamppost. Two women chatting outside a mini-supermarket in colourful saris, like butterflies, looked round. Locked in position, he disguised his predicament with a cough.

Hacking manfully, he pushed off. His hand shook as he got his mobile out and called the number he wanted.

"Hi, Simon. Can you... Can you tell Milo I won't be in? Just say I'm ill or something and I'll be back on Monday. There's no way I can make it today. Polly's..." He swallowed. *Where am I going to go?* "Polly's chucked me out."

A man clutching a whisky bottle lurched towards him like an alchemist with the elixir. *This is how people end up on the street. All the struts kicked away.* Cars and buses thundered past, going the other way. The bag bump-bump-bumped his leg. Yet he couldn't stop. He'd got caught in the press of bodies heading for the tube station.

Breathing in heady diesel fumes, he passed a bus stop. A mum knee-deep in kids called out to one in danger of being swept away: "Jack, come out of the tall people."

Greg's phone went in his pocket. Struggling to get elbow room, he reached for it, got it out and up to his ear. "Hi, Simon."

"Greg, I'm really sorry." Choppy breathing, the flap of footsteps. "What happened?"

"She asked me to leave." A Polish man and woman overtook him, one either side. "I'll tell you all about it later."

"Okay. What are you going to do?"

A bald man knocked Greg's elbow. The phone nearly jumped out of his hand. He caught it and, hand shaking, put it back up to his ear. "I don't know. Stay at a Premier Inn or

Holiday Inn, I expect, till I find somewhere."

"No, Greg, stay at mine. If you don't mind sleeping on the sofa."

Gripping the phone tighter, "Are you sure?"

"Yeah, course. I'll be around this weekend but stay as long as you need."

"Thanks, Simon."

"Welcome. And don't wander the streets. The key's here if you want it..."

Come to work and face Milo? "I'm sure I can survive a day, but thanks."

"No problem. Take it easy."

"Will do. See you later."

He'd passed the turning for the tube station. The hordes now poured towards him. He had to dodge left and right to avoid getting bustled. *Too—many—people.*

His clammy shirt stuck to him inside his jacket. Tired of lugging the bag, he took refuge in an empty doorway and sat down. *Free fall. I'm in free fall.* He lifted the bag up onto his lap. *A bag man, that's what I am.*

He tipped the contents out next to him. A phone charger and his toothbrush landed on the step. A spare pair of socks tumbled out along with some boxer shorts. Something like a fish hook caught deep in his throat. *So caring.* The photograph album and scrap book slid out one after the other. He opened up the album and flicked through pictures of them striding like giants through a model village, with a couple of the model village's model village, followed by some of them on the Epping Ongar Railway, a former tube line with fields, to stop, dead, at Polly in red in Antigua. He instantly recalled the silent lightning out at sea, that night, as they kissed at the outdoor bar. *So clever.* Opening up the scrapbook at random, he saw pairs of tickets, or stubs of tickets, for films, plays, exhibitions, a couple of restaurant receipts, a card he'd given to Polly with a teddy bear holding a flower on the front, a Post-it note from her to him, a drawing he'd done of her on her birthday. The hook tore at his gullet. *So calculating.*

He stared out through the milling legs.

The sound of a flying saucer landing issued, briefly, from his mobile.

Extricating it from his pocket, he saw the name of the sender and his heart pounded like a bass drum. What had he done now? He opened up the SMS: "The menus just arrived. Feel like crying. Hope you're happy."

He froze. If he could escape notice, perhaps he could pretend this wasn't happening.

He fell backwards.

The door he'd been resting against had swung open. A face with a beard for a toupee, a shaved head for a chin, leered over him. "Yes?"

Greg clambered to his feet. "Sorry."

Having no further to fall left only one way to go—sideways.

Greg emerged from the greasy tube station and stepped out into wall-to-wall sunshine. A woman with a large mole on her left cheek, as black as a fly, glared at his girlie bag.

At a crossroads, red buses, black cabs, crossed and turned from east and west, north and south, alternately.

He turned too.

A roofed moped revved like a chainsaw, buzzed past.

Through darkened glass, he glimpsed faces at tables.

A cluster of bellboys stood in the doorway, becapped and all different heights, like a clump of mushrooms.

Five minutes later, he arrived at work and made it inside without getting noticed.

Creeping along a corridor, he heard footsteps coming the other way. *Please, not Milo...* His breathing quickened. He looked for a door to dive through. Surely the day couldn't get any worse. Could it?

He recognized the bobbing shaved head and wiry figure, always leaning forwards when in motion as if in a hurry to get to where he was going. *Phew.* Greg's breathing slowed to its normal rate. "Hi, Rob."

"Hi, mate. There was a message for you just now."

"There was?"

"Yeah, in the fax machine."

Polly? Greg turned around and, lengthening his stride, managed to keep up with Rob. "Do people still use those things?"

"Yeah, sometimes." Rob nipped ahead, and they bounded up the stairs in tandem. In the corridor at the top, he held the first door open. "It's still in there."

"Thanks." Greg walked over to the printer-cum-fax machine. Bending over it, the niff of hot electrics, plastic and toner filled his nostrils. The blood beat in his brain. The pressure behind his eyeballs intensified as if they themselves had expanded.

"Sweet nightmares," read the message, with no indication as to who or where it was from.

He stood up. *Ow!* He'd cracked his head. What idiot put the fax machine under a shelf?

Frantically rubbing his blazing crown, he retrieved the sheet of A4 and held it up. It was addressed to him but what did it mean? Who'd sent it? Why?

The pad of footsteps behind him.

He spun round.

Rob crossed the open-plan office to pick up a stapler and returned with it to his desk.

Sleek black monitors perched on beech desks under the strip-lit cork white sectional ceiling. Pippa stared at her screen with a finger to the corner of her mouth as if trying to locate a crumb. Rob crunched the teeth of the stapler down on a document. Katissia tapped at her keyboard with her head leaned to one side, murmuring.

Backing out into the corridor through the door opposite to the one he'd come through, between white plasterboard walls, over a light blue linoleum floor, under more fissured and dotted polystyrene ceiling tiles, Greg bumped into something solid yet yielding.

He staggered and turned. "Sorry, Simon, I didn't see you."

"That's alright." Simon's face had a pale, exposed look, like someone who normally wore glasses but who wasn't wearing them today. It went with his stoop, which, given his youth, was plainly more the product of a desire to deflect attention away from his height than to avoid lintels and light fittings.

"I was just going to come and look for you."

Simon's hand dipped towards his trouser pocket. "For the keys?"

"And a quick chat if that's alright?"

Simon nodded, adjusted his tie. "Of course."

"Thanks, Simon." Greg started to turn, paused, turned back. "Hey, you didn't fax me, did you?"

Simon blinked. "Fax you?"

Greg patted his arm. "Don't worry about it. Let's find somewhere to talk." They headed downstairs and passed doors, doors. The corridor veered left. Greg halted. *But— This isn't...* "Er, Simon."

"Yes?"

"Didn't we used to come through that way? I could have sworn there was a doorway there last week."

Simon stopped and turned, this way and that way. "Did we?" The combination of a youthful complexion and scorings under the eyes gave him the troubled countenance of an old child. "I got lost on the way to the Gents' the other day."

Greg nodded. The building, an industrial shell refitted for modern office space, underwent alteration nearly every day. Prefab rooms split and halved or merged and doubled. Corridors opened up and closed.

They took the long route round to the tea room. Two sofas, one with purple upholstery, the other with red, each with corresponding cushions, faced banks of drink dispensers and snack machines.

Greg placed the bag on one of the sofas and walked over to the hot drinks machine. He pressed the button for tea, white with sugar, stared at, sniffed and finally tasted what he got— coffee, black, without.

"Stupid damn thing." He left the hot full plastic cup on the window sill.

Simon stood in the centre of the room. "What happened?"

Greg paced up and down. "I told her I wasn't bothered, about the wedding."

"Oh." Simon, who would have been the best man, followed Greg with tiny turns of the head and tracking eyes. "You mean you don't... You don't love her anymore?"

Greg stopped pacing and shifted from foot to foot. "Of course I do."

"Er... uh?"

"I was just being honest with her." He shook his head, sighed. "But apparently honesty's not a very good policy."

Simon breathed in deeply, out slowly. His eyes searched the health and safety posters, the certificates and notices on the wall.

Greg's head tipped back. He righted it. "Listen, I didn't mean I didn't want to be with her, just that if it was down to me, I wouldn't bother. With the wedding, I mean." He raised his arms above his head. Fingers interlocking, he clasped the back of his head. "It's all just plans, plans, plans. It's become this careering juggernaut." His hands came apart and one of his arms shot off to the side. "It's like she's forgotten what it's *for.*" His arm came to rest as if stuck. "I mean, a marriage is more than just a wedding." He lowered his arm. "I didn't want things to change. I was already happy."

Simon's eyebrows tilted. One twitched. "But you proposed."

"To try and make *her* happy." Greg pressed the fingertips of one hand to his forehead. "And believe me, I know, I know, if I hadn't, we'd still be together."

Simon bowed his head. *Is he praying?*

For spiritual guidance? Deliverance?

Simon looked up. "Well, maybe for her symbols are more important than they are for you. And perhaps you're overthinking it."

Greg exhaled, looked out of the window. "I usually do." He turned back to Simon. "But it's like it's all focused on that one point." He squashed his thumb and forefinger together. "And it's like trying to fit through the eye of a needle or something."

Simon smiled, and his head tilted. "Yet maybe when you do everything will be fine on the other side." His head leaned the other way. His smile waned. "Though perhaps she is putting a lot of pressure on."

"Yes." At last, someone actually understood.

"So maybe you both just need to relax. You need to think

less and communicate more, and she needs to give you some time to catch up with events."

Greg held his hands up. *"Yes!"*

He'd been living with Polly for over four years. Simon had only had one short-term relationship in that time, with a woman from Canada doing a PhD at UCL. How did he do it? How, when, had he become an expert in affairs of the heart?

Chin canted, Simon stared at him from a slight angle. "You did tell her it's just the wedding you're worried about, that you do love her? You told her that?"

"Oh, absolutely." Greg jerked his head up and down. His head slowed. "Well, I think I did." He hung it. "Oh. Maybe I didn't."

"Greg…"

"I'm not sure I had time. You know how it is. Well, maybe you don't. One minute we were talking and the next I was out on the street, carrying that bloody bag." He jabbed a finger in its direction. "I love her, devoutly. It just either comes out wrong or not at all." He pressed his palms to his forehead. "I seem to have a catastrophic tendency to say the wrong thing."

"You need to let her know you love her before she starts telling everyone the wedding's off and it becomes set in stone."

Another space-age sound from Greg's mobile.

He read the text. *Shit. Too late.* "Steph says the worst kind of waste of space is the one who pretends to be a nice guy. I mean what was the point proposing?!!" His heart felt bruised, on the inside. He started tapping a response when another one came through. "Why would I want to be with someone who doesn't love me enough to want to marry me?" Ah, the double backwards guilt thrust. *How does she* do *that?* It continued, "Just wish you could have told me before we sent out the fucking invitations."

Rob stuck his head round the door. "Simon, Milo's looking for you. Sounds urgent."

Greg darted towards the door. "I'd better get going." He bounded back. Snatching up the bag, he glanced at Rob. "You haven't seen me."

"Er, I can hear you, but I can't see you."

"I'm not here."

"Who said that?"

"Oh, keys." Simon detached his front door key from his *Doctor Who* sonic screwdriver fob and handed it over.

"Thanks, Simon. See you both."

"Bye, Greg."

Rob faced the wrong way, waving. "Bye, strange phantom."

Greg made it out of the main door without encountering Milo.

Thank God for that.

Countless bodies lay on every patch of grass like pink sea lions beached. Having seen a little too much from his elevated view over walls and into gardens and across greens and parks, Greg stepped off the bus.

Although it was a relief to escape the hot, stale trapped air of its interior, the naked sun turned its attentions on him and slowly, very slowly, baked his face. Thankfully the end of Simon's road was a few yards from the bus stop.

A warm gust of wind buffeted him as he loped up the short path to the front door of Simon's narrow maisonette. Each concertinaed house had an angled projection at the front. This particular rush of air had probably sheared off next door's façade.

Greg set the bag down, opened the door and went straight through to the kitchen-cubicle. He placed the key and his phone on the granite countertop and headed back out to fetch the bag.

Blood filled his head as he bent to pick it up. Another flurry ruffled his hair.

Slam.

He turned around. The front door faced him, shut. He reached in his pocket for the key. *No, no, no, no...* It was inside, with his phone. He pushed at the door. *No...* It wouldn't budge.

He glanced at the dead weight hanging from his other hand. *Jesus. Talk about a bag for life.*

Sweat ran down him in rivulets as, hefting the bag, Greg ignored the crunk and shriek of a siren, grabbed the cylindrical handle attached to the main door and entered work.

He trudged up one flight of stairs to his floor, then up the next flight to Simon's floor. *What the—* The layout was different on this floor and had changed since he'd last been up here. He couldn't see Simon's office. It had moved. No—the whole corridor had moved. Strip lights rendered the panelled tunnel uniformly bright. He tiptoed past a door that said "Milo Siley— Head Actuary."

Turning at the end, the corridor now passed behind Simon's office rather than in front of it. Where was the door? Where was Simon?

Swinging round the corner, he found the door that side.

"Simon Darnley—Actuary," read the nameplate.

He knocked.

"Come in." (Simon's voice, small and distant, as if from inside a biscuit tin.)

Greg opened the door, shut it behind him and leaned back against it.

Simon looked up from his computer. "Greg." He started as if he'd just taken a bullet. "What happened?"

"It's…" Given the thinness of the walls and the closeness of Milo's office, Greg kept his voice low. "I don't know how to tell you this."

"What?"

He held up the bag, fitting punishment now, only not nearly large or heavy enough. "I was just picking this up outside your place when the front door slammed shut." He tried to lick the dryness away from his lips, difficult with a saliva-less mouth and took another breath. "I've locked your key in. I couldn't even call you because my phone's in there too."

Simon raised a palm. "Greg, don't worry about it. It's happened to me too. Part of the reason my brother has a spare."

"He does?" *Phew.* "Where's he?"

"Stratford."

Oh. "Upon-Avon?"

"No, East London. Want to come, this evening?"

Confession delivered, other impulses surged inside him. "I should go and talk to Polly. She could be texting me." Reading between the lines it looked as if, unable to face the bank today, she'd thrown a sickie too.

"Good idea."

"Yeah, I think I've caused enough trouble for one day."

Simon smiled. "No, you haven't. Hope it goes well."

"Thanks." Greg edged towards the door. "And sorry again."

"Just get her back."

Greg grinned and stepped out into the corridor. Good old Simon.

The breezy air-conditioning had returned his body to a more familiar climate, yet after rushing all around town, carrying the bag, his throat felt as dry as a box of Weetabix.

He stopped at the water dispenser, filled a cup and, tipping it back, tracked the shock of cold on its way down.

He had to wait for what felt like a sharp icicle to melt before filling and starting on his second cup.

A strip light this end of the corridor hummed like a headache.

Plastic crackled next to him and he looked round to see his ex, in a trouser suit and heels, half-kneeling to fill a flimsy cup.

"Hi, Nicks."

She gave a little wave as she stood up and took a sip.

"How's the baby?" he said.

She swallowed. "Oh, on Facebook now."

"She is? Blimey. They start early now, don't they?"

Nicola hiccupped a laugh. "No, I mean the pics."

"Yeah, I saw. She's the spit of her daddy. Got his ears."

A swerve of dark, pencilled in, eyebrows.

"How's the lapdog?" he got in quickly.

"Oh, he's into squeaky toys now, when he's not humping your leg."

"Gar, that Milo, eh? I did warn you."

Her eyes executed an upwards parabola.

"How is your other quarter?" he said.

"You can ask him yourself."

Her line of sight twitched to a point just to the left of his shoulder and he spun round.

Milo stood at the head of the stairs. Set-back eyes stared at them. A generously proportioned pair of ears stuck out from his wheatsheaf haircut.

Tss, went the flickering tube of light above their heads, adding to the sense of irreality.

"Greg." A functional smile. "Glad to see you've recovered from your gastroenteritis. And so quickly too."

"It must have been something I ate."

"See you later, handsome," said Nicola.

"Bye, love of my loins," said Milo.

A wave of nausea passed between Greg and his stomach.

Milo turned to him. "We saved the P7 mortality tables for you."

"Oh?"

Knowing that that amount of desk-work would give him deep-vein thrombosis, in his head, Greg groaned sub-vocally.

They shuffled round each other, and he glanced back at Milo filling a cup at the water cooler as he headed down the stairs.

Although he tried to ignore the nameplate on his door, the engraved lettering caught the light as he opened it. It was in any case seared into his soul: "Gregory Veyor—Trainee Actuary."

Eternal Trainee. He caught himself grinding his teeth as Polly claimed he did at night. *Polly...*

His chair squeaked, bouncing a little, as he sat on it. He turned on his PC. *Polly...*

Once his machine had booted up, he searched for and found the Excel spreadsheet he needed. *I should be going to see her.* Opening up his email, he ignored the fifty-seven unread messages. *Bloody Milo.* He fired off one of his own:

Hi Simon,
Just ran into Milo, so still here. What a tosser! Sometimes I'd love just to say to him,
"Why do you have to be such an @rsehole?
Up Yours,"
Greg

He Alt-tabbed back to the spreadsheet and scrolled down so fast that it was as if the rows and columns stayed still while the percentages fluctuated within them. I did just send that to Simon?

He clicked on Sent Items to check that he hadn't copied anyone else in, and his bowels plummeted. He hadn't sent the email to Simon at all. He'd sent it to Milo.

Shit shit shit. He shot out into the corridor. His legs pistoned up the stairs.

Ahead, he made out a retreating back and a pair of radar-like ears sticking out of a blond shock of hair: Milo, getting farther and farther away; closer and closer to his office.

The light fizzled and blinked.

"Milo, just one thing..."

Milo stopped, turned. "Yes?"

"Er..." Greg cleared his throat, coughed. "I think Rob's looking for you, downstairs."

"Well, tell him to call me in my office, or come up himself." Milo continued on his way and reached out for his door handle.

He paused, turned back. "That reminds me... Polly called."

All the stronger for being from far away, Greg experienced an elastic-like tug deep within him. "She did?"

"Yes. You know, it really would be a good idea if you could keep these spats to yourself, but she asked if you could let her know the number of the DJ. She's managed to cancel everything but him." A stifled guffaw. "I hope you took out insurance." The light sizzled and flashed. "Anyway, you'd better start work. It'll probably mean staying horrendously late but then you owe several hours in any case."

Resurgent, the fluorescent tube buzzed between them like a lightsaber.

Greg went hot. "Do it yourself."

Milo's smile shrivelled. "What?"

"You do something for a change—instead of taking the credit for other people's work."

Milo swayed. "I have to say, Greg, I don't appreciate your tone. Not one bit." He leaned against the wall. "First you feign illness, now you're apparently refusing to do your job."

Greg flung an arm. "Oh, fuck off, Milo." His arm flailed back and up before slapping his side.

Milo sprang upright. "Oh, right, I see. Okay, Greg, well, if that's your attitude, there's nothing more to discuss. You can collect any belongings you have about the place and clear out. Your P45 will be in the post. Oh, and don't expect a reference!"

Greg turned towards the stairs and didn't look back. With his eyes on his feet, he cantered down them.

"You're on a real fuck-up roll today," Milo called after him.

"Check your email," Greg shouted back.

Whatever was in his desk and locker could rot. He pushed on outside. After the air-conditioning, it was like opening the oven door to hell. A blast of Gas Mark 5 or 6 engulfed him, and he didn't even pause to catch his breath.

Greg crested a knoll and bruised clouds rose to greet him. He hurried on as the very air around him darkened.

His bus had broken down on Updown Road, so he'd taken a short cut. *At least tomorrow can't be any worse...*

The fresh breeze in his face meant that he had to keep his head down, most of the time, with his eyes on his shiny shoes as they alternately skimmed over and crushed the velvety grass. Yet whenever he glanced up at the sculpted landscape—bright green here, dark green there—the cathedrals of clouds above it had got bigger, nearer.

Unexpectedly, the grass and trees lit up as the sun came out. The clouds, by contrast, turned black, before smothering the sun again.

He passed a wrinkled pond.

The branches of a copse swung.

Sea gulls? He could hear the forlorn cries of sea gulls—a bad sign this far inland, on the edge of London.

He turned up the collar of his jacket, tightened his grip on the bag. He needed to get home, to Polly.

A flap of lightening concentrated up and off to the left caused his head to jerk that way. The heavens boomed. A curtain of mist swung shut between him and the horizon.

The wind tried to push him back. He had to lean into it just to keep moving.

As he skirted a sea-choppy lake, something bounced on the

grass in front of him. A golf ball? It wasn't big enough, and now he couldn't find it. But another one landed. And another and another and another. The grass came alive with them, bouncing. It quickly turned white as far as he could see.

Hard chips of ice struck his forehead, stung him through his clothes.

He crossed a patch of longer grass. The ripping wind literally took his breath away. And the hailstones wouldn't let up. He might as well have been strapped to the wing of an Airbus A380-800 coming in to land.

Blinking, blinking, each time he raised his eyes he saw lightning flickering away like a faulty neon sign in the distance.

Then the crack of doom that accompanied a zigzag of light to his right made him jump as a nearby tree exploded. Sparks flew, as in a foundry, and he heard rustling, a creak and a crash.

Christ. Did his shoes have rubber soles? Was he going to have to lie down? In melting hailstones? In his work suit?

His clothes clung to him already.

He looked around for shelter. No huts. Nothing. It wasn't even safe under a tree.

He lifted a...

CHAPTER 2

GHOST TOWN

Greg hiccupped.

The cold soaked his body, while a sunburn-like heat penetrated deep beneath his back and down his left arm and leg. He needed a drink of water and his jaw ached from where he must have clenched his teeth. His gums pulsed.

He lifted his head and, woozily, looked around.

He lay on his back in claggy sand. Apart from a few wisps of cloud lingering like cannon smoke after battle, half the sky had cleared. It glowed with a luminous lambency, greeny-yellow rather than blue.

His ears rang.

Birdsong reached him like indecipherable code from another Earth.

He rubbed his eyes and colours kaleidoscoped before dispersing. Spots and splodges floated past, reachably close.

The birdsong became squeaky casters incessantly swivelling as white light streamed through the trees.

The sun wasn't going down. It was coming up.

Have I been out here… He sat up. It took him a while. *Have I been out here all night?*

His left forearm flopped around like a fish. *Jesus.* His heart beat to a rhythm he didn't recognize, out of time with his body. He had hot, fizzy pins and needles in his left hand.

Getting up, the soles of his shoes flapped. His right foot smarted as if he'd walked over fire, while his left had gone all spongy. Each time he shuffled forwards, that side tried to descend an invisible flight of stairs.

He turned around in the shifting sand and a deep imprint of his body yawned in it. Feeling his back, sand caked it.

He sat on the lip of the bunker, lifted his legs up, rolled over onto his hands and knees, and pushed himself up off the ground.

The bag lay several feet away. He picked it up.

His foot kept rolling onto its side. Not quite sure where his leg ended without looking, he shambled across the golf course towards Polly's.

She wasn't answering the door, so he clambered in through the back window using an upturned earthenware pot to stand on.

Hoping his backside wasn't mistaken for a burglar's, he crawled over the sink, with its edges digging into his knees, his back smarting as he stretched this way and that, and the bag sliding at, and bumping, his side. His left arm had stopped thrashing about, but his hand trembled as if he had the DTs.

Climbing down, he dumped the bag on the kitchen table.

"Polly..." He dashed through to the bedroom, only to find the covers thrown back on the bed.

He re-crossed the lounge to the kitchen. "Polly?"

No sign of her there either. *But it's Saturday... Isn't it? She should be here.*

Panting more than the effort warranted, he ran through to the hallway and out into the front garden. "Polly!" *No, no, no... Where is she?*

The Vauxhall was still there, with its familiar Portmeirion sticker in the back window.

He sprinted back inside to use the landline. Dead.

He hurried back through to the bathroom and had his first pee of the day. *Come on, come on...*

When he'd finished, he took his shirt off, turned around and checked his back in the mirror.

Bloody hell. The red fern of a tattoo festooned his skin.

He charged through to the bedroom, threw on a clean shirt and changed into a pair of jeans and trainers.

Grabbing the car keys from the dish on the dressing table, he ran out of the bedroom and kept going.

He pulled the front door shut behind him and jumped in the Vauxhall.

A squirrel ran across the entrance to the driveway as he started up the engine.

Another scurried up a tree as he eased out, between a parked yellow Polo and black Honda, into the road.

His head banged.

The tires gripped and unpeeled themselves from Tarmac as he took the corner. He checked the pavements this side, that side, and slowed to glance up turnings. Where is she?

He accelerated towards a crossroads. Traffic lights changed to red.

He hit the brakes, hung forwards in the diagonal strap and slammed back in his seat as the car jolt-halted over the line.

Breathing hard, he waited.

No cars passed, from either side.

He checked his rear-view mirror. No cars came up behind him.

None approached from the opposite side.

What's going on? Had he even seen any other traffic?

A tic started up in upper left eyelid.

The lights changed, and he set off again. He passed a succession of stationary, empty vehicles. Not only could he not see any moving cars, lorries, motorbikes, buses, he couldn't see any people. No neighbours standing chatting. No-one walking their dog. No-one out jogging. No-one heading for the shops or the gym. No-one on their way into town. Just empty streets. Endless empty streets and deserted pavements.

What time is it? His watch had stopped. But the sun was up. Where was everybody? Indoors?

Flats and houses gave way to shops, all equally dark or with metal shutters down.

He could feel the clapper of his heart, sounding the muffled tocsin. *This isn't right. This isn't right at all...*

Stationary buses crammed the bus depot, all with familiar letter-number pairings on the front that he always thought sounded more like food additives or possibly pencils.

Apart from odd glimpses of interiors, racks and racks of shoes, a corral of desks, vacant aisles, the whole street could have been a propped-up film set with nothing behind, now disused.

He shook his head, sniffed. Braking and wrenching the wheel to the side, he parked on a zebra crossing outside the tube station.

Leaping out of the car, he sprinted inside, across the concourse, past the untenanted ticket offices, and vaulted over the barriers. Clattering against a window at the back, he stared down at desolate platforms.

He pressed his fingertips to the glass.

Stretching away, crissing, crossing, as they curved this way and that, multiple sets of rails gleamed where the sun caught them—miles and miles of silent track.

This isn't— I don't— His thoughts flew like birds over water, unable to land.

He ran back up to the light and round and down to the junction. From the middle of the road, he scanned the three-storey red-brick buildings. How genteel, how Edwardian, they looked, from the second storey up. He'd never really noticed before.

He gazed up and down the high street. A pair of pigeons waddled across the normally busy junction. Their iridescent necks glistened as their heads bobbed. Otherwise, nothing moved.

What had happened while he'd been unconscious? *What have I missed?*

On his way back to the car, he passed a TV and electronics showroom and all the TVs in the window showed the same black-clad figure veering towards the camera with awful, intense, tormented eyes.

The figure turned as he turned. *Christ, I'm losing it.*

He got back in the car and, crunching the gears, roared off. *What if everyone's hiding?*

"What from?"

He slapped the steering wheel. "Great, now I'm talking to myself."

A motorbike on its side had him craning.

He was getting better at noticing things, like the shut-down bus mid-way between stops. Cars had parked badly. A lot still had their lights on. Something had gone wrong. Something had gone very wrong. And Polly was caught up in it.

The accelerator pedal creaked beneath his foot. The city blurred past.

Simon would fill him in. *Yes.* He needed to get his mobile in any case. As soon as he got his hands on it, there'd be a message from Polly telling him she was okay.

He swung up a side street.

Bouncing now, he hit his head. The underneath of the car scraped. The shock absorbers squeaked like bedsprings. "Blo-ody speed-bu-mps."

Braking hard outside a row of maisonettes, he released the lever to his right before the vehicle had even come to rest. Momentum flung the door open. He ran up the stubby red-tiled pathway and pitched forward onto his knees.

"Simon," he shouted through the letterbox.

He couldn't see anything through the swirly glass.

So he got up, lurched back out onto the pavement and peered up and down the street.

A yellow skip with orange lights dangling from it sat outside a house done up like a translucent cube. Scaffolding just higher than the ridge of the roof surrounded the building and plastic sheeting covered that.

A plank jutted out of the skip.

He ran over and pulled on it.

It was longer than he needed—much longer. The end knocked against the Tarmac as it came free, with a shudder that continued up his arms. He turned the plank side on, shuffled it along until he found its centre of gravity, lifted it under his arm, held it in place with one hand and stretched the other out to stop it seesawing.

He paused to check that he couldn't hear anyone out and about one last time before charging back round to the front door of Simon's maisonette and, jousting-style, running the plank through the glass—which shattered instantly.

He let the plank clatter to the side, reached in and unlocked the door. *He'll understand.*

Shards of glass in the carpet snapped underfoot.

"Simon..." he called, quieter now.

No answer. And no sign of Simon in the pine-floored lounge or the granite-topped kitchen. Greg picked up his phone and checked it. No messages. *Damn.* Then again, no reception either.

He raced back out into the hallway and round onto the narrow staircase with its wooden banister that, stage-set flimsy, bent slightly each time he hauled himself up. He checked the bathroom and the boxy spare bedroom that housed Simon's train set before hiking on up to the main bedroom, where his eyes travelled from the glass of water at the side of the unmade bed to the copy of *Model Monthly* ("Vintage Trains" issue) on the floor.

Simon had gone as well.

Perhaps they'd been evacuated. A twisting and tightening in his stomach. *Where?* He shook to a series of detonations in his heart. *Why?*

Greg stepped over to the window and stared down at the yellow skip with its blinking orange lights. The jumble of white appliances and sofas and mattresses it held saved him from having to confront the empty properties on this side, the empty properties on that side, the deathly stillness in between.

How many streets like this?

He took off, out of the room, down the stairs, along the landing, down the stairs, out of the house and into the car. He set off again, slower this time because of the speed-bumps but increasing the pressure on the creaky accelerator pedal as soon as he turned onto the main road.

He negotiated cars, vans, lorries and coaches, some at odd angles, many still with their doors open, as if some spectacle in the heavens had caused the occupants to jump out. He braked each time, as much to have a look as manoeuvre round but didn't see anyone. Even the vehicles with doors open still had keys in the ignition.

He flew over crossroads colour-blind to traffic lights, turned at junctions without looking the other way.

Going the wrong way round the roundabout flung him to the side. Accelerating up a ramp pressed him back into his seat. He joined the dual carriageway, heading into town. He clasped the steering wheel so tightly that he could see the whites of his knuckles. The speedometer's needle edged higher and higher—only dropping when he had to slalom around fishtailed cars.

In a desperate attempt to relieve the pressure building up inside him, he let out a laugh.

The back of his head knocked against the head rest and he knocked it again, again, again. *Keep—it—together! Keep—it—together!*

Once off the dual carriageway, he had to weave in and out of more static traffic. A bus and a lorry had wedged together. He turned the wrong way up a one-way street and re-joined the main thoroughfare a little later on.

He drove and drove and didn't see a single moving vehicle, not one pedestrian.

He shot past the entrance to work. The car park was empty. But then it would be on a Saturday.

He chewed his lip, clung to the steering wheel, stayed facing front, kept going. He'd see someone soon and they'd tell him what had happened.

The roads broadened, Marble Arch swept by and he found himself on Oxford Street, between the dirty white cliffs of facing buildings.

He'd never seen London's most famous mile and a half like this, without traffic, without the crowds. Even waiting for a night bus there had always been others. The road looked wider, longer. Signs hollered and whispered and shouted: "Marks & Spencer", "Selfridge & Co", "Bond Street Station", "Debenhams", "John Lewis."

Wrenching the wheel to the right at Oxford Circus, he straightened his outside leg, extended that foot. A succession of boutiques merged into one. Above that, 60 or more feet of Portland stone. It was like driving through the bottom of a man-made ravine. Half the street was in deep shadow, half in bright sunlight, as if the city had been hewn out of rock that had then been intricately carved.

He gripped the steering wheel round the curve. Piccadilly Circus swung into view. High up, the giant split screen slipped by like a pile of giant widescreen TVs tuned to different channels, all showing adverts. He swerved past the fountain— moving target practice for the winged god atop.

Up Coventry Street, between the Horses of Helios fountain on one side and the old Trocadero on the other. Either way ahead of or way behind everyone else in the rally circuit he'd turned Central London into, the engine roared as he changed down a gear for extra control now that the road had narrowed. Abandoned restaurants and shuttered ticket offices, fast food joints, souvenir shops and bureaux de change slid past.

Fussy street furniture necessitated a slight detour, then out onto Leicester Square—normally busy at any time of day, now devoid of people and surrounded by deserted cinemas, bars-cum-restaurants-cum-clubs, fast food outlets, gift shops, ticket booths and casinos.

His upper left eyelid kept lifting infinitesimally as if someone were tugging on it via a thread.

Right onto Charing Cross Road, past locked theatres, betting shops, pubs, banks, restaurants, radio stations, down to St Martin-in-the-Fields, where the fissure of the street gave way to—opened out into—a canyon.

He drove round the base of it, stopped, turned off the engine and got out.

The domelike blue sky, hazy here, chalky there, with feathery wisps overlapping at different levels, domed the city. Gazing up at the sun a moment too long left a black hole at the centre of his vision. Glints and blobs of gold floated from one side to the other. A sickness at the pit of his stomach spread until it engulfed his entire being.

He moved; everything else stayed still.

No engines revved. No brakes squealed. No horns blasted. No sirens wailed. He hadn't heard a single aircraft. Instead, the self-consciousness of silence.

The soles of his shoes tap-tap-tapped across the giant slabs that made up the square—now emerging from the darkness that obscured whatever he tried to focus on—and his breathing snagged on his mind and threatened to unravel. *Where are they?*

He strode past the four giant black lions, between the swimming-pool-blue basins, with their fountains, dolphins, mermaids and mermen, towards the steps to the terrace.

The back of his neck prickled.

He stopped and swung round but couldn't see anyone, apart from Nelson, aperch his column, so continued walking.

Out of the corner of his eye, he noticed something move high on the side of a building. A porcupine-spiky CCTV camera turned slowly in time with him.

Just to be sure, he walked backwards.

Sure enough, it followed him.

He stopped.

It stopped.

His eyelid twitched uncontrollably.

Was someone watching him in a control room somewhere? Several years ago, a guy at a dinner party had told him the site of what was or had been the CCTV control room for Central London—about the only interesting part of the conversation. Where had he said? Was it...?

Deep under the old Trocadero, that was it.

Greg shook his head. No, he was being paranoid. This was an electronic eye set to track suspicious movement. *No-one's down there—everyone's gone.*

He ran up the granite steps to the platform, doubled back on himself and came to rest against the parapet. The black stanchion of a lamp stuck up to either side as he stared at the paddling pools and fountains and lions and lonely Nelson on his plinth and the flags over Whitehall. Greg breathed in slowly. Cold, static, lifeless, only statues peopled London now. The flesh-and-blood hands that fashioned them, the hands of the sculptors' descendants, had gone. Heavy silence stretched out in every direction, endlessly. *What the hell's going on?* A sob-choke.

He staggered and gasped as if all the air had been sucked out of him. Concentrating on breathing, having to concentrate on it, he patted the parapet. Each inhalation came raggedly, loudly. Because would he ever feel the softness of Polly's cheek against his again? Or inhale the scent of her hair? Drown in her hazel eyes?

He filled his lungs to bursting.

"Polly," he shouted.

The silence rolled back, up every radial street, before smothering him again.

"Polly," he screamed.

The tail end of that cry bounced off walls different distances away like a snicker.

He dropped to his knees and a river ran through him, overflowed. "Polly…" He tasted, sputtered, tears.

CHAPTER 3

THE WRITING ON THE WALL

On the way back, Greg had an ache in his side like a rib missing. His eyes stung. He made it home in under ten minutes, flat out all the way apart from the odd chicane around stationary vehicles.

Instead of stopping, he kept on going. *That's where she is!* She could have left before the trains had stopped running. Her mum and dad could have collected her at the other end. She could—would—be at her parents'. *She's alive. She's got to be…*

Why her, though?

He put the question of why the odds should be stacked in his favour, and what it might mean if they were, aside.

Back on the dual carriageway, heading the other way, he tore up the outside lane at 80mph. His wing mirrors shone, the steering wheel vibrated and the engine thrummed.

Merging with the motorway, he moved over to the middle lane nudging 100mph. He'd get there in no time at this rate.

No sooner had he got out of London than, as well as vehicles abandoned at the side of the road or parked in their lanes, he came across a Hyundai scrunched up against a tree, a burnt-out Saab, an off-the-road SUV and an overturned BMW, radial tires skywards. A lorry had ploughed up an embankment and rolled back down. He braked each time. He couldn't risk any debris damage. A burst tire was the last thing he needed right now.

In between, apart from engine whine it could just as easily have been the road moving towards him, past him.

Black heathland with stubby woods undulated around him before falling away.

Reality shimmered in the heat as something gyred in the watercolour-blue sky. What was it? A murmuration of starlings?

It floated down, down, drifted across the motorway right in front of him. *It's going to hit!* He closed his eyes, had to open them again because he was driving. It descended towards the windscreen—and swept over it.

In the rear-view mirror, skeins of yellow stalks corkscrewed in the car's vortex. *Straw.* He let out a breath. Noticing a plastic packet of sweets in the central pocket, he reached for one. The bag crackled.

He withdrew his fingers almost as quickly because the air had given them a dog-lick. He wiped the stickiness off on the J-cloth he used for the windscreen.

He couldn't put it off any longer. He had to stop to relieve himself.

As he waited for the steaming stream to relent, he looked around and the "Soft Verges" sign up ahead occasioned a wry chuckle.

His smile departed almost as soon as it had arrived. *What the hell is wrong with me?* He tugged up his fly, jumped back in the car and stomped on the accelerator pedal.

When it came time to leave the motorway, he joined a road that dipped and rose but carried on straight, for miles, before swinging him this way and that. He clung to the steering wheel, hung on. *Damn.* He shot past a turning that could have been the one he wanted.

If he carried on this way, he'd arrive, eventually, at the coast. So, slowing down, he took the next turning.

Without Polly to guide him and with the network down on his phone, rendering its satnav useless, he had to rely on his inner compass.

The road unreeled in the rear-view mirror.

Half way up an incline, the engine coughed. The exhaust pipe sputtered. Everything gave out except the electrics.

He yanked on the handbrake.

The steering wheel's pattern had transferred itself to his

hands, which ached from gripping it. His fingers had lost all sensation at the tips.

Flexing and unflexing them, he glanced at the fuel gauge. *Shit*. Why hadn't he noticed the warning light?

It couldn't be much farther, could it? He'd gone over the railway line a few miles back.

He unpeeled himself from his seat and got out.

Pylons marched across a field of crops.

In the nearest corner of the next field along he spotted a stile and turned towards it. A bone-white path led across grass in the direction of velvety hills with bobbly bushes. Which would be quicker, road or path? The sun warmed his face. The breeze ruffled his hair. His collar flapped and flipped. Lazy bees sizzled in the heat.

Ambling up to the stile, he clambered over it.

All the colour drained from the day. *Fuck*. He stumbled across a stony field in the fading light. *Bad, bad, bad idea*. The chalk path had led him in the wrong direction and he'd had to double back.

Spotting a stone barn in the corner, at the top of a long gradient bounded by woods, he made for that. The grass dragged at his feet, slowing him down.

Eventually it thinned out to compacted mud and stones and he picked up speed.

Bare inside with a hard stone floor, the barn at least had an intact roof. He checked for bugs or evidence of rats or other unwelcome creatures and couldn't see any, so clumped out into the last of the light. All the pigmentation had drained from the day, leaving the barn, the grass, the woods, in black and white.

He shivered. Why hadn't he brought a sweater?

He slid down the dry, rough wall with a long sigh and ended up next to a prickly bush growing out of the barn's foundations. If Polly was alright then at some point he should have come across a cordon or road block, perhaps army trucks, makeshift camps for the displaced.

Pushing the unbidden thought to the back of his mind, he fixed his eyes on the suede-like trees at the limit of his vision.

It wasn't until he looked down that he saw it—the hand, next to him. *Another person.*

Spinning round, he rolled onto his side. Yet either the shadows under the bush were so deep that he couldn't see or... *Fuck.* He scrambled to his feet. Severed... *A fucking severed...* *Under the...*

He stood staring at the hand.

It twitched.

He leapt back. *What in—*

Involuntary movement. What else could it be?

The fingers scrabbled in the dirt. *No.* They clawed their way across it. *You can't—* Trailing the bloody stump behind them, they kept on coming. *Christ.* He had to step out of the way.

The hand stood up, like a crab on points, sideways-walking

It approached his ankle. He lifted his foot. It crawled closer.

He stamped the ground next to it. His eyes struggled to keep up with it running round the side of the barn in the spectral twilight.

That didn't happen. No, no, that didn't happen.

It's been a long day. I'm overtired.

He tottered over to the wall, slumped back against it.

He must have nodded off because he woke with a cough, tried to take a breath, couldn't. Something pincer-like gripped his neck.

Jumping up, he tore whatever it was off him, flung it away. He just made out the pale hand scuttle off into undergrowth.

He sucked in deep lungfuls of air.

The light hadn't so much sunk as risen, leaving the sky luminous and the field, undergrowth and trees dark and dense.

Swaying, fused to the spot, he couldn't account for the previous few minutes. Had he dozed off?

He massaged his sore, tight neck. *I didn't imagine that.*

He hastened inside, shouldered the door shut, lay down in the corner and curled up into a ball.

Something grazed the film of sleep.

Greg opened his eyes. Gaining ingress through tiny fissures

between planks at the foot of the door, light speared the dusty floor. It reached half way to his left flank. He lifted his head and looked down to see a dead hand on his chest.

He rolled and sprang upright. The hand came with him, tumbling across his stomach and down his side.

Oh.

He lifted it to his eyes, where it hung from his wrist.

Holding it, he squeezed the fingers. Nothing. Completely dead. So he gave the lump of flesh a shake, squashed it under his armpit a few times, then kneaded and manipulated it. As numbness receded, the hand cramped. He intensified his efforts and feeling flooded back. Even to the stiff fingers. Soon he could move them. The hand was his own again.

Dreams and reality wrap around each other endlessly.

Where had that come from?

He unlatched the door, shuffled outside and, blasted by surround-sound birdsong, took in the painterly sky. If yesterday the latter could be said to have been in watercolours, today it was in oils. Purply clouds topped the horizon off with an amorphous mountain chain.

It was only when he turned that he realized the nightmare had barely begun. Daubings on the wall, in red, stated, "You are not alone."

CHAPTER 4

TIME-STOPPED VILLAGE

The zebra-striped upper storey of a listed Tudor building projected out over the pavement like the stern of a galleon as he turned up Chantry Lane.

He passed The Pig and Stoat. Its sign creaked in the breeze. Now a row of cottages gave way to a low wall with a small red post box set in it. Eventually even this came to an end. Ahead lay the church where he and Polly should have been getting married in less than a month's time. He made out the golden stonework, the dark stained-glass windows, the lychgate and the gap between trees and headstones for the path that led up to the large wooden door. *Why didn't I just keep my mouth shut?* He turned, under the sweep of dark cedars, up a close with five, no, six bungalows.

He headed for a Rover the colour of HP Sauce and squeezed past it up the short driveway.

A rabbit nipped the lawn over by some geraniums. White tail bobbing, it scampered at his approach.

He bounded onto the front step and prodded the white button.

Ding-dong.

The sound rang through him.

Bedgley hadn't been that far away. As soon as he'd emerged from the woods, he'd spotted its church tower.

No-one came to the door, so he rapped on it. "Polly..."

Greg shuffled round to the bay window.

He planted a foot in the raised flower beds, gripped the sill and, transferring his weight onto his leading leg as he pulled himself up, pressed his face to the glass. He picked out a red sofa, lacquered sideboard, unlit standard lamp. That was it. Just... just furniture.

He ran round the property, pounded on the back door. Nothing. He peered through the window of the boxy rear room at the immaculately made spare bed. *No...*

He dashed over to the shed and grabbed the nearest thing to hand, a rake. Its tines rattled behind him as he charged towards the back door. He thrust the handle through the bottom left-hand pane, threw the rake aside and reached in to turn the key and open the door.

"Polly." Broken glass crunched underfoot. "Polly..."

He took in the mahogany waist- and head-height units and the kitchen table's four matching empty seats and made for the doorway. He careered round the corner, clattered across the parquet flooring of the hallway and burst into Mr. and Mrs. Mokes' room. Maggie's pair of tortoiseshell glasses rested upside down on a copy of *Saga Magazine* to one side of the unmade bed and Ron's folded broadsheet with the crossword showing leaned under the lamp to the other.

Greg started when he glimpsed a figure in black, with eyes like holes, in the oak wardrobe's full-length mirror.

He saw it again, just the face this time, wan and unshaven with drowned man's eyes, above the sink in the white-tiled, white-enamelled bathroom.

Lurching through to the lounge with its dark furniture, its floral, chintzy soft furnishings, he threw himself down on the sofa next to a ball of wool skewered by two knitting needles. A black and white photo of a young Ron in a dark suit and a young Maggie in a frothy, flowing white dress stared down at him from the mantelpiece.

Greg buried his face in saggy cushions as sobs engulfed him. Hot tears slid from his eyes.

Gone...

She's gone.

Am I dead? Was it even a relevant question anymore? If a working definition of death was being alone forever, then what was the difference, really?

Green leached from the rug, yellow from the curtains and red from the sofa. *Entropy in action.* Shadows crept up the wall. *Everything turning brown.*

It wasn't long before the depth and darkness of the shadows made them seem more substantial than anything else. More like presences than empty spaces, they kept him company.

Maybe this is a copy of the world, down to every last detail, and in this one it's just me. His head buzzed like a wasp trapped in a bottle. Emptiness consumed his mind.

In his less, or maybe more, coherent moments, he was convinced that Polly and everyone else disappearing was his fault—a punishment he deserved, a hell of his own making.

He got up off the sofa and the world wobbled. It had an underwater-bendiness at the edges.

His ears rang.

He paused with his hands up, out.

His stomach growled, roared. He hadn't eaten since the day before yesterday. A blackness behind the eyes had risen to the surface. He couldn't ignore the needs of his body completely. Maybe he should give his consciousness something to adhere to before it floated off. Or perhaps he should just let it drift and waft.

Take too damn long.

He staggered through to the kitchen and yanked the fridge door open. The light came on and a pair of pork chops gleamed pinkly in their packet on the top shelf. They'd do. Along with some broccoli and a carrot from the hydrator, he took them out.

He gave the door a gentle tap. The light clicked out as it whumped shut.

Preferring the room's dull monochrome, he left the kitchen light off.

He turned the oven on to warm, dragged some chips out of the freezer compartment, poured them, clattering, onto a baking tray and stuffed the bag back in the freezer.

Crows cawed nearby.

He peered out at the back garden. Even in the low, thin light, it was a shade or two brighter than indoors. Beyond the rear fence, black trees stood starkly. The silhouettes of raggedy crows flapped and took off, circled. They wheeled like fragments of burnt parchment. Some going one way, some the other, they weaved in and out of each other. For every few that alighted, others launched themselves into the air. The ghost of a plastic bag, in tatters, streamed like a banner from a branch. But what had disturbed the infernal birds? The fluttering of the bag or something out of sight in the churchyard below?

There's something out there. His hand immediately went to his neck.

The crows' raucousness intensified.

How come he could hear it so clearly? The window was shut.

He turned to the hole he'd made in the back door—just big enough for a hand to fit through.

He should have been chopping vegetables. Instead he dashed outside, under a darkening sulphurous sky, to the toolshed. He picked up a hammer from the workbench and, keeping the shed door open with his foot, scrabbled about in the stiff drawers for some nails. He found a fistful of different lengths.

He ran back inside and rifled through the kitchen's drawers. Coming across some place mats, he took one out. Rectangular rather than square, it was at least rigid. He stepped over to the door, placed the mat over the broken pane, aligned it with the frame, with the excess overlapping surrounding panes, and knocked nails into the struts.

The crow that flew low over the bungalow was its voice only as he stood and stared at his handiwork. Had there ever been a DIY job so botched?

He sighed. Everything would be DIY from now on.

Tired of the browny-yellow light, he tugged the curtains shut and flicked the switch on the wall before turning the key in the door to keep whatever was out there out.

He was alone but not entirely.

CHAPTER 5

POST-HUMAN

Another day on Earth, Polly-less.

The sun baked the interior of the car as it zipped along, while the trees in the hedgerows of the fields round about leaned and jerked as they attempted, unsuccessfully, to whip themselves. High up, the wind had shredded the clouds.

Hedgerows at the side of the road jumped out at him, rose, dipped, fell back, closed in, to be replaced by a fence, a copse, another fence corralling two horses, a much thicker hedge.

He tutted at another prissy road sign stating the obvious. "I know there's a bloody bend coming up. I can see it." The metal semaphores on poles, the em dashes of road markings turning continuous, warned him of dangers he could see, yet gave no indication of horrors that might, for all he knew, lurk just around the corner. Leaning to the side, leaning the other way, he sat up as another sign passed. "Liar! There's no tractors turning." He sank back. *I wish to hell there were.*

Although he didn't drive as fast as yesterday, instead of staying to the left of the white line, he crissed it, crossed it, as required. Taking the shortest route to the motorway, he was on his way back to London, in the Rover.

He'd left a trail of things in the wrong places. Not that property mattered anymore. Not that anything mattered.

His teeth felt furry.

The light flickered as he crossed a bridge over a gorge. He caught a flash of water plunging down a hillside.

Where had they gone, Polly, her parents, everyone? Had

they disappeared, or died? If the latter, had Polly known what was happening? Had she had to live her own death?

Oh, God. He stamped on the brake. Hanging, windscreen-wards, in his seatbelt, he swayed as the back of the car slewed to one side, the other.

When the vehicle eventually came to a halt, he rolled out and onto his feet without even turning the engine off. Leaning sideways in the roaring wind, he strode back onto the bridge.

Half way across, he curved round towards the outer edge.

He put one leg, the other, backwards over the barrier, lowered himself until his toes rested on a lip of iron just below road level and tentatively turned around. He stretched his arms out, hooked his fingers under the barrier, and clung on.

His heart thudded.

He didn't look down but, between gusts, he could hear water tumbling beneath his feet.

The wind rushed at him. Literally taking his breath away, it stoppered his mouth. He had to breathe through his nose. Although his eyes watered, he made out geometrical pines, the winking pixels of a body of water, the greyness of a town and a horizon of purplish hills.

The wind pressed him to the barrier.

Letting go, he leaned out into it.

It took his weight. He merely wobbled a bit with each fluctuation in strength. Until a particularly strong gust blew him back.

"What do you want from me?" he screamed, though to whom he had no idea.

He leaned out farther. The human race teetered with him, on the brink of extinction.

He tried to picture it—a post-human world. The animal kingdom would thrive but what about all the things that would be lost? Science, technology, astronomy, mathematics, philosophy, art, music, literature, love…

"Come on, then," he shouted.

The wind dropped, and he almost dropped with it. Just managing to grab hold of a stanchion, he swung round into the barrier.

Hauling himself back up and over, he collapsed onto his hands and knees. Tiny stones dug into his palms. *Idiot.* With the torrent rushing beneath him and the wind tearing at him, even the bridge didn't feel solid enough. He got up, sprinted off it and threw himself down on the verge.

His lungs heaved, and his eyes turned the blades of grass that speared his face dewy.

Maybe that lightning strike put me into a coma and I'm still there, dreaming this.

As if to scotch that theory, something tickled his nose.

He'd no sooner wiped it away than something tickled his hand.

He lifted his head and his vision cleared. Multitudinous ants like miniature copper-coloured aliens crawled in and out of a mound of soil in the grass. His right wrist compressed the base. He virtually had his face in it.

Ambulance ants carried away a curled-up dead ant. Soldier ants ran around, preparing to do battle with whatever threatened the nest.

"What are you all so het up about?" He got to his knees. "Oh, you think you've got problems, do you?"

He wrenched a sharp bit of flint from the surrounding soil, stood up and flung it at the nest. It buried itself in the side like an asteroid from the heavens.

He bent over and peered at hundreds of ants evacuating, carrying off the dead and injured, together with what looked like tiny white Tic Tacs. Food? Eggs? Eurgh. He kicked the mound.

Soil and ants flew through the air.

"You haven't got a flaming apocalypse to worry about."

He trod on the mound, stomped on it, jumped up and down on it.

Afterwards, breathing hard, panting, he took a step rearward and stared at a large patch of pancaked soil where the mound had been. Crushed blades of grass sprang back up around it one by one.

He couldn't see any ants.

"Oh..."

Either the change occurred suddenly or was already pronounced by the time he noticed it. A blue sky still bell-jarred the day, yet the air had darkened as if ready for rain.

Something round, or spherical, blotted out the sun. *An eclipse?* Whatever it was slid aside and kept on going.

What the...? Covering the sun with a hand, Greg made out a white orb floating in the sky with a blob in the middle of it. A jellied mass, it got bigger, nearer. He saw himself reflected in the shiny black dot at the centre of the blob, just standing there, staring. What was that in the outer whiteness? It had... It had veins.

No... He turned.

Still looking round at it, he broke into a run.

The eyeball sank towards him.

The car door hung open. He jumped straight on the accelerator pedal.

The wheels spun, and he got the hot reek of burning rubber. But as soon as he released the handbrake, the car lurched forwards. The wheels slithered from side to side until they gained traction, his door swung shut and he went up through the gears, fast, fast, away, away from the bridge.

CHAPTER 6

ROADS

Something thrashed in the bushes. Greg snapped his head round so fast that his neck clicked.

The vegetation that separated verge from woods bobbed and swayed, yet strictly in time with the breeze.

He carried on walking along the edge of the dual carriageway, between the white line and the verge, and thought of the elaborate network of asphalt, going nowhere. *Bloody Rover*. It had overheated. Since then, all the cars he'd passed at the roadside had been crumpled or burnt out.

Even in bouncy trainers, his heels throbbed.

Ahead, a blue Renault glinted in a layby. *Parked*.

Ignoring the pain, he jogged towards it. His trainers ate up the distance. He didn't stop until his hand rested on the boot.

Keys dangled from the ignition. *Yes*. He pulled the door handle and the door opened. He got in.

Oh. Automatic.

He switched the engine on, let the handbrake off, squeezed the accelerator pedal and steered out onto the main road. As the Renault speeded up, his left foot still went to a non-existent clutch and his left hand to an atrophied gear stick.

Increasing the pressure on the accelerator, he kept both hands on the wheel and his left foot out of the way.

It had clouded over. The sky turned as grey as the motorway he joined.

Wreckage was widely spaced but at 100mph, he weaved round it.

Soon back in the sepulchral city, in crepuscular light, he raced up familiar thoroughfares.

He wasn't far from home when a black Honda CR-V with darkened windows raced towards him on the other side. *My God… Someone else.*

It stopped.

He stopped.

He turned the Renault around. The Honda had got quite far ahead. Rolling forwards, he flashed his lights.

Nothing.

He tooted his horn.

Nothing.

He put his foot down.

Getting close, he'd just started braking when the car sped off. *No. You…*

Transferring his foot back to the accelerator pedal, he went after it. He was gaining on it when it swerved left.

Wrenching the steering wheel in that direction, he rounded the corner at the outermost limit, over into what would have been oncoming traffic. He was nearly level with the Honda's bumper when it took another left. *Oh, for God's …*This time he overshot and, glancing back, narrowly avoided a bicycle on its side.

Turning the Renault around, he accelerated up the residential road. "Humps for 240 yards," read the sign. He bounced in his seat. His stomach did backflips. His head knocked the roof.

The road had a kink in it at the top and by the time he reached the junction, he couldn't see the car. *Damn—which way?* He pulled up the handbrake, put the windows down, silenced the engine and listened.

Tires squealed to the right. He turned the engine back on and set off.

Braking at a crossroads, he saw the Honda off to the right again and swung the Renault round that way.

He floored the accelerator pedal and closed the gap.

It turned. He screeched after it.

A roundabout had the two chassis leaning to one side then the other, just out of phase. The road they joined came to an end at a T-junction with a high chain-link fence the other side.

A shriek from the Honda as it changed course late. The back swung right out before it straightened up with a series of decreasing jerks.

Mind and body acting in consort, he took the corner at a shallower angle with no skid and little protest from the tires.

They flew along the road as if on a race track, past buildings, car parks, with a large field on the other side, buildings the far side of that.

Where were they? A Qantas tailfin rose from behind a roof. *You're joking.*

They no sooner rounded a bend than he spotted a cockpit one side of the road, sections of a fuselage across it and, farther and farther back, a tailfin, an engine and landing gear.

A wing spanned both lanes.

The Honda bounced off the road and he went, bump, bump, after it, through the gap in the chain-link fence and out onto the field.

Rough grass gave way to smooth Tarmac. One of the back tires ahead of him flopped and flapped. He no sooner gained on the Honda than it veered off the runway.

Heart pumping and the Renault's direction bending to his will as if man and machine were organically linked—as if his blood coursed through its engine, its motor oil flowed back up his veins—he turned even more sharply to try and nip in ahead of the Honda. *Like being in a…*

Either he turned too tight or he hit a rut because he could feel two wheels leaving the ground. The Renault tilted, to his side. He leaned the other way. *Oh, shit.* He had no choice. He had to go with it. All four wheels left the ground and the car continued sideways. He fell against his door as grass pressed itself to his window. He could still hear it rustling, sliding, as, just as quickly, it withdrew. He revolved upside-down in his seat, rotated back round. The chassis thunked down onto its tires, before going again. Throwing him to the side, tipping him up, the car only stopped rolling when the roof clanged—scraped—against asphalt.

Suspended the wrong way up in his seatbelt, canted

forwards, he stared at a giant tire print.

The engine had cut out. The Renault creaked and groaned.

The roar of another vehicle, the screech of brakes, the crunk of a handbrake, followed by open-ended, unreadable silence. He tried to release the seatbelt but, probably because of his weight pulling on the catch, the button wouldn't budge. The straps cut into his stomach, ribcage and shoulder. His head whooshed with all the blood rushing to it. *Hell, hell, hell...* Maybe he should have been racing away from the Honda, not after it. He had no idea who was driving it and here he was hanging upside down, trapped.

His neck jerked. Either cooling metal had pinged, or someone had just tapped the exposed underside of the Renault.

He rocked in his seatbelt when a face swung into view at his broken window.

Long chestnut hair fell sideways from it. Hazel eyes blinked. Bow lips opened.

His heart nearly jumped out of him.

"P-Polly." His voice sounded like someone else's. Already, his vocal cords had turned scratchy with disuse. "I'm s-sorry."

Tears leaked from his eyes and rolled between his eyebrows, up his forehead and into his hairline.

Polly wrenched the door open. "I had no idea it was you. I thought it was someone after me."

Putting a hand down to take some of his weight, he managed to release the seatbelt. "Ugh." He collapsed onto the roof. His head felt as heavy as setting concrete. His bent neck ached. He was hunched over, the wrong way up, with his knees wedged under the steering wheel. He unhooked them, rolled over onto his side on the compressed roof and crawled out.

Polly helped him up.

"Is it..." Tottering one way as everything turned the other, he clutched her arm. "Is it really you?"

She threw herself at him and hugged him, tightly. "Of course it's me."

"I didn't... I wasn't sure." He couldn't quite bring himself to tell her that he'd been to the edge of insanity, and a little beyond.

They stood on the spur of a taxiway. The runway stretched

from one end of the flat expanse of green to the other, Roman-road straight. Crows cawed in the grass beyond. A flock of gulls dived and soared. The flags of tailfins festooned the terminals. A skeletal red and white dish rotated on one side. The control tower loomed like an unlit beacon on the other.

He glanced at the Honda. "That was you?"

"Yes."

A harsh crackly sound emanated from his chin as he scratched what felt like upended iron filings. "Why were you trying to get away from me?"

She lifted a strand of hair out of her face. "I didn't know it was you. And when you flashed your lights and beeped your horn, I got scared. I've been..." She swallowed. "I've been very scared."

He held his palms out, empty. "But where did you go? I looked everywhere for you."

A bird-like tilt of her head. She regarded him out of one eye. "I was looking for you. As soon as I woke, I sensed something wasn't right. I called you on the phone. Nothing."

He rubbed his shoulder.

"I turned on the TV. Nada. Radio, internet, all down."

He bent and unbent his knee.

"I went out into the street. I knocked on doors. No-one answered. When I got back, you'd taken the car."

Ignoring the crick in his neck, he nodded.

"I waited and waited but you didn't come back. So, after a lot of soul-searching, I stole a car."

Of course. He recognized it now—Raoul and Connie's Honda.

"I scoured London." She touched his arm. "There's no-one left. Finally I thought I'd drive down to Mum and Dad's."

"Thank God I caught you."

"What about you?"

He tipped his head back. "What?"

"Where did you go?"

Lowering his head, he massaged the nape of his neck. "Looking for you."

"But where?"

His mouth formed into different shapes. No sounds emerged.

"Are they..." she began.

"Gone too."

She didn't say anything, just twisted her body and flung her head around.

Her sleeve came up level with her eyes.

Taking her hand, raising it, and touching her opposite shoulder, he slowly turned her back around. "I'm so sorry, sweetheart."

Her face dipped as she came to rest against his chest and his arms enclosed her.

She lifted her gaze. "Do you think they—"

He pressed his lips to hers. She tried to push him away. He held on. She relaxed. Their mouths fused.

They continued to prop each other up as they shambled towards the apron and the planes and buildings and car parks.

"Sorry about..." He coughed into his hand. "You know... It was just pre-wedding panic."

She wafted a hand. "Oh, let's not talk about it."

He gripped her elbow. "There's no-one else I want to be with."

"It's not like there's anyone else to choose from now, is there?" A crumpled smile.

She was right. Better to leave it.

CHAPTER 7

EMPTY PLAYGROUNDS

"It's all yours," he said.

His voice crackled in his ears as if they were tuned to a different frequency.

Showered and shaved, with just a towel round his waist, he sat on the edge of the bed as she shed the slough of her tights.

"Seen my back?" He twisted round to show her.

"What about it?"

"All the burns."

"Burns?"

"These." He pointed at his left shoulder blade, before making for the mirror in the wardrobe door and peering over his shoulder at it. "Oh."

Blank.

Strange...

He stuck the tips of his forefingers in his ears and wiggled them about. "You know, three people get struck by lightning in the UK every year."

"Hm. How will that work now there's only two of us?"

He turned to her and watched the bud of her mouth set in an indeterminate pout. Her lips matched her nipples shade for shade. Her breasts shook as she made her way round the bed. Coming right up to him, she put her arms around his neck and looked at him with bottomless eyes. Each blink tugged at something deep within him.

"We're going to find out what happened," he said. "I promise. I mean, there must be a rational explanation."

A flick of her chestnut hair. "I'm not sure anything's logical anymore."

"We just have to rely on each other and not fight." He clung to her.

She clung to him.

His hands traversed dolphin-smooth skin. They moved out, round, down over her hips.

Her hands glided in the same direction. He could feel the cold hard band of her ring. Both hands just lagged behind each of his and stopped at his waist.

"You're like an angel," he said.

"Not quite."

His towel dropped to the floor.

Sunlight slashed the curtains.

He raised an arm. Polly moaned and stirred.

Lying on his back, he turned to look at her as her eyes popped open. The lids of one unglued themselves fractionally later than the other. He glimpsed white before her eyeballs rolled and realigned.

"Morning." He smiled.

She smiled back. "Morning."

"Did you sleep well?"

"Like the dead. How about you?"

"I don't know. I was asleep."

She chuckled.

Their lips touched, her mouth opened, and her tongue darted in his mouth. They kissed long and deep.

A hand settled on his upper thigh.

He pulled away. "Um, that is you, isn't it?"

"What?"

"That hand."

A fluttery laugh. "Yes, of course it is. Why?"

"Oh, no reason."

"Are you alright?"

"Yeah, love, fine, fine." He crooked an arm around her neck.

Silence lapped at the walls of the flat.

His body tautened. "What got to you?"

"Mm?"

He cleared his throat. "Yesterday, you said you'd been scared. What scared you?"

"You mean apart from waking up and finding everyone gone?" She laughed.

He didn't. "So nothing… specific?"

She ran a hand across her face. "Well, loneliness can drive you a little crazy, I think."

He nodded. "Yes. Yes, it can." She's right. That's all it is. His limbs loosened. Galvanized by competing impulses, he slid his arm out from underneath her and bounded out of bed. "You know what all this means, don't you?"

She pulled herself up on the mattress. "What?"

He flung the curtains apart. Warm sunshine poured in. "The world is our playground. We can do whatever we like."

Shielding her eyes with her wrist, she grinned. "We can?"

"Yeah. There's no-one to stop us. No government, no police. No rules at all. We don't have to pay for anything, don't have to go to work."

"Now you put it like that…"

He bounced onto the bed at her side. "The world and everything in it is ours."

The white marble of the Victoria Memorial obscured the view down The Mall. The bronze winged victory atop gleamed as the afternoon sun dispensed its riches like a cascade of gold sovereigns.

He put his arm round Polly as they pushed through heavy heat out onto the balcony, where just one cloud smudged the contrail-less sky.

Trees so full as to be almost spherical lined Green Park on one side and St James's Park on the other.

He pulled her closer as they leaned out over the parapet and the reddish gravel of the forecourt loomed vertiginously below.

They sprang upright, turned towards each other.

She puckered up. "Kiss me."

He wetted his lips with the tip of his tongue.

Her eyes drew together as they leaned towards one another.

Their mouths met and, below, imaginary crowds cheered beyond the black and gold gates.

Disconcertingly, her eyes had merged. She now had one, Cyclops-style.

He smiled as she came back into focus. "I wonder where the Queen's bed is."

The store's alarm clanged.

Greg watched as Polly dashed around picking dresses and skirts and tops from the racks and draping them over her arm. When her arm was thick with them, she ran over to the door. Carefully stepping through the jagged glass in the metal frame, she laid them in the back of the black Toyota Land Cruiser parked on the pavement outside. They'd always frowned upon such vehicles, especially in the city, but global warming was the least of their worries now.

He laughed as she bustled back in and up to the next set of racks, almost knocking over a free-standing dummy in her hurry. "I don't know why you're running. It's not like we're going to get arrested." He had to shout over the din.

"It's that alarm. It's freaking me out."

"Let's call it a day then."

"Hold on a minute. You're so impatient!"

He sighed. "Take your time." *Nothing I'd rather be doing...*

In Liberty's earlier, surrounded by salt and pepper shakers and egg timers and trivets and bottle openers and placemats and coasters and trays and tea towels and glasses and cake stands and spoons and tea pots and milk jugs and sugar bowls and blenders and kettles and espresso makers, he'd steadied himself against a display of toasters gleaming like spare car parts in every conceivable colour and thought, I'm trapped in a world of things.

More to kill time than anything else, he sauntered through the men's section.

Spotting a stand with jeans on, he picked up a pair in his size, ripped off the paper tags, slipped off his shoes, undid his trousers, pulled them off, tugged on the jeans and did up the zip. They'd do. He and Polly could remove the security tags later.

"Greg," called Polly.

He stepped back into his shoes and followed her out through the smashed door.

Alarms blared all down the tree-lined avenue of Oxford Street as she dumped her last load on top of clothes, bags and shoe boxes.

Reaching up to pull the boot down, he spied a mobile shop opposite.

The boot clicked shut and he made his way to the driver's door. "Come on, love."

As soon as they were inside, he switched the engine on, swung the Land Cruiser around and put it into reverse. It jolted one way as they left the pavement, at a slight angle, jolted the other way as they mounted the opposite curb.

"Hey, what are you doing?" Polly gripped her seat.

He flashed her a smile as the engine roared and the shop loomed in the rear window. "My turn now."

The Land Cruiser shook as it whumped against the doors. Metal ground against metal, right down the side of the vehicle. Glass clattered against the bonnet. He yanked on the handbrake. They jerked to a halt.

He switched the engine off and got out, in the middle of the shop. Glass crunched underfoot. More tinkled as it fell.

Polly's door creaked open.

"Careful, love," he said.

The Land Cruiser had been gouged right down the side. A stand had disappeared under it. Another had been shunted right across the room. But there on the back wall gleamed the mobile he wanted.

He stepped over to it and pulled it out as far as he could. "I've just got to find one of these out back. You choosing?"

"Well, even assuming we can find a network that's working..."

"Yeah?"

"Who are we going to talk to?"

"Oh." He let the phone spring back.

Standing off to the side, he watched her lean her head against the gleaming steel skin of the large round door as she twisted the dial this way and that. What was she doing, listening to the turning of the tumblers?

"You know the combination, don't you, love?" he said.

She chuckled. "I should. I've done it enough times." She kept her forehead to the door and her eyes on the dial. "Did you know that bank vaults can survive nuclear blasts?"

He stretched. "Really?"

"Yeah, two survived Hiroshima."

Faint slot-machine clacks and clunks.

She spun the wheel attached to the door as if turning a ship hard to port. Bolts withdrew. The bulky door swung open. Like the inside of an oversized mechanical watch, the back housed cogs and pins behind glass.

Yet another gate barred the way.

She produced a key and inserted it. The gate banged open.

Inside, little drawers with numbers on lined the walls.

She took out a bunch of keys and started opening them, reaching in and pulling out the contents. Cash, documents, jewellery and other trinkets started piling up on the floor.

She picked up handfuls of notes of different currencies and threw them in the air.

"We're rich," she cried, as they fluttered down.

He looked at her, at the money. "Yeah, but where are we going to spend it?"

They descended stone steps to the Thames Path. Black water shimmered in the light from globular lamps, which recast the world in black and white. Water lapped the wall below. A pair of shadow-giants stalked the buildings above.

Their footsteps echoed in the lonely night.

Furry moths clustered thickly around the lamps.

A dog barked on the other side of the river. Running feral or spooked by something?

Greg shivered.

The breeze caught him side on, making him wish he'd taken Polly's advice and put something on over his GANT short-sleeved shirt.

He reached for her hand.

She grasped his.

"Where do you think they went?" he said.

In her Joules dress, on her Ravel wedges, she looked round. "What?"

"Everybody." He glanced at some charcoaly flowerbeds. "I mean, where are they?"

"The Mardi Gras?"

Laughter erupted from him.

She smiled.

Then the smile fled her face. "Think it was another Chernobyl?"

He held his other hand out, turned it over. "How come we're alright?"

"What's that bomb that gets rid of people but leaves buildings intact?"

"Oh, the neutron bomb, yes, yeah, that's a good one. Surely we'd have heard it, though. And there'd have had to have been lots."

"I guess."

"What about a gamma-ray burst from a hypernova?"

"Come again?"

"The celestial equivalent. Thing is, there's none near enough."

"Oh." A gentle snuff.

He swallowed. "Maybe the chosen rose and we... didn't."

Her head jerked back. "What are you saying? We overslept on Judgement Day?"

He coughed. "Well, the thing we need to try and work out is..." A moth blundered against his lips. Swiping it out of his face, he dry-spat.

Bloody things.

Her hand slipped through his and out. "Oh, my God."

He stopped, whirled around. "What, baby?" Her hand cupped her mouth. "Baby, what?"

He followed her line of sight. High up on the brickwork above, something small, pale and round protruded from the mortar.

She pointed, transfixed.

He placed his hand on her shoulder. "It's just fungus, love."

"No it's not, it's..."

"What?"

"It's a..."

He could feel her trembling.

"What, love?"

"Ear."

He couldn't have heard right. "What?"

"An ear."

He positioned himself in line with it, a few feet away from the wall, stared up and had to concede that it did have the convolutions, flutes, knobbles and fleshy colouring of an ear. Yet it couldn't be. Could it?

It waggled.

"Fuck." He jumped back.

Polly let out a moan. "You know what it's doing, don't you?"

"What?" He shifted his weight from foot to foot.

"Listening."

"You're..."

She turned. "Oh, no..."

"What?" He spun round. "Oh, shit."

The lights along the river went out one by one. Blocks of darkness caught up with them.

A click from her throat as cavernous night swallowed them. "Oh, God... It's all starting again."

CHAPTER 8

IN THE WARM SEAT

"Euch, God, it's getting worse." It invaded his nose, his head, as he shone his torch left and right up an aisle of a Tesco Metro. Twice a week they visited places like this, and each time he was unprepared for the throat-choking miasma of it.

Polly, who followed a step behind, tapped him on the shoulder. "It's back this way."

He could only see surfaces, outlines, in the unlit store. The torchlight added a cone of detail.

But what was that electrical-like hum? Were the refrigeration units on? How? Leaning against the nearest, he tilted the torch downwards just as he took a breath.

The stench punched him in the stomach. His eyes watered. Furry here, liquefying there, food a vomit of colours tending towards brown heaved with maggots. A layer of flies rose up like a net. It hit his chin and he tried to bat them away. He couldn't speak, or they'd end up in his mouth. Instead he pushed Polly back. Flies blazed in the torchlight as he swung it round. She turned and they both ran. The beam jogged at their feet.

As they slowed, he flashed the torch left and right.

Grey fruit sagged in canted trays.

Tiny creatures wriggled on a stained patch of floor.

A worm-like tail whipped under a stand.

They stopped.

"Just the tins." She touched his arm. "Just the tins. That's all we can salvage."

Metal fulgurated in a sweep of torchlight. "Okay."

She took one side of the aisle, he the other. He scooped tins from the shelves into a leather holdall and tried not to think about how one day all the best-before dates would be in the past.

Bags full, they bustled out of the store, away from that awful smell.

Their loot clanked dully as they lugged it across the pedestrian square, the open-air intersection at the centre of the arcade, towards the red Golf parked in the corner.

Shrieks bounced off the dark walls and windows of the far exit.

They stopped.

Polly looked at him. "What the hell...?"

More cries echoed, closer, shriller.

Weighed down, he and Polly loped towards the Golf. He could hear his own breathing. It sounded like someone else's. They slung the bags in the boot, got in, shut the doors and craned windscreen-wards.

Three foxes trotted out into the light and paused to regard the human interlopers before shearing off up the next exit.

Polly nose-sighed. He let out a laugh.

She crinkled her brows at him.

Something no bigger than a currant passed so close to his eyes that he couldn't even focus on it.

Trapped in the car, a fly careered this way and that.

Eventually it landed, on the dashboard, crawled around on it. He slowly reached for the car's handbook, pulled it out and raised it.

He slammed it down.

Somehow the fly survived. Even peppier, fizzier, it whizzed this way and that.

Having to be careful in the cockpit of the car, he swung at it with his hand. With only six directions to choose from, left, right, up, down, backwards, forwards, it continued to elude him—perhaps getting sucked into the slipstream of his swipes.

It flew in the back out of reach.

"Fucking thing," he said.

"Just put the bloody windows down."

He pressed the buttons for all four windows and the fly got out. Only, two flew in.

"Jesus!" He didn't want to let any more in, so he put the windows back up.

One got out, leaving the other stuck inside.

He picked the handbook back up and sat still.

The fly buzzed right past his ear and, one of those hard-boiled ones, butted the windscreen.

He whacked it.

Taking the book away, he saw it hanging there, with what looked like an ooze of pus where its lower half should be.

The prick of a memory: curled-up ants. *Why all this death?*

"I just had the most horrible thought," he said.

"Yes?"

He cleared his throat. "Well, what if there's a being as far removed from us as we are from these flies? How would they regard us?"

She shrugged. "With contempt, I guess."

He shuddered as he started the engine. "Yeah, I think you're probably right."

Three days later, they cruised through Piccadilly Circus in a white Lexus with Polly at the wheel. Unnatural light, a charged glow, caused him to glance up and his mind stuttered.

"Stop the car," he shouted.

Polly hit the brakes and turned to him. "What is it?"

He stepped out onto the yellow grid.

"What are you doing?" from the driver's seat.

He stared up.

"What? What is it?" The statue of Eros' brother pointed the other way as Polly got out of the car, spun round.

"Look." He pointed up at the giant advertising screen. Illuminated, it struck him with a deep strangeness, a fresh familiarity. "How can it be on? There's no power."

Brain numbed, he bathed in its light as in a giant solarium. Grey low cloud sealed the sky like a cap on their dreams and the screen took the edge off the dullness of the day.

Polly rested her elbows on the roof of the vehicle. "Back-up power?"

"What, just up there?"

She shrugged. "I don't know." Behind her, beyond the fountain, the Criterion Theatre, Lillywhites, unlit. "A quirk of the grid?"

"We passed through here the day before yesterday. It wasn't on then."

She glanced up. "Maybe it was."

He shook his head. "It wasn't. I'd have noticed."

A memory smacked him in the face like wet washing in a sea breeze. Why hadn't he remembered before?

He stood, swaying.

The driver's door clunked shut. "You alright?"

He looked again at the wraparound screen. Had he hit upon the start of a solution to the mystery of what had happened the day that everyone else disappeared?

"Greg?" Fingernails tapped metal.

He turned to scan surrounding façades.

"Greg, what is it?" Fingernails drummed on metal.

Still turning, turning, his gaze swept up, from stubby balconies to cornices to flagpoles jutting from rooftops, and down.

Two metallic bangs. "Greg, for the love of…"

He stopped, steadied himself against the car.

Polly had her hands flat out before her on its roof.

"Do you ever get the feeling you're being watched?" he said.

She turned her hands over. "Sometimes."

He nodded, inhaled. "I know where to look."

Polly caught his arm, held him back. "Greg, Greg, talk to me." In the underground passageway, her voice had a slight stuck-in-a-drainpipe quality to it. "What are we doing down here?" She relaxed her grip a little. "I know we're looking for something. It'd just be nice if you actually told me what."

He panted.

He'd been running around at street level trying to find the way down and, resting only in the stinking lift, which, bizarrely, like the electronic signboard, worked, he'd been running around this maze of concrete corridors deep under the Trocadero. He'd battered down one wooden door with an empty gas canister he'd found up the corridor only to be confronted by another door that had required similar treatment.

He'd just dumped the canister back in the passageway. As he tried to move forwards again, her fingernails dug into his arm.

Burning up, sweating, he gulped, coughed. Trying to get his breathing under control, he bent over. "Okay. Okay…" He straightened up. "In Trafalgar Square… before we found each other… I think someone was watching me."

She looked at him with one eyebrow looping downwards, the other upwards, as per quotation marks.

"A CCTV camera followed me across the square." Her head tipped backwards fractionally as he pulled her with him. "This is the control room. And look." He pointed. "The lights are on."

Hands out, upturned. Those ironic eyebrows. "Yet no-one's home."

Strictly speaking, the lights weren't on. The wall of plasma screens was.

The locations they showed included Oxford Circus, Oxford Street, Piccadilly Circus, Trafalgar Square, the Queen's Walk. The lack of movement of any kind meant that at first he thought the shots must be stills but wavelets on a patch of Thames revealed them to be live video feed.

"So what are we looking for?" Her head jerked next to his. "They all look pretty deserted to me."

Was she really going to make him state the obvious? He gestured at the screens. "It's all places we've been."

She tutted, laughed. "Well, that's because the area they show is the area we're in."

He nodded in the direction of the main monitor. "Look, there's that supermarket." He'd only just recognized it.

He manoeuvred round the pulled-out chair and applied a little sideways pressure to a joystick. More of the plaza at the centre of the arcade slid into view. Back and up a bit and there was the sign over the entrance to the store: Tesco Metro.

He pulled the chair up to the back of his knees and lowered his backside.

He'd no sooner made himself comfortable than he shot upright in the seat. "Christ."

Polly gripped his wrist on the armrest. "What?"

"It's warm."

She took her hand away. "What is?"

He shifted, squirmed. "This seat."

"Urm... so?"

"Someone's been down here..." He pointed at the seat, then the ceiling. "Watching us up there."

"Who? How?" He glanced past her at the broken doors as she turned, gestured, this way, that way. "We would have bumped into them, heard them at the very least. The doors were locked, remember? And there's no-one out there." She indicated the telescreen showing the entrance they'd used on Wardour Street—just another empty backlot.

"Try it." He jumped up.

Slowly, she sat down.

He put his hand on her shoulder. "See, it's warm. Isn't it?"

She nodded.

He patted her shoulder. "Thank you."

"From *you*." She stood up.

He stared at her. "What?" He sighed. "Well, why was it warm when I sat on it?"

"Listen, if you'd said we were down here to rewind the video, I'd be taking this a lot more seriously."

Rewind? Of course, if they rewound the video far enough back, they'd find out what had happened to everyone. *Brilliant*!

He jumped back on the chair.

If the seat was warm now, he didn't notice. He perched on the edge of it.

His hands scrabbled at the controls.

The monitor showing the outside of the supermarket stopped, played the other way. Apart from an initial picture jerk as the camera snapped to its original position, everything looked the same backwards as it had forwards. He speeded things up. The screen went dark. He snorted when, daytime having come round a third time, a red Golf reversed in a loop around the square and stopped outside the supermarket. A man and a woman got out. The streak of auburn that followed could only be foxes chasing their own tails. The couple scooted in the supermarket with bulging bags, emerged with empty ones. They got in the car and backed out the way they'd come. He increased the speed, rewound faster and faster. Days strobed. His and Polly's cheeks drew closer as they leaned towards the monitor. She put her hand up to her neck. Back and back in time they went. Any second now there would be an explosion—of people.

"Oh, hell." He crumpled in the chair.

They'd reached the end, or the start. The video didn't go far enough back.

He should have come down here the day he'd spotted the camera on Trafalgar Square. If he had, he would know exactly what had happened to everyone.

Or maybe it was better not knowing. He slowly got to his feet.

He might not have solved the main mystery but at least he knew what the seat meant. *You're getting warmer.*

CHAPTER 9

BLACK ROSES

He lifted the net curtain of the hotel room, their new home, aside and glanced down at the empty street. He could never get used to it—the over-arching silence; the model-like stillness.

High above the classical façade of the building opposite, the early morning sun shone back, in a mosaic of fragments, from the windows of an office block.

A tap spat in the en suite. It sputtered and spurted. Pipes knocked.

Letting the net curtain drop, he brushed against the quilt as he crossed over to the cabinet his side of the bed. He tugged on the little brass knob of the drawer, plucked out the Gideon Bible and sat down in one of the two low armchairs. It curved round to enclose his backside. Resting his feet on the walnut table, he leafed through the toilet-paper-thin pages.

The loo flushed. More water ran. Pipes sang in the wall.

Polly stepped out of the inner door. Preceded by a billow of steam, clean, soapy scents issued from within.

"I don't know why you can't leave that lid down," she said. "A woman lives here too, you know."

He had to dig his front two teeth into his lower lip. *Probably for the same reason you can't leave it up.*

She'd gone in the bathroom in one mood, come out in another. Ah. Uh-oh. Her eyes flashed left and right, from the mound of clothes on the suitcase stand to the pile over the back of the second armchair, from the empty juice cartons and crisp packets that littered his bedside cabinet to the tin-can alley of the desk-cum-dressing table.

Remember, you love her, she loves you.

Pretend everything is fine and, before too long, it will be.

He sat up, smiled. "Hungry?"

"Yeah, call room service."

Polly's foot struck something metallic that rattled as it rolled across the room before knocking the skirting board.

"It's a tip in here," she said.

He looked around, nodded. "Yeah, we might have to move room soon."

Huffing, she bent and picked up a Pringles tube and tossed it in the bin, where it landed with a clang.

He smiled, with compressed lips. *Blokes cut corners. That's just what we do.*

Her gaze zigzagged about the ceiling, following a daddy-long-legs.

He thought of the half-squidged fly on the Golf's dashboard with a shudder. "Remember I asked if there was a being as superior to us as we are to flies, how would they regard us, and you said with contempt?"

She suppressed a yawn. "Yes."

"Enough to wipe us out?"

She pulled her gaze down from the ceiling. "'Us'?"

"Exactly. Have we been spared, or forgotten?"

Nodding at the Bible, she gestured expansively. "Perhaps we've inherited the Earth."

"You think?"

She swept over to the window. "Or maybe it's a special kind of punishment."

"Purgatory?"

She swiped the net curtain aside. "It certainly feels like it."

Feeling all tangled up inside, jarred, jangled, he took deep breaths. *Don't get drawn. Don't get drawn whatever you do.*

Upon laying the book down, he sat back, looked up. "You still haven't told me what you saw out there."

She let go of the net curtain. "I don't want to talk about it."

"O-kay." He got his phone out. Even though it had no bars of reception, he still hadn't quite given up the habit.

She spun to face him. "Oh, and now you'd rather play a game on your phone, I suppose?"

"Yeah, *Angry Birds*."

He regretted it as soon as he said it, and all through the silent breakfast that followed.

Maybe it was in defiance of the end of civilization, but they sat at a table in the hotel dining room eating cereal with long-life milk from white bone china bowls with silver-plated spoons.

Tinted glass all down one wall gave an anamorphic side-on view of the same street he'd observed from above, which at this time would normally have been thronged with traffic and people.

Puffing out his cheeks, he looked around at surrounding tables each set with the same polished cutlery, shiny plates, crisp napkins, unlit candle and desiccated black rose for meals that would never come.

Their spoons clicked against china.

Swallowing lumpy porridge, he studied the utensil he'd just put in his mouth. Polly spooned slower. He picked up the empty bowl, tilted it. She paused. Gripping either side of the glass tabletop, he tipped back in his chair until it was up on two legs. She put her spoon down.

"Greg, what are you doing?"

He lowered himself until his chair was back on four legs. "Is it me or is everything off about this dining room?"

Her head slid to one side. "What do you mean 'off'?"

"Well, everything's too small. I mean, look at this." He picked up his dinky teacup. He couldn't even fit a pinkie through the hole in the handle. He had to pinch the lobe to hold the cup. "And this teaspoon… I mean, it's minute." It wasn't that much bigger than a toothpick. Yet it was perfectly in proportion to his teacup and saucer, which were in turn perfectly in proportion to the cereal bowl and the rest of the dinner service out back. He touched one set of knuckles to the floor, without even having to lean very far. "The tables and chairs are showroom scale. I mean, I feel like I'm at a children's tea party or something."

She wiped her lips with her serviette. "Maybe it's just to

pack more punters in and feed them less."

"Probably. But don't you find it, well... odd?" On the narrow hotel stairs, his shoes had stuck out over the edge, clown-like.

Her head tilted the other way. "It's not really the most pressing issue at the moment."

"True. We need to try and work out what happened. I mean, nanotechnology running out of control? Deliberate genetic engineering of an invisible plague?"

"That wasn't—" Her eyes flicked away, flicked back. "But we survived."

"And that's the other side of the conundrum. The point is, there must be a rational explanation. There are forces at work here and I just can't put my finger on them." He prodded the arm of his chair. "It's—driving—me—crazy."

She snuffed. "Yeah, you and me both."

How could he miss what was right in front of him? The world had become a giant puzzle. He had the feeling that he really should know the answers if only he could dislodge them from his mind.

"Well, sorry to trouble you with the mundane boring essential things but are we going on the food run?"

"Now?"

She tapped the side of her bowl with a burgundy fingernail. "Well, unless you want that to be your last meal."

Something grazed Greg's consciousness. "Just a sec. I think I almost had it there."

She glanced outside. "It's dry, the light's good..."

"I know, I'm just trying to work out the implications of all this."

She scrunched up her serviette, threw it on the table. "And I'm trying to deal with the practicalities of it."

The serviette writhed, gradually unfolded itself.

He looked up. "Aren't you even interested in what's going on, what it all means?"

"Yeah, it's just we'll die too if we're not careful." She got to her feet.

He sighed, stood up. "Oh, fuck!" Pain cleaved his head. Either his skull had just cracked or whatever he'd hit it on had

Mark Kirkbride

He sank to his knees clutching his crown.

Blobs of colour floated by like exotic fish.

Polly's voice, getting nearer. "What is it?"

"Even the fucking ceiling's low. Or the—" jabbing backwards over his lowered head— "light fitting." He reared upright on his knees. "Oh, my God."

"Are you alright?" A hand landed on his shoulder.

"I hit my head."

"Yeah, I know you did." She leaned towards him, peered into his eyes. "You sure you're alright?"

His scalp stung and throbbed as if scalded. "No, I mean before."

She jerked in two directions, up and away.

He pictured his hand reaching into work's printer-cum-fax machine and fishing out a note.

The fax… With everything that had happened, he'd forgotten all about it. What if it was… What if it was relevant?

He turned and raised his head.

Polly stared at him from a few feet away. She had one arm bent at right angles across her stomach as if in a sling. Its hand supported her opposite elbow. The knuckles of that arm's hand supported her chin. Hands and elbows switched. "Greg, what?"

"When did it change? When did we cross the boundary from normal life to something else?"

Polly's head wobbled on the delicate construction her arms formed. "Oh, God, you won't let this go, will you?"

"How can I? We can't bury our heads." He rubbed his. "Not when we're finally getting somewhere."

She sniffed. "Getting somewhere?"

"I've been assuming everything changed the instant everyone else disappeared, that that was when we started living under altered conditions." He probed his crown with tentative fingers. Only now was the soreness wearing off enough to be able to do so. "But what if it was more gradual than that? What if there were things before then we didn't notice because we had no reason to?" He glanced up at the small black upturned dome of a security camera attached to the ceiling and dropped his voice. "I mean, take the day before everyone disappeared. I lost you, lost my job—"

"Maybe Milo felt threatened with you being footloose and fancy-free again." She flashed a rictus. "You can't really blame a pack leader for loving his mate and wanting to protect her from predatory males."

Greg sighed, lowered his pulsing head. *When you've finished the nature documentary...* He breathed in, lifted his gaze. "I even got struck by lightning. How we got separated. You name it, basically everything that could go wrong did. And it looked like bad luck, and maybe it was, but what if things started to change then?" He shuffled on his knees. "What if the clues were already there but coded, hidden in the quotidian? I think... I think I might have missed one."

"Clues?" The scaffolding of her arms collapsed. "So you're saying..."

"What if we haven't been forgotten? What if us surviving wasn't an accident? What if the whole thing was orchestrated? What if..." He swallowed so hard that his jaw clicked. "...it's all predicated on us?"

Her arms rose stiffly and fell, slapping her sides. "Now I know you've got concussion."

"It's knocked some sense into me if anything." He jumped up, with just the right degree of stoop. "I think whoever's responsible for all this..." He grabbed her hand, pulled her with him towards the door. "...tried to communicate with me."

Chapter 10

Ghost in the Machine

"Which way now?" said Polly.

He twisted left, right. Even without building work going on, his old place of work still had the power to bamboozle him. "This way."

When Simon gangled down the white corridor towards him, he had to shut out the memory.

It helped that Polly clonked along, in her ankle boots, at his side.

"So let me get this right," she said, "you think someone wrote to you?"

"Yes. 'Sweet nightmares' in a fax the very day before everyone disappeared. It has to mean something."

She turned away, shook her head. "Greg, you think everything means something." She turned back. "You're pursuing phantoms."

Phantoms? Was she in denial? Had she forgotten all the unearthly things they'd witnessed?

The heels of his shoes clicked as he stopped to let her go first, through the doorway.

Head down, he followed. "We've been looking at things the wrong way round. The question isn't why did everyone else disappear, it's why did we survive? What did we do, or not do, that caused us to be exempt?" He stared at his shoes as he scuffed across carpet tiles. "I mean, we outlived civilization. Yet why? I mean, why us?"

He bumped into her.

She'd stopped.

"What?" he said.

She pointed at the strip lights. "How come there's electricity here too?"

He jinked in front of her and led the way. "I'd like to say it's an example of the prevailing weirdness but, after the 7/7 bombings, the company rigged up a backup generator that comes on in the event of power failure. Mainly for the computers."

"Oh."

"Here it is." He blew a thin coating of dust from the printer that doubled as a fax machine.

She peered in the tray. "There's something in there."

"Yeah, I had a feeling there would be." He took it out.

"What does it say?"

He held it up, turned it towards her.

"'Go to the place where you had your first picnic and prepare to confront the person you most need to impress'?" She wrinkled her nose. "That's it? You brought me all the way over here for that?"

"It's for us."

She handed the sheet of paper back, snorted. "How do you know? It's got no name on it."

"It's the same style as the one that was addressed to me."

She folded her arms. "Who's it from then?"

"Well, that's what we need to find out."

Her arms slid undone, shot out at odd angles. "And we just forget the food run, I suppose?"

"As soon as we've checked on this, we'll go."

The hiss of a sigh as she turned.

He didn't get to tell her the question he hoped would soon be answered. *Have we been spared, or are we the unlucky ones?*

Pollen motes floated. Insects buzzed. Small pink and blue flowers threaded the long grass and blazed in the sunshine like knotted fairy lights. They shared the meadow-like park with elongated daisies, buttercups, dandelion flower heads, clocks and, here and there, banks of nettles and thistles.

They'd stuck to the pathways.

He stopped. "This is it."

He bent over with his hands on his knees while he got his breath back. The sun pumped its energy down on him. Rearing up, heat flowed over his forehead and shoulders.

Polly's chest rose and fell. "Er, you do know we sat that side?"

They stood beside a fountain on a circular pathway. Four paths radiated out from it between curving flowerbeds, segments of grass and copses. Yellow and orange marigolds held their own in the flowerbeds amid a tangle of weeds, some of which bore floppy blooms of staggering beauty. Twittering birds flitted from tree to tree.

He had his back to the fountain.

Polly faced him. "If what you say is correct and this is all about us, how do we know we haven't walked straight into a trap?"

He turned and took in the two exits on one side, the two on the other. "We're hardly hemmed in, are we?"

Her forehead crinkled. "But if you're right, what about this makes you not want to be 100 miles away from here?"

He shrugged. "We need to solve the mystery."

She heaved a sigh.

"So what do we do now?"

"Wait for a sign of some kind, I guess." He checked his phone.

Still no reception.

"Well, at least it gives us time to talk, I suppose."

He put his phone away. "What about?"

"What went wrong."

"Well, that's what we're trying to find out."

Her forefinger wagged back and forth between them. "No. With us."

His neck jolted. *Oh, not now, Polly. Please.* "Do you really want to do this here?" He lowered his voice in case they weren't alone.

She carried on at her normal volume. "Oh, am I being too impatient?" If anything, her voice got louder, and her arms swung. "Too demanding perhaps? Ah, but, yes, of course..."

The dry, hard sob of a laugh. "That's probably why you didn't want to marry me."

His chest deflated. His shoulders dropped. "If I hadn't been scared then I wouldn't have been taking it seriously." He breathed in. "Besides, I thought we were in a safe space where I could express my feelings." He drew himself up to his full height, turned his hands outwards. "You asked me, I was honest."

"Yeah, I guess it was totally unreasonable of me to check that you actually did want to marry me."

He threw his head back. "This is what I mean." Spinning round, he shot glances down each of the other pathways to check no-one was heading their way. Polly came back into vision. He stopped. "You tell me to communicate, then when I do, that's when everything goes wrong. It's like the world turns... spongy."

"Spongy? What's that supposed to mean?"

Jesus. Numbers never let him down like this. "I struggle to say the right thing, alright? Period."

"Oh, my God!"

Damn. He held a hand up. "No, no, I didn't mean... All I meant..."

Her gaze widened, veered from side to side.

His hand fell away as he looked to the left and watched brown leaves fall from the trees in ones and twos and threes. Some got whisked away by squally gusts. Others circled, rose up and sank, came to rest and then got whipped away again.

"What's—"

He glanced back to Polly, who stood staring in the opposite direction.

He turned the same way and saw bare trees with juicy shoots and bright buds. Two brilliant green parakeets streaked by. Wave upon wave of birdsong filled his ears, with, lower, closer to, the druggy buzz of a bee.

His gaze shot back to Polly, who this time gaped over his shoulder.

He whirled around.

On the other side of the fountain, it snowed. Flakes as

big as feathers rocked to and fro as they fell from a grey sky. The ground whitened. Already, budless, leafless trees stood trimmed with snow along the upper surface of every branch and twig.

Nearer to, precipitation slipped from the sky as sleet.

"This isn't right." She swallowed, with a dry click. "It isn't right."

"What do you mean?" Crossing one of the radial paths, he kicked through crackly leaves. The tree-stripping wind goosebumped his arms. "It's…"

Crossing the next path, he experienced the shock of cold. "Am-m-mazing." He hugged himself to keep warm as the snow came down thicker and thicker. Large flakes attached themselves to his T-shirt.

The fountain sprayed every way but his. Ice glazed this quarter of the basin.

On the opposite side, Polly stood with her back to lush green trees bathed in vivid light.

In his quadrant of the park, the covering of snow acquired an extra dimension that his footsteps compressed.

He scraped together a handful, shaped it into a ball that was ice-cream cold and lobbed it over the fountain.

It fell just short of her.

She folded her arms. "I really believe you're enjoying this."

She spoke to him as if he'd recently murdered a close member of her family.

He let his arm drop. "I wouldn't go that far."

"Oh, come on, you must be chuffed to bits."

He turned away.

Even if every answer led to another question, he'd proved the faxes were relevant. The printer was the key. They weren't alone. But he didn't expect congratulations. She disagreed with him on principle.

Caught in his thoughts, he'd wandered several feet. Sucking sounds came from the path he'd just crossed. Leaves swirled around him. The wind cuffed and biffed him.

"You see? This is your trouble, you just don't care."

What the hell—?

He swung round. "And this is yours, constantly carping."

Her neck gave a whiplashy jerk. "God, you can be insensitive sometimes."

"Me insensitive?" *Bloody brilliant.* If the mixer tap of emotions usually went off halfcocked somewhere between hot and cold, now it blasted out hot. "You're the one bleating 'me, me, me' all the time. And you don't communicate in plain terms. Oh, no, that'd be too simple." He batted away a dead leaf. "It's like, something's wrong, so everything's wrong. Well, what—is—wrong?"

"You." He was the one to jib this time. "You're an arsehole."

"Fuck's sake, Polly."

"Please don't shout at me!"

"Oh, yeah, I forgot. I'm not allowed to say anything, and you can say anything you like." She seemed to think that whatever she said was a true expression of her feelings at that moment and therefore okay. He threw his hands up. "And now I suppose you're going to use your get-out-of-jail-free card."

Her mouth made a succession of plosive sounds that consisted almost entirely of b's and p's. "You really... Do you... Oh, what's the point?" She about-turned in her boots.

"Hey, where are... Where are you going? You can't just walk off."

"Watch me."

"I'm sorry the world's ended," he wanted to shout. *No doubt that's my fault as well.*

"Why now, Polly?" he called after her. "Just when we're finally getting somewhere." He gestured at the park. "We're so close to solving this. And I'll happily discuss everything with you. Just not today, okay?"

She'd stopped, turned back. "Greg, do you know what day it is today?"

He sighed. Is this *really relevant*? "Tuesday."

She shook her head.

"Thursday?"

"It's our wedding day—in a parallel universe where you actually loved me enough to go through with it."

As had happened so many times throughout their

relationship, what they were arguing about wasn't really what they were arguing about.

"Oh."

The ground had shifted, with him on it. Maybe that was why he'd ended up back in snow. It had got in his shoes and melted, soaking and numbing his feet. He clamped his raw hands under his armpits.

She stood half akimbo with one boot out behind her, ready to pivot. "'Oh'? That's all you've got to say?" A coruscating look.

He hung his head. Off to the side, at the junction between summer and autumn, the flowers died by degrees.

His brain beat like a heart.

All around him, the wind whined and howled like the ghost of a dead dog. Flakes blizzarded. Lying snow deepened and duned.

By the time he looked up, she'd gone.

He pulled the fax out of his pocket, unfolded it and read it again: "Go to the place where you had your first picnic and prepare to confront the person you most need to impress."

It had been a confrontation alright, just not with the person he'd expected.

He screwed up the piece of paper, threw it on the ground. The wind caught it and carried it away.

The seasons passed in quick succession as he strode through them.

CHAPTER 11

DRAFTS OF THE FUTURE

Greg let himself in at the main entrance and charged across the foyer, up the corridor, up the stairs. He burst into Admin and stomped over to the printer. Yes, he'd walked right into the park fiasco, but the no-show had been a set-up.

Maybe Polly was right, and he was a monomaniac who concentrated on one thing at a time at the expense of all else. Yet they faced a power beyond comprehension, which, although, so far, had merely toyed with them, had demonstrated that it could do anything it wanted. Anything at all. Who knew what it ultimately had planned for them?

He leaned over the side of the fax machine.

A stack of A4 paper filled the tray. *Bloody hell.*

He lifted it out, read the cover note: "First Draft."

Strange.

He turned the page.

"*Someone else's dreams.* Greg couldn't remember them now but that was what they'd been like—someone else's dreams."

His heart ba-boom, ba-boom, ba-boomed. What the—? His maw threshed. What kind of sick joke was this? He read on. About the fax. The lightning. The CCTV camera tracking him. The disembodied hand. The gnomic messages. The floating eyeball. The wall with an ear. Piccadilly Circus' lit advertising screen. The warm seat in the CCTV control room. The manuscript even came right up to date: four seasons in one park. How had whoever had written this got it down so quickly? How had they known everything that had happened including—and this was the creepiest bit of all—his feelings? He ploughed on. The fountain altercation didn't happen. In this make-believe version, he won Polly round.

The old ache in his side returned. A pang for what might have been.

Twisting at the waist, he leaned back against the printer, rested his elbow on it.

It chuntered into life.

Internal fans whooshed.

Had he hit the start button? Was it reprinting the whole thing again? What came out followed Draft 1 word for word, yet the cover said, "Draft 2."

While it printed, he flicked through the rest of Draft 1, which described how their lives might have gone if he hadn't messed things up a second time. The ending saw them settling down and doing their level best to repopulate the world beginning with a small seaside town. On the last page, they strolled along the pier hand in hand with a baby boy strapped to her chest, a little girl's hand in his, brightly coloured lights dangling between Victorian lampposts and stars coming out above and around them. Visible through gaps between planks, the sea rolled in as they walked out.

He let the last of the manuscript fall and, along with it, this tantalizing glimpse of how the future might have unspooled.

What was its purpose, to torment him? The walk on the pier that had never happened left a chasm inside him. Was the power behind the printer trying to split them up or get them back together?

Hungry for answers, he snatched up what was ready of Draft 2. Hot off the press, it had reached the bit about the park. His soul curled up at the edges as, this time, the exchange played out exactly as it had in real life. Polly left him standing by the fountain; he came back here, found Draft 1, read it; the printer went into overdrive with Draft 2 and after skimming through Draft 1 and reading the ending, he switched to the new draft, read that instead—the manuscript he held in his hands now.

He spun round and glared up at the bug-eyed ceiling camera.

Taking a step towards it, his foot slipped on the papers carpeting the floor and he fell back against the hot fax machine, which continued spewing text.

He pulled himself up, turned back round and plucked out the next page, which described his stagger and recovery.

Bloody hell. Is it predicting the future?

"Christ. Is it predicting what's going to happen?" he read.

He flinched, dropped the sheet of A4.

The printer stopped.

He patted it, laughing.

Of course, how could it actually know the future?

He wiped his brow with his handkerchief, and noticed a button flashing on the control panel.

The printer hadn't stopped. It just needed more paper.

He placed another wad in the feeder tray and put the flashing button out of its misery. Pickup rollers, cogs and clutches clicked and clunked, and the machine was off again, projecting their lives forwards from this moment, this time plausibly. Endless fights. Elemental obstacles. No author had ever held his attention so raptly. Yet the printer churned out copy faster than he could read it. First he had to skip whole chunks, then whole pages, as he kept falling behind. He lifted out the final section. The printer had stopped. The fans had cut out. What did it hold for Polly and him? As far as he could make out, it ended on a hill, the one near where her parents had lived, with the two of them surrounded at sunset.

In a world without other people? By what?

His heart shook him with its pounding. He wanted to find out more but needed to warn Polly.

He set off at a sprint.

"Polly," he called.

He leapt from toehold to toehold up the hotel's stubby stairs. He thudded round landings and the bend half way up each flight.

"Polly."

He slid the key card down its slot and pushed the door open against its oil-dampened spring.

"Polly, you won't believe—"

She wasn't in the bedroom.

"Polly?"

With the tip of a finger, he tapped the bathroom door ajar, on darkness.

He left their room and thump-thump-thumped back down the stairs—all three flights.

Momentum carried him as far as the lobby, where, heart pumping, he stopped, stood swaying.

"Polly," he shouted.

Nothing.

This wasn't what the last book-length fax said would happen. *That's good, isn't it?* Draft 2 was wrong. They wouldn't die on the hill.

That still left him with a major problem. *Where's Polly?*

Standing on paper, he leaned into the printer's invisible heat-field. *The world's ended and I'm still coming to work...* But his hunch paid off. Another manuscript filled the tray.

He snatched it up, Draft 3.

He flicked through its warm pages. *Come on, come on, come on...* Polly going off had rendered Draft 2 obsolete. *Where is she?* Radical action on their part could nudge fate in a different direction. *Tell me.* While unstable over time, short term the manuscripts' predictions proved accurate. *A clue. Something. Anything...* With the right information, he could use Draft 3 against itself.

Yes. It worked. He found out where she'd gone.

Oh, God, not there.

Not now...

For a moment he could see himself from the outside, clasping the manuscript—the story of their lives, written.

Rearranging his grip, he noticed he'd smudged the cover page.

His thumb came away with a black mark on it. *The ink's still wet.* He left the manuscript on the side. *There's still time to change things, if I hurry.*

The car's sun visor creaked as Greg lowered it.

Don't worry, love. Foot on the accelerator pedal of the Alfa Romeo he'd commandeered, he extended his right leg and the vehicle whined like a Formula One car. *I'm coming.*

His head bumped against the cushioned headrest.

A white plastic bag floated across the dual carriageway like the ghost of a small child as the heath erased all trace of London. *Now I'm even commuting.*

Why did she have to head down to Bedgley?

Where else would she head for? Bedgley was home.

How come she ended up on the hill, the very last place she should go with whatever it was that was out there, that was coming? Draft 2 had them sat on the hill watching their last sunset together. In Draft 3, Polly watched that same sunset alone.

A shudder ran down him. Where was he in that version? *Already dead?*

He gripped the steering wheel tighter.

Hopefully he'd averted that scenario. Her heading down there would bring them both to the hill. The original prophecy would have its fulfilment. Yet he could only think of one thing worse than dying together.

Dying apart.

A hawk hung as if on a string, tilted its wings and dived.

Black bin-bag-like shreds fluttered from barbed wire next to fuzzy bits of wool. Beyond, black-legged sheep flocked this way and that.

Each time he came over a hill, he fixed his eyes on the furthest bit of dual carriageway he could see. If the hill was high enough, this was where a band of Tarmac disappeared over the horizon. He willed himself towards that point.

He and Polly had deviated from the script and changed things before. They could do so again. He had until nightfall to win her back.

Sun flared from above.

Another creak as he lowered the visor a little more.

Heart thumping, breathing all out of kilter, Greg made it to the top of the hill. *Oh, God.* Now that he could see the sun again, he looked down on it, or felt as if he did. It dazzled him, turned tatters of cloud pink. Those across it caught alight. They blazed yellow, orange, gold.

Polly sat on the grass facing the sun exactly as Draft 3 had described. He took in the hut he'd spent a restless night in a few fields away and, the distance between the two foreshortened from this vantage point, Bedgley's church tower beyond that. He couldn't see it, but he could feel the pull of the sea from beyond the horizon to the left.

He strode towards Polly. "What are you doing?"

"What does it look like?" She continued staring at the fiery sky. She must have heard the car. He stopped at her side. She did look round then, if not up. "How did you know I'd be here?"

"I had a little help." He could explain about the printer later, once he'd got her away from here. He held a hand out. "We have to go."

Her face swerved back to the front. She remained sitting with her knees drawn up, her arms round them and one hand gripping the other wrist. "It was too lonely in the bungalow. I used to come up here as a girl."

With an eye on the sinking sun, he extended his hand farther. "Love, we really do need to go."

"See, you're not even interested."

He lowered his head to scratch the back of it. "I am, love, I am." He lifted it. "But trust me, we have to leave or that…" He pointed at the conflagration. Even small outlying clouds now glowed like hot coals. "…will be the last sunset we ever see."

"Why?"

"Just come down to the car. Please. I'll explain everything on the way. I promise. We just need to—"

"On the way where?" Holding her hair out of her eyes, she looked up at him.

He grabbed her other hand. "Anywhere but here. Believe me, you don't want to be up here when that sun goes down." He pulled.

"Why?" She stretched her legs out, dug her heels in, hung from his arm.

He shuffled to the right. "Because..."

Her backside swung in an arc several inches off the ground. He shuffled to the left. "Can...?"

She swung back the other way.

Apart from gouging out a divot of earth, her heels hadn't budged.

Still pulling. "Can you please, just for me..." Panting. "Even if just for today..." He paused. "Concentrate on the fact that I love you and forget that I express it so badly."

"I don't dispute that you love me." A cracked smile. He could hardly believe it. *Progress.* "I just don't think you love me enough."

Letting out a sigh that lowered her back onto the ground, he glanced behind him.

Lava flowed in the sky.

He should have brought the MS. Then again, would he really want her reading his thoughts?

He cleared his throat. "Listen, okay? The fate of the human race depends on us getting it right instead of arguing over trivial stuff."

"'Trivial stuff'?" She wrenched her hand away.

He straightened up. "I mean trivial in the grand scheme of things..." Another glance over his shoulder at the molten sky. *Damn, damn, damn.*

"So you're acting purely in the interests of the human race now?"

"We are the human race!" He could feel the muscles in his cheeks tautening and slackening as he ground his teeth together and breathed in and out through his nose. "Listen, together we live, hopefully, alone we die, definitely."

"And that's the only reason you want to stay with me?"

"No!" He shook his head, violently, and sighed. "This is coming out all wrong."

She looked at him.

He looked at her. "I..." He closed his mouth, opened it. "You were right. We need to rebel." Her face whipped away. Even he knew that he might be permanently damaging his personal cause by appealing to logic instead of love but if they stayed up here any longer then they wouldn't have lives singly or together. "Listen… The printer at work started printing manuscripts. They accurately predict the future." Her face half turned towards him. "Our future, according to existing conditions." He saw her blink. "Each time we deviate from the plan, the current manuscript has to be completely rewritten to accommodate that change." Her eyes widened. "So the bad news is that we die on this hill shortly after the sun goes down. Because whoever's doing this to us isn't interested in getting us back together or even in splitting us up. He wants to kill us." She shook her head as if trying to shake out the thoughts he was busy planting there. "The good news is that if we leave"—he glanced out to the west—"right now, then maybe, just maybe, we can sidestep our destinies."

Her head wobbled.

Her mouth goldfish-blebbed.

It worked. She clambered to her feet, kicked off her ankle boots and picked them up. One elbow went up and out and she dashed with him, down the hill.

She even took his hand at one point where the slope steepened and the creases in the hillside got close enough for them to be able to jump from one to another.

At the bottom, in the shadow of pylons, they ran, rustling, through wheat.

She said something to him as they approached the road, only he didn't catch it.

"What?" he shouted.

"The car…"

"Car what?"

He looked up. Ahead of their old Vauxhall was the Alfa Romeo, on the move.

It went past, without a driver.

It's started…

He threw a hand out.

No, we can't be stranded. He sprinted towards the wooden fence. *Not…* He vaulted over it. *…here.*

Even as he gained on the car, he couldn't hear the engine. Just the tread of the tires and choppy breathing—his.

Catching up with the vehicle, running alongside it as it rolled up the hill, he tried the driver's door. *Bloody—* He got his keys out, unlocked the car, pulled then pushed the door, hooked an elbow over it, hopped onto the sill of the opening, shimmied in, yanked on the handbrake. He slammed against the steering wheel.

Prizing himself off it, he got the door open.

It had shut itself.

He climbed out.

Bent over with his hands on his knees, trying to get his breath back, he looked up. "I left the... I left the handbrake off."

Polly picked her way along the lane. "But it rolled upwards."

"I know."

Spotting a red Coke can on the verge, he picked it up and lay it down on its side in the road.

It wobbled a bit as if deciding what to do before that too started trundling up the incline.

"See?" he said.

She ran up to, stood over, the rolling can. "What is it?" She peered up the lane, down it, turned to the hill. "An optical illusion?" She leaned to one side. "The surrounding landscape makes the road look like it tilts one way when really it tilts the other?"

"Some kind of magnetic anomaly maybe?" Greg shook his head. "It almost doesn't matter anymore. Normal conditions are breaking down."

Dense shadow fell across the field like early twilight or a first draft of darkness. *It's coming.*

He swallowed. "Polly..." Running back to the driver's door. "Polly, get in the car. We have to go, now."

CHAPTER 12

GOD GAMES

Birds flickered above the field opposite. They wheeled, gyred. Up. Down. Some black, others white. Those on the ground strutted a few steps, rotated, so as not to bump into one another. Seagulls on one side, crows on the other, intermingling in the middle, ranged out like a vast chess game in progress.

"Which way, which way?" he said.

Polly turned her hands over. "Where to?"

They'd stopped at a junction. Right led to the sea, left to the motorway. The seaside had featured in one of the earlier drafts, yet they couldn't afford to be predictable. Besides, London had the printer.

He took a left.

They barrelled down a curving green tunnel. The roads had narrowed because the verges had widened. Fronds, whole bushes, overhung Tarmac. Higher up, beeches either side of the road embraced. One day the roads would shut completely. They'd have to force their way through or find a way round—if they survived that long.

As they left the trees behind and the road straightened, a blood-orange sun stared back at him from his mirrors.

It had dipped beneath the streamers of cloud, staining them red. Now it closed with the horizon.

Skeleton hunched, he gripped the steering wheel tighter, extended his right foot farther, getting the two of them as far away as possible before night fell.

Why's he doing this to us? Did their continued existence after the end of the world constitute a wrinkle that needed smoothing out?

Polly hooked her elbow over her seat, stared out through the back window at the distant bump of the hill.

A glance at him as she straightened up. "So, are we safe again now or what?"

Gazing into his rear-view mirror at the sun a little too long left a cut-out at the centre of his vision when he looked away.

He wrenched his head up and down. "For the time being." Anything more than that would be a lie.

Her fingers pitter-pattered on her knees. "And how long is that exactly?"

Jesus. Normally she didn't want to talk about all this stuff. Then again, normally he did. As far as he was concerned, he'd already told her how things stood. Now he had to make up time, distance. "The next draft starts being printed pretty much as soon as the present one becomes redundant, so it's probably being prepared as we speak." *We can get away from the hill. We can't hold back the night.*

The sun balanced on the horizon. With every mile, shadows lengthened.

She folded her arms across her seatbelt. "What's going to happen now?"

"I don't know."

"You must have some idea."

Let me at least get us out of here first. He ungripped and gripped the steering wheel, sighed. "That's the whole point. We haven't just changed the course of events this time, we've given our own personal deaths the slip. We're in some kind of nether region."

They joined the dual carriageway. *I'm wearing this road out.*

Slowly, the sun merged with the horizon.

He put his foot down as far as it would go.

"So let me get this right…" Polly picked husks of wheat from her dress. "Each draft is a revised version of our lives as they're actually going to pan out unless or until we throw a curveball or a wobbly?"

"Yes." He looked round at her. "You've actually been doing

a pretty good job of that so far."

Her head turned sharply towards his.

He faced front. "The park was him revealing his hand to us." He veered onto the hard shoulder to avoid an upside-down van. "But that was benign. Nice even. What you have to imagine is that kind of power deliberately setting out to do us harm."

"Why him?"

"What?"

"You said 'him'. How do you know it's a he?" She slapped her thigh. "Oh, no, wait, you're right, only a man would show off like that."

He peered, at an angle, into the rear-view mirror.

The sun had disappeared for the time being behind the shoulder of a nearby hill.

He flicked the headlights on.

The dual-carriageway ahead shimmered like a carpet of fish scales.

"What's that?" he said.

Polly sat up. "It looks like..."

He braked. Polly shot forwards. They went over whatever it was. He braked harder. Polly braced herself against the extension of the dashboard. Slithering one way, then the other, they slewed towards the central reservation. Polly clung to her door, folded up against it. The moment hung, endless.

They rocked to a halt.

Polly pushed herself off her door, he let go of the steering wheel.

"What the hell is that?" he said.

As the throaty engine idled, the thin layer blazed in the headlights like inside-out stockings.

He put his window down, leaned out.

Closer to, in the gap between the car and the central reservation, the unidentified items looked more like tubes of bubble wrap.

"Wait, I've seen them before," she said. "On a TV program."

"And?"

"It's snakeskins."

"Snakeskins?" He glanced out of the window, looked at her.

"Well, where are the snakes?"

She nudged his arm. "Drive."

"What?"

"Drive." Jab, jab. "Go!"

"Alright, alright." Something out of one of her nightmares? He knew all about those. Only now they didn't even have to fall asleep.

He straightened up. They roared off.

In his mirrors, he had a clear line of sight to the horizon through flying snakeskins tinged red. From the sun?

Where's the...?

The sun had gone.

Other than the car's front beam and rear ruddiness, the dashboard provided the only other source of light.

They joined the motorway. Colour drained from the landscape. While it remained daytime in the sky, the angle of light tilted upwards, tipped backwards. The lit portion of the sky retracted like a huge canopy closing, leaving nothing but blackness ahead. Had he really thought this through? The flight away from the hill meant a rush towards darkness.

The advance of ink-black clouds extinguished the first pinpricks of starlight one by one.

Only the faintest of glows from the rear horizon provided any evidence that the sun had ever been there.

The day closed like an eyelid.

Night came and still it kept on getting darker.

The headlights only illuminated so far.

In the splash of full beam, something separated from the verge. It slid, whipped, towards them across the road. The tires squealed as he braked, and they leaned one way, the other, as he swerved to avoid it. All head and tail, no arms or legs, it reared up at the side of the car, stared with lidless eyes and flicked its tongue at them as if it had a fish tail in its mouth.

He returned his foot to the accelerator pedal and they left it behind.

"Christ," exploded from his mouth. His head jerked with the force with which he uttered it.

Polly shuddered. "Was that a...?"

"I think we can safely say we're no longer in his blind spot. We're into a whole new script now." He splayed his fingers, drove with the heels of his hands for a moment as his thoughts skipped, skirred like stones thrown across water. "Who was that... Who was that philosopher that said if one knew all the conditions, everything could be predicted?"

"Holbach?"

"Holbach, yes." Greg nodded vigorously. With his hands stuck to the wheel, it was all he could do. That and look round. "Well, that's how he operates."

"So he knows where we're going?"

"He knows everything."

Her voice shot up an octave. "He's omniscient?"

He nodded. "With a built-in delay. We have to live in that moment."

A dip-flash up ahead.

He craned forwards. *What was that?*

A moment later a vein of light pierced the sky.

"What if he's omnipotent as well? What if..." She twisted to face him. "What if free will's an illusion and he's controlling our minds? What if everything we do, everything we say, everything we think, is determined? Like human robots."

He slapped the wheel. "No, he's not omnipotent. The scrapped drafts prove that. And we do have free will."

She faced front. "Within limits."

He let his head fall back, roll forwards. "Within limits, yes, but there wouldn't be any point if we didn't have any. He'd be playing against himself." A quick peep at her profile—dimly visible in the glow from the dashboard. "He can control pretty much everything else. We're the wild cards."

A distant rumble.

"So what do we do?"

"All we can do. Keep on trying to stay one step ahead. Assert our free will." He turned back to her. "What's that Old English proverb? 'The snake can swallow its body but not its head.'"

Her eyes drilled into his. "How can someone remove everyone else, leave just us"—even as he looked away, her eyes continued boring into his face—"know what we're going to do before we do it and do all those things? And how come we never see him? Who the hell is he?"

Light speared the sky.

"I don't know."

"But he's..."

A detonation cracked the firmament.

He ducked involuntarily. "Playing God, yes."

She left a pause. "Just playing?"

"Unfortunately for us, either way the consequences are the same."

Lightning forked from dark clouds. Thunder boomed and reverberated.

He had to shout. "The apocalypse missed us before. Now I think it's about to catch up with us."

Outside the wind roared, buffeted them. Thankfully the Alfa Romeo responded like an extension of himself. Fighting back with twitches and yanks of counter-pressure, he wore it into battle like a suit of armour, an exoskeleton. Its snug interior made it easy to forget that, any second, road could rend metal, metal could tear flesh.

Lightning flashed, illuminating cows in a field off to the left, what was left of them. They weren't just dead. Their bones had been stripped bare. *Eaten?*

By what?

Polly groaned.

Lightning strobed. Ribcages on the slope opposite—smaller, or just farther away? —clawed the sky.

Polly clapped her hand over her mouth.

Rain pelted the car. It rapped like small arms fire against the windscreen, drummed on the bonnet and roof. How come the windscreen didn't break? Forced to slow down, he flicked the wipers on full.

Whenever they passed under a bridge, the fusillade stopped for a moment, before battering metal and glass again.

The rain turned red. Thick crimson streaks hit the windscreen and the wipers smeared them left, right, left, right.

"Fuck, fuck, fuck." He had to slow right down.

"Is that...?"

"The blood of all the dead."

Polly's head shot round.

He dipped his. *Christ, where did that come from?*

"What's happening?" she shouted over the din.

Eyes on the road, eyes on the road... "We disobeyed his plan. Now he's visiting hell upon us."

Greg found the windscreen washer, used it.

In a pulse of light, accompanied by a massive boom, he glimpsed a silhouette on a motorway bridge as stationary as an Antony Gormley statue.

"See that...?" He swung round to Polly.

Blood spattered the windows. Thunder rolled in, out.

Polly gripped her seat.

She hadn't heard him.

The wipers metronomed but he had to use the windscreen washer again and again in order to be able to see anything at all.

The rat-tat-tatting stopped as they passed under the bridge. It didn't restart. Slowly, the windscreen cleared.

Thunder came from behind them now.

The blood-storm had passed.

"We survived," she said.

"Somehow I don't think things have even started yet."

Her face bobbed in his peripheral vision. "Well, what was that, then?"

"The prelude to the backlash." Peering from mirror to mirror, he deployed the rear window washer. Thanks to the rear wiper temporarily compounding the smears, he couldn't even see the bridge, let alone anything else.

"Look out," cried Polly.

He'd crossed over into some roadworks. At least, he was in between two sets of traffic cones. He must have veered to the left because cones that side went flying. Then he must have overcorrected because cones his side flipped and bounced. Or were the cones either side getting closer?

Running out of lane, he hit the brakes.

They stopped. He pulled up the handbrake. "What the hell..."

Polly shrugged out of her seatbelt. She opened her door. "That's it!"

She jumped out.

He leaned across her seat. "Hey, where are you going?"

Polly kicked a cone out of the way. "If he can communicate with us, maybe we can communicate with him."

"What are you talking about?"

She ran across the hard shoulder over to an orange SOS phone and picked up the handset.

A few more squirts of the rear washer and the back window had cleared. He could make out the gantry of the bridge, just about. Only, the gaps between lightning flashes had grown longer and longer. In the meantime, in a contest with only one possible outcome, darkness had won. It infiltrated everything.

He turned back to Polly and the black pines behind her.

"What do you want from us?" she shouted. "You sick bastard. Who do you think you are? Why can't you just leave us alone?"

He checked the mirrors just in time. In the play of distant lightning, he could see the outline of the bridge. He should have been able to see the figure on it. It wasn't there.

His heart punched him from the inside. "Polly."

"I know you can hear me, you—"

"Polly!"

"What?"

"Get back in."

"What? Why?"

"Hurry. Now. Get in."

She held the receiver to her ear for a moment, hung up.

"What is it?" She ran over, jumped in.

"Did you hear anything?"

"What?"

"At the other end."

"Yes."

"What?"

"Breathing."

He slammed his foot down on the accelerator pedal. The uprights of their seats caught them. Their headrests knocked them on the back of the head. Cones scattered like skittles. Others got crumpled under the tires.

In one smooth motion, Polly pulled her seatbelt in from the outside and looked at him as it slotted into place. "What is it?"

"I think…"

"Yes?"

"I saw someone."

"What? You mean we're not alone?" Her voice rose. "But that's fantastic."

He didn't reply.

"Isn't it?"

"Not necessarily."

"What do you mean not necessarily? You think it was *him*?"

"I don't know."

"Well, why are we…" She gestured at the rushing motorway. Her hand came to rest on his arm. "Greg, who was it?"

"God knows."

Her hand dropped to his leg. "It might be another survivor." She patted his thigh. "We should pick him up."

Keeping his hands locked on the steering wheel, he gave a quick turn of his head. "Trust me, okay? Something about him wasn't right."

"Maybe the loneliness sent him crazy." She took her hand away. "I can relate to that."

Another glance. "Well, me too." For a moment, she'd almost sounded positive. He hadn't heard her like that in quite a while. It's just, he'd read the manuscript and there was one word in particular he couldn't get out of his head. "*Surrounded.*" "Listen, something's coming. I don't know what. All I know is, things won't be as they were before."

PART 2

CHAPTER 13

THE OTHER SIDE OF THE MIRROR

A hand jiggled his shoulder. Polly's voice: "Greg, Greg, they're back."

Head humming with numbness, Greg had no idea what she was on about. He groaned a response and kept his eyes screwed shut. Now he just had to catch a lift on a passing dream.

Sleep brushed him but didn't take him.

The mattress bounced, he bounced on it, as Polly shook him. "Did you hear me? I can hardly believe it. They're back."

His mouth struggled to form words as if unfamiliar with their precise shapes. "What—do—you—mean? Who's—back?"

"Everyone. Well, they're coming back."

He opened his eyes.

Polly must have undrawn the curtains. Light flooded the hotel room.

She pointed at the window. "Look."

Another delay as he processed this.

She pulled him up into a sitting position and kept on pulling. He shuffled to the side of the bed, strode off it and stumbled round one of the armchairs over to the window. She stopped at the last second, propelled him towards it.

Oh, God. What now?

With one cheek pressed up against the glass, he swivelled that eye downwards.

In the street below, he spotted a person moving along the pavement. Then another. *My God…* And another. *She's right.* A pause that went on and on. *That's it?* No, two more in tandem.

People. Not a lot but a trickle.

Hair brushed his other cheek as she joined him at the window. "You see? It's finally over. We can go home."

His brain woke up. "Wait, what, no. We were supposed to die on that hill yesterday. He wouldn't just…"

"I don't understand it any more than you do." She opened the window. "But the important thing is, they're back." She stuck a shoulder out.

"What are you doing?"

She started waving. "Hey, we're up…"

He yanked her away by the elbow.

"Oi… Ow."

"Ssh, stay down. Stay down."

"Greg, you…"

He peeped around the curtain. The only figure on the street, a woman, carried on her way.

"Polly, we need to be sure first."

She shook his hand off. "Sure about what? You're just being paranoid."

"No, I'm not. I'm…" He let his hand drop. "Okay, how about this? We go out in the car and just observe to begin with. If all seems well, then we'll do it your way."

She sighed.

"Okay."

Ten minutes later, they raced up the dark ramp from the hotel's carpark and, stomachs vaulting, chassis flumping on the front suspension, out into daylight.

"Where are they?" he said.

"There's some." She pointed.

He locked the doors of the Nissan 4x4 and set off in the direction of a blond man, brunette woman and red-haired little girl. All three of them had an unironed appearance, and their hair looked as if it hadn't seen a hairbrush for weeks.

Hugging the curb, he tried to stay well back. The Nissan's overdrive insisted otherwise.

Now he had to brake so as not to get ahead of them.

Polly folded her arms. "This is a waste of time. We could

be out talking to them, asking them what happened, where they've been."

"Trust me, okay?"

At the next crossroads and without speaking, the child turned left, and the woman turned right. Only the man carried straight on.

Greg followed him.

After the crossroads, an Indian restaurant and a row of shops, the man turned up an alley. Concrete bollards barred the way.

Damn. Greg kept on going.

Polly's fingers tapped her kneecaps. "What are we doing exactly?"

He increased the pressure on the accelerator pedal and the Nissan went back up through the gears. "I want to find out how many there are and where they're going."

She sighed. "Wouldn't you be better finding out where they're coming from?"

On the next street, one loose group walked up one side of the street, another down the other.

He had to admit, she had a point. He took a couple of lefts and spotted one, two, three loners. Yet heading towards him, they passed even quicker. He had to guess which way they'd come.

He glanced in the rear-view mirror at their receding forms.

"Have you noticed that not one of them has paid us any attention?" he said.

"Well, you did choose a vehicle with tinted windows."

"I know but they've ignored us completely."

"They seem tired. Besides, they probably don't know we didn't go with them."

The numbers thinned out and he went from monitoring them to monitoring the sludgy movements in his head. "What did you see?"

Polly's head swung round. "When?"

"When you were alone. You saw things."

A flick of her hair. "You don't want to know."

"No, tell me. I do. That's why I'm asking. What did you see?"

She scratched her neck. Her hair flicked the other way. Her head tipped back, forwards. "Okay, well, one time I was passing this charity shop window and there was a mirror in it, you know, facing outwards. I stopped, glanced at myself in the mirror and, behind me, I could see busy streets, heaving with people. Yet when I spun round, there was no-one there." Her breathing had a hitch in it. "It was like I was on the other side of the mirror and they were all carrying on without me." She put a hand up to her forehead. "It was like... I felt as if I was..."

He touched her elbow. "What, love?"

"It was like I was dead." A bar of shadow crossed her body as she lowered her arm. "Like the living and the dead had swapped places and I was on the wrong side of the glass."

He swallowed and just missed catching her eye. She obviously didn't need anything so crude as a printer.

She lifted some strands of hair out of her face. "Afterwards I kept thinking, 'Well, maybe they are all still there, I just can't see them.' And 'Can they see me?' It wasn't..." She clamped her hands between her knees. "It wasn't a very nice feeling."

He didn't know what to say.

Her hands fluttered free.

He reached out, caught one, gave it a squeeze.

She glanced out of her side window, jerked her head his way. "Oh, my God, that's not what you're thinking, is it?"

He took his hand away. "What do you mean?"

"That this is, that this is the same. That they've been there all along and are only now coming back into view." She kept her gaze fastened on him. "You think that's why they don't look at us, because they can't see us?"

Mis-swallowing, he coughed.

Her head tilted closer. "Is that why you don't want to talk to them, because you don't want to know?"

Her gaze warmed his face.

He kept his eyes on the road. "I can't explain them coming back anymore than I can explain them disappearing. But after what he had in store for us yesterday, I know this can't be the end." Now he did look at her. "There's no way he'd let us off so easily."

CHAPTER 14

WRATH

"Where are we?" she said.

He looked out at the empty red-brick Victorian houses bathed in sunshine all down one side of the street. A red-brick wall facing them and blocking the view cast its shadow across a grass verge. "No idea."

Spreading out across the city, the other survivors hadn't reached this far out yet. So Central London provided the point of ingress, only, which bit? And where had they come back from? By what form of transport? A couple of coaches? A half-filled train?

"Hey, stop."

He pulled over. "What?"

Polly pointed. "There was a ginger cat walking along the top of that wall, now it's gone."

"Maybe it jumped down."

She shook her head. "It was coming this way but disappeared backwards. Cats don't jump backwards, do they?"

"Where's Wikipedia when you need it?" He smiled.

She leaned outwards, craned.

"Anyway, it's probably turned feral by now," he added.

She snuffed. "Well, I didn't want it as a pet. Cats are half feral at best." She put her window down, stuck her head out. "Hey. Hey, listen."

He turned the engine off. "What?"

She undid her belt, opened the door and, as she got out, said something.

He couldn't hear what, so got out too. "You what?"

"Ssh, ssh. Listen…"

What was that? Something scratching or scraping? It came from the other side of the wall.

She cupped her hands around her mouth: "Hello?"

The scraping, or scratching, stopped.

Then, if anything, it intensified.

He joined her on the verge. "Probably the cat."

"No, wait, ssh, ssh."

Was that… Was that a human moan?

"I'm going to climb that tree," she said.

"No, let me do it. My trainers have grip."

She shrugged, stepped out of the way. "On your head be it."

Catching hold of the lowest bough, he hung from it, walked up the trunk and, hooking a leg over it, hauled himself up. He'd no sooner got to his feet on his perch than he picked his way upwards. He hadn't climbed a tree since childhood. Although the gain in height meant that he could reach farther, branches creaked and protested.

"What can you see?" called Polly.

He was higher than the wall now, or his head was.

Typical. Leaves blocked his line of sight.

"Hang on a minute."

Spotting a hole in the canopy above him, he climbed three, four makeshift rungs. His feet came level with the top of the wall. Propping himself against the trunk, he peered out. In the leafy gap, crosses and headstones leaned this way and that. "It's a cemetery."

"Who's making the noises then?"

Clearer from up here, the sound defined itself. Digging. His ears popped and crackled. Leaves still restricted his view.

Grabbing hold of a neighbouring branch, he turned on the bough he stood on and, opening and closing the gap between his feet, slid them along it.

He could see Polly's upturned face. *So small.*

His crooked handrail bobbed and swayed.

Breathing, loudly, through his nose, he shuffled along the tapering bough. The farther out he got, the more it bent. It came to rest on top of the wall just at the point that it fanned out. Carefully, he transferred his weight to the wall.

"What are you doing?"

Leaves brushed him. Twigs clawed.

"Trying to get a better view."

The top of the wall sloped to either side. With his trainers at a forty-five-degree angle, and bandy legs, he made his way along it.

He emerged from the clutches of the tree. Resting his hands on the fronts of his jeans, he twisted round to scan the cemetery.

Row upon row of headstones and crosses stuck up, punctuated by the odd tomb, yew or oak.

"I can't see a soul," he said.

He concentrated on ground level instead. Not that he could see much. Gravestone surmounted gravestone.

What was that?

Probably nothing.

On the next sweep he spotted a spray of earth in the same place, so fixed his eyes on that patch. The ground sloped. Even more sinister than cemetery subsidence, something moved between two headstones.

A hand.

Thin, grey, it scrabbled around. *Oh, God, not again…*

Thank you. This one had an arm attached.

What was left of one. *No, no, no…* Withered to bones, ligaments, slack cords of muscle and tendons, it only had scraps of skin.

A skull with meaty bits adhering to it overtopped the right-hand headstone. It clicked in his direction.

"What the—" Wobbling on the wall, he put his arms out to steady himself.

"What? What is it?"

Twisting back to the world on the other side of the wall, he noticed three men chasing a lame dog out from a distant side road.

One of them pounced, caught it, held it down and ripped a leg off.

Before he could form words, or point, on the cemetery side

a stick-thin figure the colour of bone darted, leapt and clutched at his foot.

Leaning back, knowing that if he looked down, he'd fall, he reached for a branch to grab and found nothing. His arms threshed air.

"Greg," screamed Polly.

Too late, he was going.

His arms flailed in reverse as he went.

Polly's voice drifted out.

Drifted in again. And the wall stretched out above him rather than below. *What happened*? His body remembered, even if his mind didn't. Pain seeped up from the ground. Of course, the fall. He stretched. Grass rustled under, between, his fingers. Another, louder, burst of speech from Polly arrested a precipitate withdrawal inward. *Who's she talking to*?

To sit up, he had to lever the world the right way up using only his elbows. No gravestones. *No creatures*. Instead, the shadowy side of the street outside the cemetery. He felt his head for bumps. *Did I imagine that*? Had he simply passed out? The car sat empty. He turned the world with just his head.

Polly stood in the middle of the road, in streaming sunshine, with her arms partially extended, hands out.

He shuffled round on his backside and saw them, the three figures, walking towards her. The one at the back dragged the dead dog.

"Thank you, thank you," she called out. "I think he's unconscious."

No... Couldn't she see? Blood smeared the entire lower half of the face of the one at the rear. *The dog's*. The man let the animal drop in favour of something more appealing.

"Polly."

Doubtless because she didn't expect to, she didn't hear him.

Having strode out to meet them, she was half way between them and him. Yet whereas he lay on his back, they closed the gap.

"You speak English?"

Her rising note of uncertainty had some way to go yet.

Wincing as he forced himself up—just a sprain, hopefully—he limped over to the car, hopped in.

He switched the engine on. Polly whirled round.

Letting the handbrake off, he hurtled towards the dog-men. They lunged towards her.

Mouth an "O", she dashed his way. Stopping, she spun in time with him as he swerved to place the vehicle between her and them.

He leaned across to release the door handle as he braked, hard.

"Get in," he yelled.

Metallic thuds.

The heel of a hand smacked his window. With a squeak, it left a stained-glass-effect daub of blood.

Polly climbed in and her door shut as they screeched off.

He took a left, quickly followed by a right.

She pointed back over her shoulder. "What was wrong with them?"

"I've got something to tell you and you're not going to like it." How to describe what he'd seen on the other side of the cemetery wall? "They're—"

"Look out," cried Polly.

A young girl in a pink dress with hollow eyes jaywalked out in front of them and he didn't slow down, he speeded up.

"Greg," screamed Polly.

A double jolt as first a front tire went over her, then a rear.

"No," she cried, twisting round. "Stop, damn it! Stop!"

While he did slow down, he didn't stop. "Darling, it's alright."

"You just killed a girl." Her voice cracked. "And you didn't stop." Tears welled up in her eyes. "Oh, God, you too? What's happened to everyone?" She gesticulated at the streets sliding by the wraparound windows. "Am I in hell or what?"

"Love, listen, listen…"

She clapped her knee. "That's a hit-and-run!"

"It doesn't matter."

"'Doesn't matter'?" She flayed him with her eyes. "My God, I can't believe I was going to marry a monster that runs over—"

"Polly, I didn't kill her." He nodded out of the window at a group of them. "Look at their eyes." He turned to her. "See any humanity there?"

Her head bobbed and wagged. "What do you mean?"

"I can't kill any of them."

She snuffed. "I would hope not."

"Polly, he's bringing them back to finish the job."

She threw her hands up. "Who?"

"You know who. Him."

"Finish what job?"

"It's not us who's dead, Polly. It's them." He pointed at one of the figures on the street. "They've been dead a long time and they're..." A lightning flash of memory. Half-eaten cows. "...hungry." His neck jerked as he looked at her. "We haven't descended into hell. It's risen to meet us."

CHAPTER 15

THE DISEMBARKATION OF THE DEAD

In his peripheral vision, she shook her head.

With his hands on the wheel, he glanced at her. "What?"

"I can't believe you didn't even slow down."

He slapped the steering wheel. "Jesus. How many more times? She was already dead."

The glance Polly threw him lodged like a grappling hook in his soul. "But she was just a child."

"You'd rather I'd have let her eat you?"

"How do you know she'd eat me?"

He gestured at streets no less devoid of life now that they were no longer empty. "Cos we're the hottest buffet in town. I mean, you saw them coming for you."

A tall woman with long white hair stepped out into the road.

He swerved round her to avoid an argument.

"Well, how come they don't hassle us in the car?" Polly put her window down.

He pressed the button to put it up from his side. "I don't know. It could be the tinted windows. Or maybe they go by sense of smell or body warmth." He turned to see her staring at him. "Think of it like driving through a safari park. All that's left is the basic, cunning animal part of the brain."

"What are they doing here?"

"They've been sent."

The volume of her voice shot upwards. "Sent?"

"Yes."

Her voice dropped to a whisper. "By him?"

Greg nodded.

They knew who they meant even if they didn't know who he was.

Her nearest eyebrow quivered. "Why?"

"They're a proxy."

Her eyebrow stalled. "What does he need a proxy for?"

"There's an anomaly that needs... rectifying."

"What anomaly?"

A few waggles of his finger took in the two of them.

She blinked. "What do you mean?"

"Well, we survived the end of the world and..."

"And?"

"Shouldn't have."

Her head sank.

God damn it. Can I never lie? Not even just once?

He cleared his throat, squirmed upright in his seat. "But look..." *Two on this street; one on the last...* "There's not that many of them. It's, it's manageable."

A shadow spread across the road.

"What's that?" she said.

"Must be a cloud."

She looked this way and that. "That big and only one?"

The shadow changed everything. It rendered road and pavements and buildings drab, which instantly became the new norm.

Several yards ahead and behind, sunlight gave the street a fresh lick of paint.

The band of dullness only widened as they drove across it.

He spun the car round at the next crossroads and stopped.

They both looked up.

"Holy hell," he said.

"Oh... my... God."

A gargantuan black airship floated in the blueness.

An engine pod stuck out from each side with a giant float beneath it. The fuselage went on and on. Now another set of engine pods and floats crossed the street. More blank fuselage. Until the black craft retreated to just the horizontal and vertical stabilizers of its tail.

"Look, look, there's another one," cried Polly.

Three or four times longer than any airliner and fatter than it looked side on, the airship above turned and, at the end of the street intersecting theirs, a second nosed into view.

He followed her line of sight as she looked the other way and her eyes widened.

A fleet of titanic Zeppelins darkened the sky.

"What the hell's going on?"

"I don't know."

She thumped his arm. "But you should know."

"Oi!"

One airship dipped as it turned. It assumed the attitude of a colossal bomb.

He put the car into gear and set off not so much after it as heading in the same direction and endeavouring to keep up with it. He didn't want to lose it. Nor did he want to get too close.

Their focus wasn't on the street anymore, and it wasn't on the inside of the car. It was directed a couple of hundred feet up.

They lost sight of the dirigible behind flats stacked on top of launderettes and newsagents and betting shops. He had to second-guess the extent of its turn and descent. Then, in gaps between elegant Georgian façades, he caught glimpses of tilted black hull slung slantwise across side streets, a little straighter each time.

The park they'd met in, and, later, fallen out in, meant a massive detour. He had to put his foot down to keep up.

In the mirrors, the front of the airship levelled out into wind, came in low over a line of trees.

He screeched round a corner and slowed right down.

So far it had been impossible to take in the whole of the airship in one glance. Now they could. It was pointy like a rugby ball but elongated like a cigar. In perfect profile, it had three sets of engine pods with floats attached this side and presumably the same number the other side. It had a gondola slung beneath it where the airship started to curve upwards towards the nose. The belly of the beast had a passenger compartment with two decks and each deck had windows and hatches.

What were those blobs at the windows? Not tiny faces?

The propellers unblurred and the giant craft stopped, right over the park.

She touched his arm. "Stay back."

He pulled up, tugged the handbrake on. "Don't worry, I am."

The propellers flickered into life again, rotating just enough to keep the airship in position.

A hatch popped open. Then another and another and another and another all along its considerable length.

Rope ladders unreeled from these hatches, with a corresponding complement drop-swinging on the far side.

Figures appeared, climbing down them with slow, stiff movements.

As soon as one was on the way down, another took his or her place at the top of the ladder.

One lost its footing and fell, thirty or more feet.

Polly gasped as it got up and joined the others.

Lines formed, curving round trees, bushes, flowerbeds and the fountain, streaming towards the exits of the park as if according to some prearranged plan.

"Let's get out of here," she said.

"Good idea." He stamped his foot and their necks jerked as the Nissan leapt forwards.

They drove in silence. Neither of them had uttered a word since setting off again. Not that the tickertape machine of consciousness ever let up. It chuntered on regardless.

The population of the dead was about to explode. So how had the early arrivals, those that hadn't dug or clawed themselves out of their own graves, got here? The car weaved around the streets of this new London, twinned with Hell.

Greg turned down Constitution Hill. Foreshortened from this angle but visible above the canopies of the trees and through the trunks that flashed by, an airship hung over Green Park like a pregnant whale. Another edged into view behind it over St James's Park.

He swung past Buckingham Palace, raced up The Mall. Rope ladders unfurled all around the car as, here too, death spawned.

The dead commanded the skies. Soon they would claim the earth.

In these last few minutes while he still owned the streets, Greg did as much reconnaissance as possible. The engine boomed as they passed through Admiralty Arch. Out the other side and up to the roundabout.

The sinister mass resurrection continued apace as, to the left, cadavers stalked both the square and the terrace.

The wrong way round the roundabout and up Northumberland Avenue. Left onto Victoria Embankment with its plane trees and the wall that curved as the river curved. He covered distances in no time at all, while he still could. The dead swarmed across Waterloo Bridge. He peered up at them until the bridge itself blotted them out.

Out from under the bridge and now he had to brake because the dead thronged the road. Like sleepwalkers moving en masse, they shambled towards the car with a curious plodding gait, slow and twitchy, yet determined. He drove at the speed they parted. Now, ahead and on both sides, he glimpsed bloodless, almost solid-looking faces and hard, empty eyes.

All it would require for this to be a revolution would be for the dead to march in step.

Shuffling, so much shuffling. On and on it went, all around them. The hairs on the back of Greg's neck stiffened. He gripped the steering wheel so tightly, his knuckles whited. His ankle ached from keeping his foot at the same angle on the accelerator pedal. He revved the engine and little surges of speed had them making better progress.

In the distance, a tall black ship loomed on the Thames. A conning-tower, funnels, turrets and signal masts stuck up above intervening bridges.

Another black ship manoeuvered behind it.

"Where are they all coming back from?" said Polly.

Even though little more than a whisper, her voice made him jump.

"The place from which no traveller is supposed to return." He glanced round and met her eye. "The mirror's well and truly broken."

She gripped her knees. "Where does that leave us?"

Still edging forwards, he put his head on one side. "Well, if this were a computer game, I think you could safely say we've just gone up a level."

"What do you mean?"

"I told you, our survival threw the apocalypse out of kilter and he's trying to restore the balance. If we won't go to our deaths, he'll bring death to us." The knee of a supernaturally pale young man with cavernous eye sockets and a shadowy beard knocked against the off-side front wing of the car. Greg braked. "He wants us dead, like that."

The young man leaned in with a punky bend of the neck and peered through the window with iced eyes.

Polly bolted upright in her seat.

Greg turned his head away.

Polly slunk back down and shuddered. "So what now?"

"We find out what we're supposed to do—"

"And do the opposite."

"Exactly. We need to find out what our new fate is in time to dodge it."

Chapter 16

Apocalypse Adjustment

Greg screeched to a halt outside his old place of work. They flung the Nissan's doors open and, to the chugging of the generator in the background, ran inside.

Their shoes clunked on the lino. They bounded up the stairs and through to Admin.

Had they broken the curse of the hill? The first thing he did was press the standby button on the fax machine.

The small screen lit up and, according to that, something was already queued for printing. He pressed the green button to set it going.

Sure enough, the cover read "Draft 4." Sheet after sheet of print followed. He checked the warm pages as they came out and the past they detailed was of course exactly the same, only now there would be more of it. He laid these first pages down and, minding his head, peered back in the output tray. "Come on, come on…" His fingers drummed on the lid of the scanner.

The printer stopped, as far as he could see, at his second trip down to the countryside. It needed more paper.

He had the drill down pat now and its fans soon went into overdrive.

Stepping away, he stood up straight and looked about. Panels of the white ceiling had fallen to expose wiring and puffy silver lagging enclosing ducts. Had they been like that before? They must have.

Polly leafed through the portion of the manuscript he'd discarded.

He coughed. "I guess the very act of reading the future changes it."

"Hm?" Polly turned a page of the manuscript.

"Because, you could say, free will is not knowing what one is going to do before one does it."

"Mm-hm." She stood with her head down, legs crossed at the knees and one foot slightly ahead of, the wrong side of, the other.

Among other things, the manuscript documented his thoughts. Would the glimpses inside his head it afforded make her love him again, or hate him more?

He leaned over the tray and checked the page coming out: "A fleet of titanic Zeppelins darkened the sky." *Yes, come on…*

A door thunked up the corridor and this time he nearly did bang his head. *One of them.* It must have blundered inside the building.

Polly's hand holding the manuscript dropped and she looked this way, that, before looking at him.

She laid the manuscript to the side. He clutched her hand and pulled her with him through the nearest doorway.

At right angles to the one they'd come through, the door had a small window crisscrossed by fine wires. They stared back in.

Beanpole-thin and basket-player-tall, a male figure lumbered in and stopped right where they'd been standing just moments before. The printer carried on whirring and clanking.

Slouching, the man turned and surveyed the room.

Greg recoiled with such force, his neck clicked.

In an attempt to uncrick it, he gripped and massaged his nape.

Polly's elbow dug him in the ribs. "Hey, hey, it's Simon."

He crouched over. "Was."

"What?"

He straightened up. "Was Simon."

"Oh." Nodding.

The face might have been Simon's but the saturnine set of it wasn't. Even from here, Greg could see that his friend's personality had been unseated, leaving only this deathly automaton.

"The real one wouldn't hurt a fly," he said, in a cracked

voice. *Sorry I couldn't save you, Simon.*

"Is there another way out?" whispered Polly.

"We can't leave. We need to know what the next draft says, now, while it gives us the advantage." He watched "Simon" head towards the door opposite the one he'd come through, at the other end of the room. "Let's wait till he's gone."

Shoes dragged behind them, beyond the double set of fire doors. Greg swung his vision that way, in time with Polly's head. *Another one!*

His gaze shot back to the office.

Simon still hadn't reached the exit.

Behind them, the footsteps grew louder, closer. The fire doors could open at any moment.

He gripped the handle. "Come on, come on..." An eternity of seconds. "Yes!"

Simon exited.

Greg pushed Polly through the door.

He took up position between her and the printer. "Check the manuscript."

They heard the creak of the double doors, then the clack.

"It's not finished," said Polly.

"We'll just have to..."

The door burst open. A whiff of rotten eggs.

"Christ, it's your ex," said Polly.

Nicola's eyes rolled and blinked. Her make-up had run and smudged. The smears and blotches gave her visage a crooked, cock-eyed appearance. Her hanging-open mouth drooled. A rope of saliva swayed as, with tight turns of the head, her eyes took in both of them.

"Well, it's an improvement," said Polly.

Nicola shut her mouth with a snap of her teeth.

She bared them.

Greg turned to Polly. "It's alright. She's a vegetarian."

Nicola lurched towards them.

"Are you sure?" said Polly.

Nicola stopped.

They followed her eyes to the doorway they'd come through first.

Milo entered.

He lifted something brown and furry to his mouth, and bit into it. It wriggled and squeaked. A worm-like tail whipped his face. He crunched through bone and the small creature fell quiet, limp. He tore out a hunk of its belly with his teeth. Through blood running in rivulets, Greg could have sworn he caught the ghost of a smile.

Milo tossed the bloody creature to Nicola. Spinning, it arced through the air. She caught it.

Tipping her head right back, she lowered it into her mouth, head first. The skull cracked, and she kept on chewing, disposing of more and more of it.

Soon all that was left was the tail, which she threw away.

It landed on Katissia's desk lamp, looped over the upper joint, ends swinging.

Milo's eyes turned their dark light on Greg.

Low gutturals escaped his lips, and Nicola responded in kind. It was as if they were trying to communicate but couldn't. It came out as growls and groans instead.

Milo and Nicola shuffled closer. Greg backed away with Polly beside him. The printer carried on printing.

"What do they want?" whispered Polly.

"Well, I don't speak the language of the dead but I'm pretty sure they've been sent to protect the printer and its prophecies. That and... get things back to how they should be."

He gripped her hand.

She gripped his. "You mean...?"

He leaned towards her. "I've a horrible feeling that rat was just an appetizer."

"I don't..."

Milo and Nicola charged.

"Run," he shouted.

Polly tripped, went down.

He turned to her, swung back to Milo.

Tuberous fingers waggled towards them at the ends of outstretched arms.

Tipping documents and files off a table, Greg picked it up and swung it round, metal legs protruding. He jabbed at

Milo with the legs before thrusting the entire table at him and throwing it.

It knocked him off his feet.

Greg turned to Polly. Before he could get back, Nicola reached her.

Polly seized the nearest thing to hand, a metal bin, and swung it at Nicola's head.

A resounding clang sent his ex crashing backwards over a desk.

The blow would have killed anyone who wasn't already dead. Instead, Nicola's bluey fingers scrabbled at the edge of the desk and gripped it.

Greg helped Polly up. They dashed towards the third door, the one Simon had passed through, and clattered down a white corridor.

"Where—are—we—going?" she panted.

"Out of here."

They needed to get away before any more dead ex-colleagues showed up.

"Which way?" she said, as they came to the end of the corridor.

He skidded to a halt, veered left, right. "Er... I don't know."

"What do you mean you don't know?"

Simon stepped out of a door to the right. "Left!"

They ran round the corner at the end to find a staircase leading up, leaving them with no choice but to ascend.

Once at the top of the stairs, they didn't turn left or right or take the next flight. They went thumping down the facing carpet-tiled corridor. Their breathing had a choppiness to it increasing all the time but also a jumpiness susceptible to sounds. Only, now the noises drowned out their breathing. Creaking, cracking and smashing emanated from one side of the passage.

Greg pictured bodies behind the doors, in cubicles of death, hatching.

The partition next to them split, burst, fell away, and Milo emerged from the fragments. Springing back, they ran the other way.

Footsteps thundered to head them off.

Ahead, more and more of Simon came into view from the top down as he climbed the stairs. He stepped onto their floor, which sent his head bobbing up towards ceiling, just as they reached the end of the corridor.

Nicola smacked into him and they both went sprawling.

They rolled over one another in the diffuse shadowless light.

As dead hands reached for their ankles, Greg and Polly leapt to the side. Again, even though it would take them farther away from the carpark and potential safety, they headed up.

In the corridor above them, on the top floor, a number of the strip lights had gone out. The first fizzed and flashed as if taking their photo. By the time they reached the top, Milo was on his way up, with Simon close behind.

Greg wrenched a red fire extinguisher from its bracket on the wall. He tore it open and fired in their direction. Foam sprayed from the nozzle and covered them both in seconds. Simon's arms flailed in the stairwell. He fell backwards. Milo surged forwards.

"Run," shouted Greg, hurling the extinguisher at him.

Milo caught it but the weight and momentum of it knocked him back down the stairs.

Ahead, darkness hung like a rope bridge from the ceiling. With no intersections or exits, when the corridor turned, they turned with it.

A light out at the next corner warped the corridor out of true.

Polly's elbow nudged him as she lifted her hair out of her face. "Where does this go?"

"There's another set of stairs at the back. I'm hoping it links up with them."

She took a band off her wrist and tied her hair back with it. "Hoping? What if one of them's coming the other way?"

Their breathing was all over the place. It snagged on darkness' fuzzy edges, filling the void.

"Ssh." She grabbed his arm.

They stopped.

Footsteps pounded behind them.

Like an echo, footsteps pounded ahead of them too.

Damn.

"Quick, in here." He opened the door of a small office. Daylight flooded the corridor.

They dived inside, and he shut the door with the merest of clicks.

Both sets of footsteps drew closer. They stopped right outside.

Heart thumping, Greg held Polly close. He stared into her eyes. She stared into his. Holding his breath, he puffed out his cheeks to get her to do the same and he felt the thuds of her heart.

She rapidly turned red.

A meerkat standing to attention gazed at them from a calendar on the wall as one set of footsteps headed off to, or back to, the left. The second set tramped about outside.

Finally they continued, or turned, the same way as the first.

Both he and Polly released their breath as if deflating.

The last set of retreating footsteps stopped, turned back.

"Shit," mouthed Greg.

He pushed Polly to the hinged side of the door and stood in the middle of the room with his back to the window.

The door swung open, to reveal Nicola, and conceal Polly.

What was that bauble dangling from his ex's soft blobby face? About the size of a golf ball, it rolled around her cheek.

Nicola pitched into the cube of the office.

Even as she left the shadows of the corridor behind, one of her eye sockets remained in darkness. It gaped.

Oh, Jesus. He flinched. The spherical object was her eye. It hung by its optic nerve. The other side of her head had a dent in it. Polly must have hit her even harder than he'd thought. The Nicola he knew would never have been seen dead looking like that. Now she was. Then again, death had never been so eventful.

His fiancée peeped round the back of the door.

Dragging his attention away from the dark cave of Nicola's eye socket and the eyeball swinging as she approached, he threw his arm up and around his head before, glancing behind her, flinging it off to the right.

Polly tiptoed over to the far right-hand corner of the room. *No, no, no, down the corridor.* She reached for something, picked it up. It looked like a metal… No, *get out of here.* What was it with her and bins? Go, *for Christ's sake!*

Nicola advanced.

He retreated.

Raising the bin, upside down, Polly crept up behind Nicola.

A few steps behind her now with one foot out, Polly put her foot down. The floor creaked.

Nicola stopped.

Polly froze with the bin aloft.

Pinching the dangling eyeball between forefinger and thumb, Nicola pulled it out to the side. The optic nerve stretched.

Keeping one eye on him and swivelling the other between her fingers, she looked round her own ear.

Before she had a chance to react to what she saw, Polly rammed the bin down over her head. Nicola's hand got knocked out of the way, and her eyeball with it. The eye dropped and rolled across the floor like an oversized marble.

"Out of the way," shouted Polly.

He leapt to the side

Polly lifted her leg, placed her foot on Nicola's backside and thrust off with it. Except it wasn't Polly that moved, it was Nicola. Propelled forwards, her bin-helmeted head dipped, adding to her momentum. The base of the bin struck the window, shattering it, and over the lip she went.

The clang of the bin hitting the ground three floors below had an extra dimension to it like an egg breaking in a can.

On the way out of the office, Greg trod on the eyeball, squishing it.

"Oh, God!" He rubbed the sole of his shoe on the carpet tiles.

"Quick, come on."

They ran all the way round to the flights of stairs at the back of the building, down them and out of a fire door, then round the outside of the building to get back to the carpark.

When they got there, they saw Nicola's body not far from the Nissan.

"Sorry, Greg," said Polly, over the 4x4's roof.

"Don't apologize to me, apologize to him." He pointed up at Milo leaning out of the broken window impervious to the remaining shards of glass. He and Polly got in the car and he accidentally bumped shoulders with her as they reached for their seatbelts at the same time. He started the engine. "We should have got here sooner."

She plugged her seatbelt in and looked at him. "Why?"

He put the gear selector into drive, let the handbrake off and London revolved around them for a moment before straightening out. "Because now the printer's out of bounds."

CHAPTER 17

ELECTRIC MEAT

"I was thinking," came Polly's voice, on the way down to breakfast.

Swinging round a bend in the stainless-steel tubular banister to turn back on himself on stairs composed half of shadow, he glanced up at her. "What?"

Half a flight behind him, darkness competed with his peripheral vision to claim her. "If we can receive via the printer, maybe we can send via it too. We could get a dialogue going."

"Brilliant." *Twenty-four hours ago.* "There's just one thing…"

"What?"

The handrail levelled out, curved round and bent smoothly downwards, delivering him to the final half-flight. "We can't get to the printer."

She leaned out over the banister above him. "It really is that bad?"

"Bad?" He cast his eyes down. "We're buggered."

Knee bending as if trying to push his foot through the floor, he dipped to one side as his forward foot ended up on the same level as his rear one. He glanced ahead at the foyer where mirrors and glass doors slowly brightened as light came in like the tide. Brass fixtures glimmered.

He swung round.

When the first light hit her face and he saw what his words had done to it, with the cheeks caved in by shadow, lending a skull-like effect, he wished he'd learnt to lie.

She scrunched up her mouth. "There must be a way…"

"They're protecting it, guarding it, with their... Well, whatever you want to call it." He thought of Milo leaning out of the window. "And they'll be more of them by now. No, the printer's off limits." He pictured his old rival's almost human eyes. "In any case, I have a feeling it's all turned rather... personal."

"You mean it wasn't before?" She shot him a look.

"I just mean..." He blenched. "We have to avoid Milo. Like the plague. You saw him, staring down at his corpse bride."

"Rather I killed children?" she muttered.

Just before she reached him, he pivoted.

They crossed the lobby, with its gathering light and rock pools of darkness, in tandem.

He stood aside at the entrance to the dining room and tortured a smile on the rack of his face as she passed. "Oh, don't get me wrong. I'm glad you've got over your squeamishness." His heels clicked as he turned after her. "It stood in the way of our survival."

Her shoulders drooped in front of him as she exhaled.

He inhaled.

They wheeled round towards their table.

Suddenly she stopped.

Outside the long window, figures stumbled past, in both directions, in the bluey charnel-house light.

She turned her head slowly.

He placed his hand on her shoulder. "It's alright. They can't see us. The window's tinted, remember?"

They continued to their table. Bending by degrees, she sat down.

He remained standing. *Carry on as if everything's normal.* "What do you feel like today?"

Her gaze flicked from him to the window and back. "It's like..." She leaned closer, lowered her voice: "It's like the early morning commute out there." The dead moved as if underwater. "Don't you think we should go upstairs?"

"Come on, we've got, well..."

"Tea and those tinned sausages and some baked beans."

"Coming right up." He spun away and headed for the

saloon-style doors of the kitchen.

The drowned pushed on beyond glass.

He'd nearly got to the swing doors when the low chandeliers, with all their jewel-like dangly bits, ignited into life.

Electrical equipment beeped in Reception.

Everything stopped in the aquarium of outside. Yet they were the ones that fish-mouthed.

The dead turned, to see them clearly illuminated.

"Oh, shit," said Polly.

"They fixed it."

"How?"

For a moment the living and the dead stared at one another. Then it was as if someone had banged the dinner gong. The latter knocked on the window, pummelled it with their fists. The glass shuddered with the blows.

"Run," he shouted.

She caught up with him and they dashed out into the lobby. "Down to the carpark."

"All the keys are upstairs," she cried.

Damn. She was right. They'd collected them from other rooms, sorted them out and only kept the ones for vehicles that had enough fuel.

Dead came in through the revolving door, the slowest getting spun back out but the strongest coming straight in.

At the other end of the lobby, the lit-up lift disclosed its interior.

They ran towards it.

The relentless pounding reached a crescendo. The dining room window came crashing down. Glass crunched under feet and a battle cry went up. Or was it a cry of hunger?

He and Polly squeezed into the mirrored compartment of the lift and he jabbed the button by the 3.

Nothing happened. He jabbed it again.

"Punch the button," she shouted.

"I am," he cried.

The doors juddered in their grooves as dead charged towards them.

More dead poured into the lobby from the dining room.

Come on, come on, come on. The doors trundled in from the sides.

As quickly as the doors could crop them, the dead stampeded up the lobby. They were a little way back yet, but the doors were taking their time.

Greg clasped Polly's hand.

Racing the closing doors, dead stuck their arms out as if in anticipation.

He and Polly huddled against the back of the lift.

As the gap narrowed, lots turned to some, some to a few, then the glaring eye of one. Polly twisted her face away.

A finger made it through the gap as the doors met.

The doors sealed themselves shut. The finger dropped to the floor.

Polly's hand flinched away.

She hopped and sprang around the finger as fists thumped at the doors.

The hairy finger wriggled and jerked before coming to rest as whatever malevolent energy animating it drained away.

Groaning, the lift lurched upwards. Greg's stomach sank. He felt like a ghost passing through physical barriers as his head rose to where his feet had been only a moment before and kept on rising.

Polly leaned against the side. Her head sank. Stepping over to her, he rubbed her back. He watched himself looking at himself rubbing her back to warped infinity in the facing mirrors as the banging that carried on below receded, receded.

She spun round and stared at the finger.

He let his arm drop.

"It's like there's a current flowing through them or something." He shuddered. "I guess that's what they are."

When she turned her hands out, her mirror doppelgangers copied her. "What?"

"Electric meat."

"No, whatever that is—" She pointed at the finger, from all angles "—is not natural. Meat is food."

"Ah, you mean us."

She glanced sideways at him with her eyebrows out of kilter

before her gaze zigzagged to the numbers.

The lift stopped. The doors opened and, to the thud of footsteps on the stairs, they reeled out onto the third floor and round to their room.

He grabbed a handful of car keys from the dressing table.

"Oh, my God, look."

He joined Polly at the window. Below, a sea of dishevelled heads surged in the direction of the hotel's main door.

"Why are they coming after us?" she said.

"Because resources are scarce."

She put her head on one side. "Resources?"

"I told you." He pointed at the two of them. "Meat, brain burgers." He grabbed her hand. "Come on, let's get out of here."

Out in the corridor and back round the corner, the number above the lift changed from 1 to 0. Then it changed from 0 to 1.

He peered down the stairwell and saw the same wild-haired bunch one and a half floors below. No, one floor. *Shit, shit, shit...*

"Come on." He led the way up the next flight.

"Upwards?"

"We haven't any choice."

They arrived on the fourth floor.

The lift bell pinged on the third. The dead had now reached that floor too.

"Come on."

They had to keep going.

The next floor up, they ran out of stairs. The corridor stretched off to either side. Doors faced doors.

Turning the same way, they ran towards the end.

Round the corner—Yes!—the floor dropped away in the form of a staircase.

The thunder of feet from below.

"Poll, quick!"

They sprinted back the other way, past the head of the main staircase. He saw them, the dead, turning onto the last half-flight.

"Run," he shouted.

They'd just passed a laundry trolley and had nearly got to the other end when a foot-dragging chambermaid rounded the corner, followed by a hell-bent bellboy.

Greg tried to stop without toppling into them. Polly grabbing the back of his T-shirt brought him up short like an arrester gear.

Invisible tendrils of putrefaction speared his nostrils, infiltrated his skull.

These withdrew as they backed up at a trot.

Polly kept a tight hold of his T-shirt as they wheeled round.

The same smell smacked him in the face. It enveloped him. Polly wrapped the crook of her other arm round her mouth and nose. But they were panting, even if the dead weren't, and it was impossible not to breathe it in—the compound unpleasantness, like off meat wrapped in used nappies, getting worse all the time. Its wisps and coils reached down his throat, gave his inner linings a lick, making him gag.

Dead running up the stairs slowed to walking pace as they joined the band from the other end of the corridor. The half-bridge of the landing echoed with their stiff-jointed tramping.

He and Polly retreated, slowly.

They rotated back the other way.

Twelve or so dead hobbled behind the chambermaid and bellboy, with more and more rounding the corner all the time. Pale, rigid visages harboured sunken eyes.

He stopped.

Polly stopped.

The amount of free space shrank by two steps at a time, one from each side. For he or Polly to move either way now would be to hasten their end.

He reached out and tried a door.

Locked.

Polly tried the one opposite.

He turned side on, raised his elbows. No, no, no, no, no…

Legs scissor-walked quicker and quicker. Arms extended, hands reached. Dry mouths clicked, open.

"Greg," screamed Polly.

CHAPTER 18

DEATH'S COUP

Something dug Greg in the soft flesh above his left hipbone.
He'd bumped into the handle of the laundry trolley.

He grabbed it and, yanking Polly, pulled her behind him. He spun the squeaking trolley this way and that, in a sweeping motion, to ward off the advancing horde.

When the trolley collided with the wall, a couple of bulging duffle bags rolled off the top, one white, one blue. Polly reached for them, picked them up and lobbed them at the dead.

The bags failed to knock the dead over but fell at their feet and tripped them, which caused them to trip over each other.

"Greg, look."

He glanced back.

Where the laundry trolley had stood hung a brass flap in the wall not much bigger than a cat-flap.

"Go," he shouted, jabbing at the dead with the trolley.

Polly climbed in, feet first. When she was in up to her waist, she lifted her arms and slid out of sight.

He swung the trolley the other way. The bellboy caught it. They tussled. Quickly realizing he wasn't going to get it back and with dead closing in on both sides, Greg ran it at him.

He whirled round, leapt and landed in a crouch. Dropping onto his behind and rocking onto his back, he put his feet through the flap, raised himself up and pushed off.

Cold-blooded fingers brushed the skin of his hands, then metal slid around him, faster and faster. Unable to see anything or sit up, he helter-skeltered down and round an endless slanting hairpin. After what seemed like minutes but was probably only seconds, the chute straightened up, bent downwards and his stomach dropped away as he plummeted. Just as quickly, the chute bent back up, came level and he shot out as if from the mouth of a cannon.

He landed on a soft pile of laundry bags, rolled over onto his hands and knees and pushed himself up. His head swooped with each pitch and roll as he picked his way over the lumpy landscape.

Once on solid ground, his feet did a ridiculous little jig as he tried to correct for a tendency to veer to the right.

He joined Polly and they ran up the concrete steps.

Hinges squeaked as he pulled the door open.

He kneeled in the gap and leaned out into a corridor just off the lobby.

The smell had largely lifted. Unearthly groans came from other parts of the hotel.

Feeling hands on his shoulders and a knee resting against his back, he looked up and saw Polly's head above his. Twisting the other way, he read the sign above the door: "Staff only". He'd passed it many times.

Checking that the lobby was clear, they snuck the other way up the corridor and crept down the stairs.

The low-ceilinged underground carpark was mercifully free of the dead. He and Polly had their pick of vehicles but the first central locking that yelped when he pressed a key fob belonged to a Mazda.

They got in and belted up, then tore up the ramp into gathering light and the demesne of the dead.

Sunlight decanted itself over east-facing eaves into streets heaving, teeming, with their new denizens. They spilled out into the road and he and Polly drove through them.

Maybe it was because the car didn't have tinted windows, or maybe it was because of the lack of food, but heads turned in their direction. While the dead may not have run after them, they kept up with them with their eyes.

"Is your door locked?" he said.

"Yes."

On Oxford Street, the dead thronged, milled and crossed.

"I had not thought death had undone so many," said Polly.

He peered at her. "What?"

"Nothing."

Dead weren't just on the street, they were entering the stores, or emerging from them, with bags.

Catching a middle note of sewer to add to the top note of morgue, he reached forwards to shut the air vents.

"Are they..." Polly glanced at him, then stared back out of her window. "Are they shopping?"

Greg shrugged and kept a steady pressure on the accelerator pedal. He ignored the thuds as anyone who didn't move quickly enough got bumped out of the way.

"Look," cried Polly.

A black cab came towards them on the other side of the road.

"My God. Someone else?"

"Oh."

As it got closer, they saw the familiar blank fish gaze. The man driving was no more alive, no less dead, than any of the others. The passenger in the back had Milo's haircut, or lack of one. *Can't be.*

Ahead, a bus blocked the way. It had swerved and gone into a bus stop.

Even though the driver hung slumped over the steering wheel, the passengers, on both decks, remained in their seats.

A policeman stepped out into the road with white gloves, a pale, sunken face and hollow eyes. He put a hand up.

The bus driver lifted his head and smiled.

"Ambush," shouted Greg.

He stamped on the accelerator pedal.

The policeman fell back, went under the wheels.

Greg thought he heard bones snap. The car rocked, and Polly clung to her seat as he swung up a side street.

She gaped back over her shoulder, before looking at him. "How could they know we'd come that way?"

"I don't know."

He turned a random succession of lefts and rights. Only, the streets narrowed to such an extent that if a vehicle came the other way now, they'd be in trouble.

They rattled over cobblestones.

Up an alleyway, neon signs proclaimed, "Adults only" or, more simply, "Sex". Black windows and doorways with chains like dog leads dangling from them concealed garish interiors. Spot-lit windows featured headless torsos in lingerie. Round the corner, a woman with long blonde hair leaned over a counter to the side of an entrance. When she looked up, her hair slid aside to reveal a growth on her cheek the size of a grapefruit. In the angled, mirrored corridor behind her, women lolled in various states of decay.

"Jesus Christ," said Greg.

Back onto wider thoroughfares, where window displays blazed showcasing dusty handbags and shoes, traffic lights worked, and the city had woken, if you could call it waking, to the miracle of electricity. The dead made their way along the pavements, this way and that, crossing here, entering doorways there. *What are they up to?*

Above a coffee shop, gift shop and Whittard's, stringy dead pumped weights by means of contraptions, or ran towards the floor-to-ceiling window without ever reaching it.

"What the hell...?" he said.

The streets filled with light and on and on it went, ceaseless activity, even beyond the boundary of death.

Greg only slowed when he came to a man sitting eating on the curb with his feet sticking out in the road.

The man's tattered clothes fluttered in the breeze.

Amid an outcrop of skyscrapers, at least one of which loomed like a giant electrical appliance, he gorged on raw sausages. He had an endless string of them. As soon as he finished one, he pulled on the streel and bit into the next.

Greg braked hard and he and Polly lurched to a stop.

In a face composed of pale, discoloured skin, eyes rolled in the man's sockets as he focused on them.

When he stood up, the coiled heap of meat in his lap unravelled from a hole in his stomach and more and more of his intestines slapped the ground.

Polly folded in two, clapped a hand over her mouth and retched ineffectually between her knees. She only lifted and turned her head to shout, "Get out of here."

A surge of acceleration slammed her back against her seat. Greg wrenched the wheel round and she rolled against her door.

A gang in dark suits piled out of the entrance of one of the thrusting towers and bounded down its steps. They swooped like carrion birds on the man and his glistening repast.

"Oh, Jesus," cried Polly, gagging again.

When she'd quieted and after a decent enough pause, he put his hand on her arm. "You alright?"

She nodded.

To their left, the Thames still flowed—a rare constant in a world full of abhorrent variables.

"Think these are older dead?" he said. "They definitely look a bit green around the gills."

"Green, grey..." She waved her hand, swallowed.

Repopulation complete, the black ships had withdrawn along with the airships.

Spokes clearly visible, the giant bicycle wheel of the London Eye slipped by on the far side of the river.

With the Houses of Parliament coming up ahead, he braked. He turned right onto Bridge Street, left onto Parliament Square.

Outside what had once been the seat of Government, a fight had broken out between three or four factions of the dead.

His fingers clenched and unclenched the curve of the wheel. "I think I know what they're doing." He'd realized it. He just hadn't wanted to believe it. "They're returning to their old walks of life."

Polly's hair swished in his direction as she peered round at them. "You could say that."

As she faced front, he nodded in the direction of another band chasing a bloodied fox across the green. "Well, a debased version of them." Polly craned past him. "It's almost like a revolution."

The flicker of Polly's gaze. "What, 'Long live the dead'?"

Feeling as flash-chilled as he had with the snow piling up

around him in the park in the middle of summer, he shiver-shuddered. "God, I hope not."

Yet they couldn't ignore it. The dead had colonized London. The coup was complete.

CHAPTER 19

ESCALATOR TO HELL

Foot down, hands firmly on the wheel, he piloted them through the crowded streets. They sped like death tourists through the city.

They flew over a crossroads.

Off to the side, he caught a glimpse of something like a fissure in the road, yet glinting rather than dark and a foot or two off the ground. Doubtless a reflection in the window of something much higher, perhaps strung between two buildings, it was so attenuated as to barely be there. He didn't even bother trying to focus on it.

Without him doing anything, they decelerated so abruptly, it flung them forwards. Bracing himself against the steering wheel, it took all his strength to raise his head as the car groaned and the front of the bonnet buckled. By some bizarre concatenation of cause and effect, a lamppost came down in slow motion off to the side. They slewed out of the way. The streetlight's cover smashed just behind them. They bumped up onto a curb facing a jeweller's. To the grinding of metal, they came to an even more rapid halt and rebounded in their seats.

The car creaked as he turned his head. "Are you alright?"

She stared straight ahead. "Did you do that on purpose?"

"What? Why would I?" He reached out to touch her. "Are you okay?"

She yanked her arm away.

"Are you... Are you hurt, baby?"

"Hurt?" she cried. "Why in God's name would I be hurt, Greg?"

"I just mean…" He glanced out of the windows and checked the mirrors. Dead shambled towards them from all four exits of the crossroads. He put the car into reverse and the engine roared, yet they didn't move. Were the front wheels off the ground, or had the drive shafts broken?

With hungry eyes, the dead got closer.

Polly stared at the shop window and its cove of treasure in canted trays that gleamed silver, gold, platinum. *Shopping—now?*

"We need to get out." He'd no sooner opened his door than he spotted the cable lying snaked around the car. "It's a trap," he yelled over the roof. He ran round to her side. "Come on, quick, we need to go."

Walking down the middle of each street in loose rank and file, the first of the dead bobbed and wambled just meters away.

From the corner he and Polly had crashed on, they could try and escape up either of two inside pavements. He picked one at random and set off at a jog.

Unable to hear her footsteps, he checked behind him.

She'd gone the other way.

"Polly!"

Running after her, he had to stay close to the wall to keep out of the clutches of the dead. The nearest swivelled accordingly.

He had to duck behind some scaffolding to avoid a woman whose hands brushed him. She stuck her tongue out as if tasting air. The whites of her sclera rolled.

Sprinting to make it to the other end before the dead did, he caught up with Polly, overtook her. Why wasn't she running?

Wires hung out of some kind of junction box. He leapt over them.

Grabbing the handlebars of an abandoned rickshaw, he placed his foot on the pedal and tipped his head back in the direction of the rear seat.

A man with something crawling in his beard made a beeline for Polly and she swerved out of the way of both of them down some steps.

Spinning the rickshaw around and shoving it at the bearded

man, Greg managed to mow down him, trip another and enmesh a third.

He followed Polly down the steps. No, not down here. She strode across the concourse to the barriers.

"Polly, where are you going?"

She produced her Oyster card, touched it to one of the readers and passed through.

"Polly!"

They needed to get out while they still could.

Dead shuffled down the stairs. Oh, just great.

He ran over to the barriers, vaulted over the access gate and plunged down the moving metal staircase.

Way ahead, Polly had reached the bottom.

Above and behind, the dead banged into and rattled the barriers. They grunted and growled.

Yet they weren't held up for long. By the time he neared the bottom, they thundered through like racehorses from a starting gate.

At some point he must have bashed his foot, which, pulsing, felt about three times its normal size.

Listening out for Polly's distant footsteps ahead, largely drowned out by the stampede down the escalator behind, he limped along cylindrical tunnels tiled like latrines.

Polly, Polly, Polly...

He hobbled down a flight of steps, deeper and deeper into hell.

Following the echo of heels, he stepped out onto the long curve of a platform.

Polly stopped right at the far end and turned to face the track.

He loped along the platform as fast as he could.

Upon reaching her, he halted. "What's got into you?"

She stood with one leg straight and the other bent, rocking slightly between them. "You crashed into a jeweller's and you don't know why I'm upset?"

He glanced back at the opening. Twisting and dipping passageways funnelled footfalls—a hundred or more, overlapping.

"Listen, can we not do this right now?" he said.

She folded her arms. "Oh, not important. I see."

"No, it is important because it's to do with you. It's just, we've kind of got more pressing things to worry about at the moment."

The smell of decaying organic matter invaded the platform. *They're coming.*

He flapped an arm. "If you wanted to get away from them, why down here? We could have taken the rickshaw."

She stared at a poster of a beach on the opposite wall. "I wasn't trying to get away from them. I was trying to get away from you."

Throwing his hands up, he spun away.

Dead spilled out onto the platform.

He spun back. "You can't." She did look at him then. "Even if you want to, we're stuck with each other."

She chucked her chin up and off to the side. "Oh, thanks very much."

"But why down here? A dead end." Another glance behind him at ex-Londoners dragging themselves up the platform.

"I'm waiting for a train."

His head recoiled on his neck. "What?"

She pointed up at the digital readout behind him, which said two minutes till the next arrival.

"You're jok…"

Sure enough, over the moans of the dead, he caught familiar scissory switching sounds from the rails.

Oh, God. Now he and Polly couldn't even use the tunnel.

Dead streamed along the platform.

One minute, read the countdown.

The choking smell of off meat made it harder and harder to draw breath without the gag reflex kicking in.

A pinprick of light in the tunnel grew bigger, nearer.

Polly pulled a face with her tongue out and to one side. If any smell could suffocate a person, this one could.

The electrical hum of a train filled the tunnel.

He didn't need to look behind him anymore. The shadows of the dead loomed on the wall.

He craned up the tunnel. "Come on, come on, come on…"

A hot gale blew the stench away.

A smack of air and he jumped back as the train emerged.

The hunched driver went by with his hand on the dead man's handle. Behind him, to a succession of hissy screeches, commuters leaned into the direction of travel, lurched back, leaned, lurched back. In carriage after carriage, bluish hands help up newspapers, unkempt heads looked up with wires coming out of their ears connected to their electrical devices. As well as passing slower than the one before, each carriage contained fewer dead. The back two, thank goodness, had none.

The red, white and blue train had no sooner stopped than Polly banged the button next to the nearest door of the rear carriage.

Feet away, stiff legs twitched, one in front of the other.

Ghost-walking, the dead had their arms out before them.

As the door slid open, Polly shot through it. With dead barely more than a snarl away, he dived after her.

He spun around, grabbed the horizontal pole, hung from it and double-kicked as the dead tried to follow them on.

The one in front fell back against the rest.

Polly jabbed the button and, before the dead could rally themselves, the door shut.

With the carriage half in the tunnel, half out, they only had two doors to worry about.

He sprinted up to the other as, beyond the window, dead surged towards it. He swung round a vertical pole and kicked out as they tried to pile in.

Hard on his heels, Polly reached round to shut the door.

He had to deliver another swift kick, just as the door shut, to stop the dead getting a leg or arm in.

Growly motors roared, and the train got off to a stuttering start before they swept down the platform to a rising DC hum punctuated only by dead thumping against the windows.

Inches from the glass, walls enclosed the lit train in greyness.

Greg swayed next to Polly. *We made it.*

She nudged him, somewhat harder than necessary, and he followed her line of sight up the train. In the next carriage but one and farther and farther back, as far as he could see, dead got to their feet and pivoted in their direction. *Oh, you've got to be joking.*

Turning to face them, he adjusted the weight he put on each foot according to changes in the direction and gradient of the track.

The dead got the connecting door at the nearest end of the next but one carriage open, closely followed by the connecting door at the far end of the in-between carriage.

Greg backed away level with Polly.

Mirroring the progress of the dead up the adjacent carriage, they kept on going. Clanging into a pole, he stepped around it.

He touched her elbow. "Don't worry, we'll get off at the next stop."

Lights blazed. The tunnel opened out on one side. Static and flat, the living flashed by in posters immediately to the left, while ambulatory and 3-D dead, sporting briefcases and handbags or rucksacks, navigated each other to the right.

"No, no, no," cried Polly.

"Don't worry." He clutched her wrist. "The next one."

She shook his hand off. "Don't worry?"

The dead had nearly reached the last set of doors.

His and Polly's heels hit the back of the train.

Greg watched as the dead negotiated the doors and entered their carriage. The reek of rotting meat, sickly sweet, wafted their way.

The train bounced and rocked. He and Polly had to hang on. Had the driver speeded up?

"What am I to you, Greg?"

He looked at her. "Now? You really want to do this now?"

Feet thumped up the aisle.

"Now might be the only time we have."

He gave a few turns of his head. "Trust me, okay?"

She refused to release him from her gaze. "What am I?"

He turned away, as the advancing file of dead reached the halfway point of the carriage. "You're my fiancée."

"*Ex-fiancée.*"

He snapped his head round. "What do you mean?"

Her chin jerked. "So what am I?"

He thought for a moment, which, with the smell as invasive as snogging the dead, was probably all he had. "You're my not-self."

Spotting the lights of the next station coming up, he leapt to the side and yanked the emergency stop handle.

"'Not-self'?" screamed Polly.

The train braked, hard. He swung round, into her.

"You're my anti-self!" she shrieked, right in his face, as dead reversed up the aisle, quicker and quicker.

Unable to keep up with itself, one went down.

As soon as it went down, they all went down—tripping backwards over it.

The train squealed to a standstill.

Polly tugged off her ring and flung it at the floor.

"Opposite fucking species!" she cried, as it bounced around the carriage.

The door opened, and she scuttled off the train and up the exit.

"Jesus Christ," he shouted after her. "I don't know who's worse, you or the flesh-eating dead."

He gestured over his shoulder at the pile of dead as the ring rolled right past him and over the lip of the door.

Ting.

Even amid the cries of the dead, he heard it.

Oh, that's just bloody...

He ran out and jumped down to the back of the train. Reaching under it, he scrabbled about next to live rails as dead feet shuffled up the platform towards him. *This is why men die first.*

He felt the engagement band and quickly retrieved it.

Ohhh, wedding rings... "Jeweller's... Of course." Why couldn't he have crashed into another shop? Any other shop.

Puffing a sigh, he dropped the ring in his pocket and climbed onto the platform just as the first of the dead reached him.

Dancing round a London Underground employee, he shoved him onto the rails and paused to watch the electric crucifixion before leaping out of the way of a fellow commuter as more dead piled off the train.

Then he was off, trying to catch up with Polly, pumping up long brightly-lit tunnels connected by stairways or tight bends. On some of parts of the Underground, one footslogged half the way.

Finally he came to a wider space with an escalator, a double one, stretching up and up. It wasn't working. Yet heels clattering on the metal blocks, Polly neared the half-way point.

Footsteps echoed in a neighbouring tunnel. A band of dead approached the opening. He sprinted past them before they had a chance to cut him off and he bounded up the escalator. He couldn't hear them anymore but didn't slow down till he reached Polly. Only then did he look back.

They hadn't bothered following him up. Instead, they stood in a gaggle around the base. *Phew.*

He fell into step beside Polly and was just about to open his mouth when their walkway lurched, pitching them forwards. Before they'd even got up, it trundled the other way, taking them with it, downwards.

Glancing—between his legs—at the dead, he realized they'd clustered around the escalator's control panel. *The crafty...* He could see them, eying and awaiting their catch.

Clambering to his feet, going backwards all the while, he helped Polly to hers.

"Run," he shouted.

"I am," she screamed.

Running uphill against an escalator going the other way wasn't easy. Had the dead tampered with the speed? He had to run twice as fast as before to make any headway at all.

He and Polly must have run the equivalent of several flights just to make it to where they'd been before.

She'd obviously hit her leg because she ran with a limp and started to struggle. As much as she kept trying to forge ahead, the escalator kept trying to carry her back down.

He grabbed her upper arm to encourage her to keep up the pace, but she shook him off.

"I'm trying to stop you ending up as lunch," he shouted.

All he caught of her response was a skein of f-words.

Puffing, panting, he suddenly saw everything in the starkest possible terms. Without Polly's cooperation, neither of them would make it. Soon he would tire too. Already, angular pains lanced his sides. He had to make a dash for the top now while he still had the energy.

He had to do it. He had to leave Polly behind and go on ahead.

CHAPTER 20

ENEMIES IN HIGH PLACES

He extended his stride, stiffened his leg muscles, thrust off harder with his feet. The walls moved by at a slow walking pace. Leaning forwards, hunkering over alternately stretching and bending legs, he pushed on.

His lungs heaved. And was his heart about to explode out of him?

Before too long he could see where the escalator flattened out. He checked over his shoulder. For all Polly's pounding of the uphill treadmill, she only succeeded in slowing her rate of descent.

It gave him the extra impetus he needed.

Grimacing as he crested the escalator, he slapped the big red emergency stop button. The stairway shuddered to a halt and he flew off the end of it. He heard a clank as Polly went down again, followed by cursing and a clatter as she got up.

He kicked in the cover of the panel at the head of the escalator and wrenched it back to access the controls. He hit the upwards button.

Listening to Polly's footsteps, and several more behind, he waited at the head of the escalator.

Polly hurtled towards him. Smiling, he opened his arms wide.

She punched him in the stomach.

"Oof."

Doubled over, he clutched his abdomen until the flare of pain subsided.

"What was that for?" he gasped.

"Well, one, I bashed my other shin." She pointed at the red mark. "Two, you abandoned me!"

"I didn't abandon you. I left you temporarily." He straightened up. "Listen, which is better, a good product and terrible PR or good PR and a terrible product?"

"Are you saying I'm a terrible product? Is that why…"

"No!"

Multiple pairs of footsteps thunked closer.

"We need to go," she said.

He waited for the dead to come into view, then reached for the controls.

The dead fell forwards as the escalator ground and screeched to a stop before going the other way.

Having got up, dead bobbed back into view. At least, their heads did. Despite their best efforts, they couldn't outrun the escalator and gradually receded.

He gave them a wave.

Polly tutted as she strode off.

"Right, that's it," he said, catching up with her. "They're not as dumb as they look. You're going to get me killed if we don't even the odds in our favour."

"What do you mean?"

"You'll see."

Polly touched in with her Oyster card.

He shook his head.

Nine dead pursued them, two in police uniform. He kept checking over his shoulder. Polly's leg injury can't have been that bad because she kept up with him with a steady running action.

Under their arms they carried the weapons they'd stolen after deliberately crashing a truck into the armoury of a barracks. Every now and then, they stopped and turned to fire off a shot.

"They're not dying," cried Polly. "How can we kill them when they're already dead?"

"Aim for the head. They may not need hearts, but they must need brains."

The knapsack on his back bounced up and down.

Pausing to aim and squeeze off a round, he took one of the policemen's ears off, which didn't even break the officer's stride.

Two more dead joined the chase from a side street.

"All our shooting's only attracting more," she shouted as he caught up with her.

Yeah, he hadn't thought this gun business through.

Although the dead didn't move particularly fast, they could keep going and going and going. He and Polly weaved and staggered. They'd been running for miles, it felt like.

"Shit," panted Polly. "The Thames."

Catching sight of the glinting water, he pulled up. "Oh, God."

She swung round. "I said not to come south of the river!" The muzzle swayed in his direction, arced across his chest, back the other way.

He put a hand up. "Hey, mind where you're pointing that thing." He lowered the hand. "Though I know you'd probably like to blow my head off."

"Don't tempt me."

He hadn't taken the river into account at all. He couldn't even see any bridges.

"We could take the Blackwall Tunnel," he said.

She shook her head. "No, no way. You're not getting me into a tunnel with that lot."

She pointed over her shoulder where the soles of the dead's shoes slapped and scuffed Tarmac and, gradually increasing in size, their moon-faces dipped and rose.

Turning the other way, he spotted cable cars slung over the Thames, shuttling. "It's alright. Look. Come on, quick."

They dragged themselves through the barriers and round and up the steps. The dead weren't far behind—not because they'd speeded up but because he and Polly had flagged.

The cable cars of the Emirates Air Line bunched and moved slowly here for passengers to board, so they scuttled to the furthest one. Fifteen or more dead lolloped along behind them.

He held the pod steady for Polly and jumped in after her.

Swaying gently yet barely off the ground, they inched forwards. The doors slid together equally slowly as dead ran round to their gondola. The gap closed. Bodies slammed against the side as the two halves met. Long fingers clawed at the seal. Mouths hissed.

He and Polly shot upwards, sideways.

She leaned against the window with her forehead resting against it. "Phew, that was close."

"Er, yeah." Too pumped up to take a seat, he stood with his hands pressed against the glass.

Machinery whined as they climbed. Receding, the dead jostled each other. He checked the next car—empty, thank God.

Another empty gondola descended towards them.

It zipped by.

They climbed past the spiky white dome of the O2 Arena.

Downriver, he could make out the piers of the Thames Barrier.

A rumble and vibration as they reached the first tower.

Ascent over, the car sank a little as the slender cable drooped slightly. *Don't look up.* His gaze fell and continued to fall to the Thames beneath. Like beaten metal, it changed in the light. How had they got so high? He leaned forwards and his stomach turned over as a seagull flew under him two hundred feet below. *Don't look down.*

Now his stomach hung from the wire or felt as if it did as it registered every rock and sway.

The whine had faded to a background hum. Apart from the wind and the faint truckling as of wheels above them, peace closed around the compartment and he started to move with it rather than against it.

Polly steadied herself. "I was thinking, I might go and see if my parents are... back."

He clutched her wrist. "No." She looked at him. "Promise me you won't. Promise me you won't go and see them, ever." He let go before she pulled away. "They won't... They won't be the same."

She nodded slowly as she stared back at him. "I just need..." Her eyes flicked to the city. "I just need some time to think."

"Yeah, we need somewhere we can rest a while." He scanned the area out to the east, where, left behind, a black airship tethered to a pole took up a huge chunk of City Airport. "Somewhere where we can see them, but they can't see us." He turned upriver. Between the pointy tower at Canary Wharf and its flat-topped neighbour to the left, the Shard just edged into view. He tapped that window. "Look."

She turned in time before the closer buildings obscured it again.

"Yes, maybe."

He glanced ahead. "Oh, shit."

"What?" She spun round and followed his line of sight along the cable. Her head recoiled.

Another cable car glided towards them. It was as empty as those before it but one of the dead had got onto the roof.

"What the hell's it doing?" she said.

"The gunfire must have drawn it, I guess."

She shook her head. "No, I mean up there. Out there."

The dead man's long hair thrashed in the wind as he crouched on the roof of the approaching gondola.

Greg trained his gun on the man's head. He turned it quicker and quicker as the two cars closed on each other. Polly ducked out of the way. His forefinger looped around the trigger, ready to pull. The long barrel's muzzle knocked against glass. Damn. The window... The dead man passed out of sight.

A thud and their gondola jolted. Polly screamed.

A pair of legs dangled at the window in raggedy trousers.

The legs shook, swung, in time to thumps from the ceiling.

Both of them glanced at the spot above them. The dead man's feet walked up the side. He let them drop, raised his knees and slammed into the window.

The glass held.

He walked back up the side—higher this time. They could see the rubber soles of his trainers. Bent double, he stamped on the window, once with one foot, twice with the other. He jumped, laterally, to stomp with both.

The glass shuddered but didn't break.

What force animated these things? No living person would

have attempted that leap or made it.

Grunting from above.

Raising his gun, Greg pointed it at the source.

"No," shouted Polly. "The wire!"

He lowered his weapon. He didn't want them plunging into the Thames any more than she did.

The dead man dropped a couple of feet, then stopped. Arms vertical, he stared in at them, expression blank yet set.

He head-butted the glass.

Greg flicked the switch on his gun, aimed, squeezed the trigger and kept it squeezed. The window split, splintered and the spinning fragments fell amid the din of spat-out gunfire and casings jinking. Bits tore off the overripe body as he raised the gun upwards towards the head.

The man lifted his feet as if about to jump in through the jagged hole.

Oh no you don't. Greg continued firing up through the head then switched to firing just above it—back and forth in a sweeping motion. The arms disintegrated to mere strands until a gap opened up in the middle of them. The torso fell away backwards and the forearms dropped out of view after it.

Greg let go of the trigger. The gun had turned hot in his hands.

He and Polly leaned out and the wind tried to claim their faces.

He missed the splash but saw the water closing over the body.

Polly turned and sat down. "I thought you said not to use that setting."

He pulled his head back in. "Well, yeah, where possible we need to conserve our ammo." He sighed as he sat down opposite her. "I think we're going to need it."

"Wow…" she said, as they reached the top of the flight of stairs, stepped out onto the deck with its widescreen windows and stared out at streets and buildings ranged out before them like microchip circuitry. "I never knew London could be so beautiful."

With the gun slung over his shoulder, he put his hands in his pockets. "I guess it is if you get far enough away."

The red globe of the sun sank out to the west.

Greg's gaze tilted from the green horizon to the city at his feet. Curves of track gleamed pink. Had that train jack-knifed? No, it was just stationary across points. Red buses stood wedged in streets. Small dots covered open spaces.

Polly shuddered. "Thank God the entrance is so tucked away and none of them saw us."

He rested his hand on her shoulder. "Yeah, even we had trouble finding it."

She stepped away.

"What are these?" She stopped by one of the screens on stands with handles either side, like games consoles.

"Electronic telescopes, I think."

She tipped and swivelled the screen.

Joining her, he peered over her shoulder as she pressed "+" to zoom in.

If in miniature, they saw people, actual people, as they used to be, staring at a shop window.

A sharp intake of breath. "My God."

He leaned closer. "It can't be…"

She adjusted the angle of the screen, glanced back over her shoulder. "There, more. Look."

Tiny couples sat at tables outside a restaurant.

His heart bobbed like a helium balloon in his chest. Had normality returned? Had the nightmare finally ended?

The streets outside the window filled with darkness. These streets were bright. How?

He reached round to take control of the screen and must have jogged it because a bubble of text appeared over a public building.

Of course. These were augmented reality telescopes, with stock images of the same views for different times of day digitally stitched together to recreate the sensation of movement. The screen was in day mode.

He switched to the live video setting. Now, in the greyness of impending twilight, dead surged in the streets. They swarmed and crawled over cars and street furniture.

Polly sighed. "I thought it was too good to be true." She peered around. "Are we even safe up here?"

He massaged the back of his neck. "I hope so. At least we'll be able to see if there's a pack of them heading towards the building or something."

"But it's almost too high to see properly."

He patted the telescope. "We've got these."

Her eyebrows arched. "Those lifts rise in, like, a minute."

"I know. We'll just have to sleep with one eye open. Better still, we can take it in turns to see if anyone... anything's coming in." He patted her back as she turned away. "Let's have a proper look around."

They went up the next flight of stairs, to an open-air viewing platform. The jagged geometry of the Shard rose above them, sticking up into the luminescent sky. Even if they couldn't feel it, they could hear the wind whistling. And he didn't know if he imagined it, but he thought he heard the groans of the multitude seventy-two levels below. Or was that his stomach?

"You know we haven't eaten all day?" he said.

Travelling as light as possible, they hadn't packed anything in their knapsacks apart from ammunition.

"We'd better go and search for something."

He nodded. "Yeah."

After scouring the floors immediately below, he returned to the observation deck. Night's curtain had dropped. Crisscrossing lights denoted the streets. Buildings consisted of pinpricks of light on darkness or, closer to, cubes of light inside a more velvety blackness.

Twinkling, the configuration of lights changed over time.

What are they doing?

He strode over to one of the hi-tech telescopes, turned it on his workplace and, biting into a Snickers that had only recently gone out of date, zoomed in. He couldn't see any of his ex-colleagues, couldn't see any activity at all.

That was something at least.

"Greg, Greg..." She pushed him off her shoulder.

The wall hit the back of his head. "Ow."

Already? At night they wrapped themselves in each other's bodies. By day they were at sevens and sixes.

He rubbed his head, opened his eyes.

Blinded by brightness, he quickly shut them.

He heard footsteps.

This time he did manage to open his eyes. Sprawling sideways in the right angle between two planes, it was as if he occupied a different medium to her. His was all planky flooring, hers light, air, sky. She paced up and down in front of the floor-to-ceiling window.

She stopped, spun towards him. One arm went up and out. "You were supposed to be keeping watch." Her arm slapped her side. "Now we can't even see if they're coming."

"What?" He scrambled to his feet, stumbled towards one of the giant panes of glass and looked out at loose rolls of milky whiteness that stretched as far as the eye could see.

The whole of London had been expunged, overnight. Only the tops of taller buildings, like those clumped together to form the City, poked through.

Humphing, she stalked off.

The click of her boots receded down the stairs to the floor below.

"It's just fog." He glanced out to the east, where the eye of the sun deterred inspection. "It'll burn off. There's nothing to worry about."

Could she still hear him? Was she even listening?

What was that? Had she called his name?

He stood very still. "Polly?"

"Polly," he shouted.

"Greg..."

He picked up his gun, ran round to the stairs, skedaddled down to the floor below, found her standing there. "What? What is it?" His heart knocked.

Her lips formed words, but it took him a moment to register what she'd said: "The lift. It's moving."

The numbers were changing. The lift was coming up. He grabbed her hand, dragged her back up the stairs to the viewing platform.

She pulled away and, knees bent, stretched her arms out, palms upwards. "You said we'd be safe up here." Half turning, she gestured at the head of the stairs. "Now we're trapped like... like bugs in a jam jar."

"Mm."

He didn't have time to give her latest, no doubt justified, grievance any more attention than that. He positioned himself at the head of the stairs, with room for her if she wanted to join him.

She'd resumed pacing up and down. "We should have stayed on the ground. At least we had a fighting chance down there."

"Mm."

The lift doors opened.

How long before they ran out of bullets?

Groans echoed.

Feet dragged and thudded.

Polly clamped a hand over her mouth as dead turned up the stairwell.

He let off a few rounds to keep them at bay but not before recognizing Milo, Simon, head and shoulders above the rest, and a reanimated Rob.

Polly gasped at his side. "How did they know?"

He lowered his weapon. "I..."

Canted sunlight fell upon the faces of his ex-colleagues and the seven or so others.

Was whatever had breathed life into the dead rapidly wearing off or was prolonged contact with the air taking its toll? Milo's skin had a blue-grey tinge. Simon's looked as if it had been coated with clay dust. And the smell... Greg had to turn away as it licked his face, the inside of his mouth, his throat, like gone-off garbage in a metal dustbin left to bake in the sun for days and days.

Retching, he pulled Polly with him up the next flight of

stairs, to the open-air viewing platform.

Despite the steel structure and glass walls closing in, they kept on heading upwards.

Panting, she clattered against the side of a gantry. "You really think this is a good idea?"

He threw a glance over his shoulder as he yanked her round and up the next set of stairs. "What about this makes you think I'm not making it up as I go along?"

Just as they were running out of stories, he spotted the open side and lines of rope.

Ignoring the hard hats and cleaning equipment, he picked up a harness and pair of gloves and thrust them at her. "Hurry."

"You're having me on. A thousand feet up?"

"It's that or..." Dead spilled out onto their level.

She stepped into the harness.

Stuffing a pair of gloves in his pocket, he donned another.

Milo and the others thunked closer.

Greg raised his gun.

Milo stopped. The others filed past him.

Rob, recognizable more by his spongy, toddler-with-soiled-nappies walk than his waxy countenance, headed for Polly.

Greg tried to aim for Milo's head but Simon, gangling towards him, blocked the shot.

"Shoot," shouted Polly.

Greg jabbed his thumb over his shoulder.

The two of them retreated towards the edge, clipped themselves onto the lines. He connected the loop on his leg strap to the lower clip on the rope, obviously some kind of safety feature, and watched her do the same then pull on the gloves. Behind them, unbroken air and the longest, steepest of slides to the ground.

"Shoot," screamed Polly.

Raising the gun, Greg's hands trembled, and Simon getting closer and closer left him with even less margin for error.

Polly scrabbled for the weapon slung across her back.

Greg lunged towards her, pushed her off the edge.

A yelp stifled her scream.

Rob and Simon converged on him.

Greg slung his gun over his shoulder, tugged on his pair of gloves and took a step backwards, over the side. He didn't so much grip the rope as wrap his body around it and fireman-pole down it. Air squirrelled up the hems of his trouser legs. Portions of his shirt bulged and rippled. The building widened but with nothing to latch onto, he bounced, slid, past glazed galleries.

Tightening his grip on the rope and clamping his knees, he slithered to a halt.

He shivered.

It wasn't cold. He just wasn't used to having emptiness all around him.

The gloved hand he'd put out picked up vibrations in the window and he peered into a different medium. Dead thumped at the panes.

He loosened his grip and zipped down several feet, a process he repeated.

The white horizon shook with each jump.

Thanks to longer bounces, he gained on Polly.

"You alright?" he called down.

Catching the word "bastard", he peeped at her through dangling legs. "Er, what?"

Her head tipped back and the look she gave him made his head and body jerk. "Pushing me off the edge like that."

"Oh."

"Yeah, 'Oh.' You know what?" She let go of the line, started to tilt, grabbed it again. "I hate you more than I hate them!"

He jumped out farther and longer. "We'll talk about it later."

"There won't be a later!"

"Ugh." He slammed into a window and prized himself off it. "Don't say that."

She jerked upwards. *What*—Had he imagined it?

No, she rose another few feet.

He leaned back till he could see Milo, Simon and Rob. They hauled her back up hand over hand.

"Greg," she screamed.

His bent-back toecaps slipped off the window and the lumpy cloudscape whirled one way, back the other. *Fuck…* His heart hammered. The flight from the dead and the stillness of the air had dulled his senses to the peril he'd put them in, dangling from a glass cliff-face with the false bottom of the clouds scores of levels below.

Polly screamed again. He had to do something, or she'd pass him. *No… Polly…*

He raised a foot. It knocked against the window and he managed to steady himself.

Noticing a giant hole in the angled wall of glass down to the left, he dropped a few feet, side-stepped towards it. He swung, grabbed hold of the lip of it, pulled himself in. Just within, a cradle hung from a giant mechanical arm. He slipped out of his harness and climbed into the cradle.

Polly's cries got closer still. Soon she'd be level with the opening. He had to be quick or she'd pass out of reach. He operated the arm's controls. The cradle extended out over the city. *Christ.* A little too far. He brought it back in line with Polly, and just in time. Her head bobbed level with his foot, then shot upwards half her height.

He leaned out, grabbed her round the waist and hooked her legs inside.

"Undo the belt." He held on tightly. "Now, Polly. I've got you." She slid up through his arms till all he had hold of was her ankles. "Now!"

Just as she was about to slip through his grasp, she dropped, and he fell backwards.

"Oof." The back of his head throbbed. His jaw ached from where she'd managed to smack him in the mouth. Her knee dug into his stomach. *We did it.*

They hung on to the side of the cradle as they got up because it rocked with a violent kink.

Her harness tumbled past them.

He put his arm round her, squeezed her to him. "You made it."

She waved a hand, clutched the side. "Just get me down. Get me down, get me down."

The top of the building receded. The dead had fallen back.

"How the hell did they find us?" she said.

He clapped a hand to his forehead. "Oh, God."

She met his eyes. "What?"

"Oh, Jesus Christ." The wispy rolling clouds spread out around them rather than below them. His stomach sank along with the rest of him as he remembered spotting someone that resembled Milo in the back of a cab just before the attempted ambush on Oxford Street. "You know what this means, don't you?" She shook her head as mist spilled over the sides. "Milo's using the printer's predictions to intercept us."

Everything whited out.

CHAPTER 21

GRAVE BIRTHS

The sensory world retreated to the shape and size of Greg's mouth. He probed a cavity with his tongue. "Where are we?"

They'd just shaken off a band of dead in the fog. He couldn't see any farther ahead than he could behind but they'd tramped past boutiques, cafés, newsagents, restaurants.

"I don't know," said Polly. "I can't see a thing."

He peered into opalescence. "More to the point, where are they?"

Polly's face shot round. "Why didn't you kill them? You said they'd been sent to kill us."

"Milo and the others?" He stretched the fingers of one hand. "I know them."

"You know me." She might as well have lasered him with her eyes. "Yet you don't have any trouble pushing me off the top of a skyscraper."

His knee jerked involuntarily, causing him to stretch his leg, stamp his foot. "Well, we had the upper hand and we lost it. This isn't about the nameless faceless dead anymore. This is personal."

"So it's all my fault? Because I killed Nicola, you mean?" She turned away. "Yes, I'm sure you won't forgive me for killing your ex."

"Ssh." He pressed a finger to his lips.

Ahead, items clattered and rolled. He and Polly swerved to the opposite pavement. Then they saw him, a grey man in the greyness. He was on his knees, emptying a bin on the other side of the road.

He got to his feet. They sprinted off.

The trouble with running in milky, curdy fog was that it wasn't until you got near something that you could see it and they could just as easily be running towards dead as away from them. Since reaching ground level, they'd already survived several encounters and used up numerous magazines.

Greg came off the end of the pavement.

Judging by the traffic light, they'd arrived at a crossroads.

"Right, which way?" she said.

"Well…" He halted in the middle, on the diamond-shaped yellow lines, turned his head left and right, and listened.

Tutting, she strode over to him. Raising her gun, she fired in automatic mode up each of the exits.

He had to run round her, behind her, to avoid getting mown down. "Great. Finished attracting their attention?"

Feet shuffled to the left. Moans broke the silence to the right. Heads popped through quickly followed by shoulders shrugging off mist to reveal whole torsos just feet away, on both sides.

Oh, sod it. He fired one way, Polly the other. It was easier to get the head in automatic mode because they could see where they'd missed each time bits flew off the bodies, raise their aim and take a couple out with each spray.

Bodies crumpled like marionettes with their strings cut.

"We know which way is clear now." Polly smiled. "Come on." She plunged straight on.

He shook his head, caught up. "I'm starting to worry about you."

Had the dead been waiting in the fog or were more and more of them simply joining the chase? He and Polly blazed away at any they came across. Whenever a head and shoulders lurched into view behind them, they put on an extra spurt and the figure dropped back into pearly light as the sun tried its best to burn through.

The numbers on their tail swelled as letting off bursts of rounds drew yet more. They scuttled over another crossroads firing opposite ways.

His breathing felt like trying to fit square shapes into round holes.

Both their chests heaved.

How long before they needed to change magazines? They couldn't have more than three or four left.

A pub reared out of the fog. He swerved round the jutting quoin.

Metal trap doors clanged under their feet. He stopped, spun round, scrabbled at and lifted the flaps. He grabbed Polly's hand. She scurried down the steps and he shut the horizontal doors after them as he followed her down. They sat up to their necks in darkness at the bottom as multiple pairs of feet rounded the corner and bang-bang-banged over their heads.

He sank back against a stainless-steel keg as the rumble of shoes receded.

She whispered, "They found us at the Shard because of the printer?"

He took off the knapsack. "Yeah, they're reading the manuscripts." Unbuckling the flap, he stuck his hand in. "They know what we're going to do before we do it." He rummaged around inside. *Hey*? He and Polly only had one spare magazine between them. *How*? "Which puts us at a critical disadvantage. Milo's got the heads-up now, not us, and he's using it against us."

Darkness swallowed the entire lower half of her face as if she had no chin, no mouth, no jaw. "So what you're saying is, wherever we go, he'll find us."

He nodded, slowly.

Her mouth came up for air. "So how come they ran straight over us?"

"Because there's a delay while the next draft is produced, remember? The whole thing has to be projected into the future according to the latest conditions." Putting his arms through the knapsack's shoulder straps, he lifted it, with no effort whatsoever, onto his back. "They need to plot a point far enough ahead that they can be sure of a convergence. That's the space we have to try and survive in." He stretched, grazed his knuckles. "However cramped."

"Look, in here." She pointed at the tall spiky black iron gates.

He paused. "A park?"

"To get off the streets, away from them."

He followed her through the small gate next to the large gate set in a wall like the façade of a mini-castle, only with nothing behind it. "Is this private property then?"

She shrugged. "Does it make any difference?"

The narrow Tarmac road, or wide path, stretched ahead through dripping trees to be erased, like everything else, several yards away.

It wasn't long before ahead resembled behind.

"Hey, don't forget I need a new magazine," she said.

"Oh. Yeah." He slipped off the knapsack, reached inside and pulled out the last one. "But…"

She clutched the other end. "Yes?" Her face had taken on a rounder aspect now that damp hair plastered her head.

"Don't use them all at once."

"What? Okay."

He let go and she clicked the magazine into place.

Dangling from his fingers, the knapsack dragged at his feet. When she wasn't looking, he let it drop.

Either the trees strained the fog, the sun succeeded in thinning it or it parted with the ground because, gradually, they could see farther. At least, the fog had caves, caverns, that they could see more-or-less normally in and which slowly drifted.

Polly jabbed him in the arm with her elbow.

Turning, he saw the pale statue of a woman wreathed in mist. "It's just a…"

A tall man in a dark suit emerged from behind it. Up to his shins in thick mist, he veered left, right.

Soil dripped from his hair.

His indirect, chess-like moves brought him closer and closer. Something small, white and segmented poked out of one nostril.

It wiggled.

The man stopped, plucked the grub out of his nose, popped it in his mouth, and swallowed.

"Oh, fuck..."

Greg heard the shudder in Polly's voice.

He clapped a hand on her shoulder. "Come on."

They got ahead of the man before he could cut them off.

To the left, a woman reclining on some kind of stone bench that he took for another statue, because equally grey, suddenly detached herself from it. When she turned, she had holes where her eyes should be.

Farther away and as if black and white because likewise blending in with the mist, he made out corpses of varying ripeness. What could have been a man with straggly hair, but which might have been a woman with exposed ribs, shuffled round. A skull-face with barely any skin snapped their way.

These weren't the new dead. They were the old dead, the already dead, resurrected.

As the fog rolled back, he made out stones and crosses, standing, leaning, and mounds of earth, gaping holes, with tombs broken open and statues significantly more lifelike than the ambulatory dead.

The earth had disgorged its tenants.

"This isn't a park," he leaned towards Polly and whispered. "It's the very last place we should be."

From the side of the path, click-click-click, knitting-needle busy.

He leaned out over a trench.

At the bottom, a pair of clackety skeletons assembled themselves from kit form.

"Let's go back," he said.

But when they stopped and turned, dead stood behind them.

They set off again and the dead moved with them, in slow procession.

He kept stealing glances rearwards. "Why aren't they trying to attack us? It's like they're herding us or something."

"Stop being so paranoid."

He stuck a thumb over his shoulder. "In a cemetery followed by ravenous dead?" He half coughed, half laughed. "Paranoia'd seem to me to be a ludicrously laidback response."

The pathway diagonally crossed another path at what could have been the centre of the cemetery or just the centre of this part of it.

A shaft of sunlight poked through the middle of the clearing like a spotlight from heaven. *Not now.*

"Which way?" she said.

Something flitted between the trees ahead.

"Quick, Poll..." Dropping to a crouch, he yanked her down beside him.

They squatted behind a pair of headstones.

"What?" She looked around. Thankfully, their unwanted entourage stopped too. "What is it?"

He pointed. "Look, there. There... And there. Oh, shit. And there."

More recent, fitter dead loitered in the mist at the edges of the clearing.

"Okay... We have to make a run for it." She stood up.

"Polly, get down, get down."

She set off up one of the pathways, turned back. "Er, you need to see this..."

"No, I don't. Get—"

She pointed at the headstones. "No, Greg, you really do need to see this."

He peered round, couldn't see, so got up and slunk round.

Sunlight illuminated the letters scored in the headstones: her name on that one, his on this; each with a pair of dates. His birth date. Hers. Identical "to" dates. When was that? Tomorrow? *Oh, my God. No...* It couldn't be. "That's..."

"Today!"

He rocked back.

A pair of planks demarcated each grave.

She edged towards him, over the first plank.

"Don't make a sound but we need to get out of here, now," he whispered.

She sidled closer, screamed as the earth swallowed her up.

"Polly!" He darted towards the opening.

The earth gave way under him, quicker and quicker. He sank up to and over his head and crashed onto one shoulder.

Fighting off the bristly artificial grass matting that had blanketed the grave and which now shrouded him, he scrambled to his feet. A cross-section of damp earth hemmed him in on each side, claustrophobically close, and at both ends. He glanced up at his headstone and shuddered.

"Polly," he shouted. "Are you okay?"

"No! Get me out of here!"

One of the planks stuck out over the edge of his grave. He leapt, grabbed it and pulled it down with him. It clattered in the hole. He dragged it back, turned it so it lay flat, jumped on it and scurried up.

As soon as he was out, he dashed round to Polly's grave and lowered a plank into it. She yelped before running up the ramp.

Whether by choice or chance, she smacked into him. Feeling her hands in the small of his back, he put his arms round her.

He whispered in her ear, "Don't look now but..."

"What?"

They came apart, turned opposite ways.

With hands together and heads bowed, dead stood around them in a wide circle. One by one, they looked up, and some had faces he recognized. The woman with holes for eyes... Maggot Man... Skull-Face... Lots of skull-faces. Oh, hell. Milo.

"Quick," shouted Greg.

They turned and half fled, half charged. Concentrating fire on the opposite quadrant of the circle from Milo, dead fell away, and they broke through.

Polly's arms flailed as they ran. "They dug our..."

"I know."

One arm shot out behind her. "With our names on the..."

"I know."

"How come they found us so soon? You said we had time." She slapped a branch out of her face.

Wet leaves sprang back at him.

He wiped the droplets from his face. "I don't know. Because we stopped to talk at the pub or..."

She swerved to avoid a cherub. "Or what?"

"The convergences are coming quicker."

They weaved round tombs and headstones in the gauzy light.

She leapt over a vacated grave. "So what are we going to do?"

He landed with a thud, kept on going. "Death's coming for us. That's clear. We can't escape it, only outrun it."

She glanced round at him. "Can you outrun death?"

Breathing fraying at the edges, he glanced over his shoulder. "I think the question's how long can you outrun death for?"

CHAPTER 22

HIVE MIND OF THE DEAD

Knees bent, heels not even touching the floor, they climbed the ramp's steep spiral. Patting the top of the low concrete outer wall as if in thrall to some desperate superstition, Greg looked out at higgledy-piggledy rooftops as the mist lifted and colour seeped back into the city.

A laugh from Polly echoed hollowly.

He turned to her. "What?"

"Now the dead are above ground, they want us under it." Her eyes scorched him. "And instead of my wedding, I get to go to my own funeral."

He swung his arms round himself, one over the other, alternately. *Does everything relate back to weddings?*

He cleared his throat. "Well, he's changed the scenario now, scheduled our deaths. We've seen our own graves, with today's date on. We need to get out of here—as far away from that damn cemetery as possible."

They reached Level 3, exactly the same as the lower levels, with metal barriers, low ceilings and dark even with daylight beyond.

"I know. You do that side, I'll do this."

Stepping and bending, he peered through drivers' side windows. The cars were all neatly parked in bays with either bonnets or boots pointing outwards, yet with a sporadic quality: one here, one there; a preponderance of empty spaces in between.

He looked up. "Any luck? We need to find one."

Her head popped up from between a Dacia Duster and a SEAT Leon hatchback. "Don't you think I'm looking? It's just getting harder and harder to find one with keys in."

"It's almost like they're..."

"What?" She stopped altogether.

He glanced out of the semi-open side at the half a mile or so they'd covered since the cemetery. The mist had lifted. "Like they're removing them."

Her body jerked from the shoulder. "Would they do that?"

"I don't know." With the thumb and fingers of one hand, he massaged under his chin. "I hope not."

Either they speeded up or there were fewer cars after that because, pretty soon, they'd checked them all.

They climbed the next ramp of the multi-storey, straight this time but equally steep. With even less cars up here, they had farther to walk between each one but exhausted them in no time.

"Damn," he said, banging his fist on the bonnet of a Maserati.

Step away from the vehicle, said a voice in an American accent.

When he didn't comply, an alarm went off, a tocsin, a siren, a whoop, a toot—every conceivable earthly aural warning.

His eardrums vibrated.

"Jesus," he said, though drowned out by the din trepanning his skull. "Talk about overkill."

Polly threw her arms up and out. She let them flop to her sides as she groaned. "It'll be overkill in a minute."

He swung his head round. "Oh, shit."

Shuffles and moans rose up from the ground floor. *Already?*

"They're coming from the far side," she shouted.

They dashed down the ramp they were on.

She grabbed his arm. "Stop."

They peered over the edge. Heads bobbed in the gap, two floors down, on the way up.

They turned around, headed back up to Level 3.

"Exit upwards," read the sign.

Polly tutted. "Exit upwards in a multi-storey carpark?"

He shot her a glance. "I know. Wrong on so many levels."

She shot him a scowl. He dipped his head. They kept on going.

"Let's check the cars," he said, when they reached Level 4.

She glanced round. "No, no, there's no time."

Footsteps thundered up the ramp below and the one on the far side.

"Go, go, go," he shouted.

They raced up the next ramp and emerged out onto the tarmacked roof. The layout was different up here with a much smaller surface area but an extension at the other end.

Lungs heaving like bellows, he spun round. "No fucking cars."

They sprinted across the open-air deck.

Dead surged up from both the helical ramp ahead and the straight ramp behind.

Stopping and swinging slowly from the hip, she sprayed them with bullets.

A few went down.

He stopped too. "No, single head shots!"

"There's too many of them." Half way through the return sweep, her gun gave out. She pulled the trigger. Nothing, just click, click, click. She held her other hand out. "Magazine."

"That's it."

Still with her hand out, she looked at him. "What?"

"That was the last one."

Her hand dropped. "What? Why didn't you tell me?"

"I didn't want to worry you."

"Oh, great, well, thanks. I really enjoyed my bubble of security." Her gun clattered to the deck as she threw it down. "It's just a pity it's burst!"

The dead closed in from both sides.

Polly screamed as one tried to grab her with the wizened claw of a hand. She swerved out of the way. Greg kicked it in the shins.

He drove the muzzle of his gun into the grey face of another, where it remained as the man sank to the deck.

He and Polly ran the only way they could, towards the floor's extra wing. His breathing jumped around all over the place. *No...* Why hadn't they smashed up their gravestones when they'd had the chance? *Not today.*

Once round the corner, he spotted a jutting bit of wall with a panel with a window in it and a handle below that. *A door...* The sign next to it read, "To the shops".

He tapped Polly's arm. "Quick."

They altered course because it was almost as if the exit had materialized especially for them.

Plunging down the grimy concrete stairwell confirmed that it had been there all along.

Greg eased the car, with its gleaming black bonnet, out into the opposite lane. Overtaking a bus went on and on. Dead pounded at its long windows. A schoolgirl licked the glass.

"Ignore them," he said, waving a hand as if erasing them from his vision. He got a little ahead, yanked the steering one way, the other, then nipped in front of the bus. "I told you we'd get transport."

"Yeah." Turning his way, her head canted forwards even as it slid back. "It's just a shame you had to choose this."

He glanced behind him at the long platform with its wood-effect laminate finish, stainless-steel runners and rubber rollers.

If the dials on the dashboard had included gauges for blood pressure, his would have tipped over into the red. He tried to keep his voice steady. "We broke in the back. How could I know it was a funeral parlour?"

She held her hands out, shook them. "But a hearse, Greg. Of all the different kinds of vehicle to choose from, a hearse?"

"I'd no idea what we were getting till I ran round the side and pressed the key fob."

"No idea? Really?"

He shrugged. "You never know, it might come in handy."

A terse laugh. "For us or them?" She pointed out of the window at streets teeming with dead, who only parted because they had to. "I thought we were trying to escape our own funeral, not hand ourselves over on a platter."

He sighed through his nose.

Polly shifted, edged forwards.

All elbows, she peered out of the windows from one angle, jerked to another, switched to a third. "Greg?"

"Yes?"

She clutched the corner of her seat. "Why are we down by the river?" He smelt tangy Doritos as she leaned towards him. She'd found a packet in the funeral parlour's office. "We're supposed to be getting out of here."

They barrelled over a bridge.

He gestured out of the window. "How high does the water look?"

"Very."

"Good." He nodded, privately. "We are leaving, don't worry. There's just something I need to do first."

Navigating his way through menus, Greg sat clicking on a mouse in front of a flat-screen monitor. As if for inspiration, he paused to glance past a dead plant at the view beyond the window of piers lined up across the Thames like stationary craft. Each one had steel housing enclosing front and back in the shape of an armadillo's shell. An open middle section featured the yellow beam of a crane and a pair of yellow hydraulic arms of the kind usually found on JCBs. Shut gates all the way across divided the river in two.

He'd dispatched the skeleton staff easily enough with a spade from the hearse but if a woman hadn't come out when she had, they'd never have got in in the first place.

"I can't believe the dead still smoke," he said.

"Why, you think they'd stop for health reasons?"

"No, I …" He checked his watch. "Never mind."

Polly pivoted in her boots on the carpet behind him. "I still want to know what the hell we're doing here."

"They've closed the barrier. So they must be expecting a very high tide."

"But surely it's closing the barrier that's caused the high levels." Leaning over him, she gestured out of the window. "I mean, it's not even raining."

"Just because it's not raining here doesn't mean it's not raining upriver. Perhaps there's a major storm sitting off to the edge of London." He glanced round and up. "You wouldn't want the extra water from that and a tidal surge meeting head on."

She spun away. "I don't care whether it's raining or not, I just want to know what the point is."

"I'm trying to give Milo and his cohort something to keep them occupied to give us a better chance of getting away." He carried on clicking. "Do you know, we could get 14 years for this."

"I think you'll find that's the least of our worries." Polly resumed her pacing up and down.

Finally, one of the nearer gates started rotating.

"Got it," he cried.

She stopped at his shoulder. "Good, come on, we need to get out of here."

"Soon. Just nine more to go."

Harumphing, she twisted away.

Polly placed a hand on the dashboard as they swung round a corner near to his old place of work. "I mean, I could have understood it if we'd stopped at your office but..."

"That's good," he said, "because that's where we're going now."

"What? You're joking! I thought we were finally on our way."

He indicated. "We are." Tutting, he clicked the lever back to the neutral position. "Just a quick pit stop while Milo's out. Er, hopefully."

"Oh, you have got to be..." Polly put her other hand out as they swerved into the car park. "Greg!"

He slammed on the brakes.

She peeled herself off the dashboard. "Unbelievable..."

He got out, fetched the spade and hammer from the compartment at the back.

Lips pursed, alternately sniffing and breathing out through her nose, Polly joined him.

He handed her the hammer and they entered the building.

"Listen," he said, "it might give us a vital heads-up about their intentions."

"We know their intentions!" She pointed back over her shoulder at the hearse. "They want us dead on arrival."

They turned the corner.

"Worst-case scenario, even if we can't get anything out of the printer, we can always smash it up." Walking level with her up the corridor, he checked for the flicker of a response. "The link between them and him..." Another glance. "So they can't use it either."

Nothing.

They climbed the stairs.

At the top, he stopped outside the door to Admin, gripped the handle and, leaving a space for Polly at his side, peeped through the wired window.

"Oh, Jesus," he muttered.

Hundreds of dead formed a massive horseshoe around the printer. Every single one of them faced it, which meant that the ones this side had their backs to the door.

Polly's shoulder attached itself to his. Her hair brushed his ear.

A breath leaked out of her.

"What are they doing?" she whispered. "Protecting it?"

He shook his head. "I don't know. Worshipping it? Waiting to receive orders?"

"It's... creepy. Like their lair or something."

Her shudder communicated itself to him.

"I know."

A flyblown face slid in from the side to fill the window.

He and Polly jerked back.

It peered out just as they'd peered in.

Katissia...?

The skin moved, independently.

The mouth opened. Gutturals emerged.

Heads turned behind.

"Oh, shit," said Greg. "Run!"

He and Polly flew down the stairs.

They'd made it two thirds of the way along the corridor when they spotted Simon and Rob slouching the other way.

"Uh-oh," said Greg.

Footsteps clattered down the stairs behind them.

He couldn't be sure that the doors either side weren't just doors to cupboards.

They kept on going.

He lined up with Simon on his side. Polly lined up with Rob on hers.

"You have to do it this time, Greg." She leaned towards him. "As much for their sake as for ours. I mean, they wouldn't want to be like that. And you said it yourself, it's not even them anymore."

Was he right? Had the Simon he knew ceased to exist, become separated from himself, become something other, or had part of him survived?

Taking the hammer, he handed Polly the spade.

Polly held it out before her.

One swift clunk to the head dispatched Rob.

Greg raised the hammer. *What kind of world is it where you have to kill your friends?*

Simon bared his teeth, snarled, and lunged.

Before they kill you. Greg brought the hammer down on his friend's skull.

A crack. Simon jolted.

With the next blow, he slumped against the wall.

With each successive blow, he slid down it.

Greg could hardly see for the tears spilling out of his eyes.

"Sorry," he cried, with each whack.

"Sorry!"

"Sorry!"

"Sorry!"

One-sided streets, concrete embankments and giant stores and warehouses sped by as, riding the dips, rises and bends of a dual carriageway, he and Polly headed out of town.

He pulled the chauffeur's cap he'd found between the seats down low over his eyes and piloted the hearse with lead-heavy, automaton-like limbs, and a gnawing black hole in his chest. "When did I become a murderer?"

Polly touched his elbow. "You didn't kill him, you know." She squeezed his arm. "It was his body that got brought back, not Simon." Greg kept his eyes on the road. "Even if it doesn't feel like it, we did the right thing. We had no choice, or we wouldn't even be here." She removed her hand, sighed. "Though we could have been well on our way by now."

The hearse vibrated, and Greg corrected for a drift towards the side of the road. "Hopefully the barrier sabotage will slow Milo down a bit, if not drown the bugger."

She swung round. "What? Nothing happened. It was a complete waste of time."

"Well, you can't expect anything to happen instantly."

She craned forwards. "What the hell's that?"

"Fell off the back of a lorry? I don't know."

Piles of tables and chairs, with metal legs sticking out, filled the opening of a bridge.

He veered up the ramp, came level with an office complex, crossed the bridge and followed signs for the next route out.

They'd joined the motorway and rounded a bend when, ahead, they spotted the blackened hull of what must have been a tanker blazing right across this side. Lifting the peak of his cap, he stopped and stared at the pullulating hoops of fire. "We could go round, find another car farther up..."

"On foot? With no ammo?" She jogged his elbow.

He followed her line of sight. What, at first, he'd taken to be a couple of scarecrows lurched through a field, with more and more standing up in the tall grass.

He checked the rear-view mirror.

The first dead clambered over the outer barrier and into the road.

"Hang on." He swung the car about, put his foot down and swerved and counter-swerved round the lumbering dead. The bumper caught the shins of one and it went down. The back wheel jolted, and the skull crunched. "We'll go up the down carriageway."

"No, we can't. Look." Polly pointed out of her window.

On the other side of the central reservation, a jack-knifed lorry had wedged itself against a coach, completely blocking all three lanes along with the hard shoulder. He hadn't noticed on the way up, or not consciously.

He put his foot down. "It's deliberate."

Polly's head shot round. "What?"

He came back off the motorway and they leaned to one side,

leaned to the other, straightened in unison as he traversed the roundabout.

"Hey, this is heading back into the city." She slapped his arm. "Oi, we're heading back in. And what do you mean, deliberate?"

"They're blocking all our exit routes."

"Because we wasted so much time!"

"No." He shook his head. "How would they know, out here? There's something else going on, something even more disturbing."

Polly clutched her seat. "What?"

His hands flexed on the steering wheel. "They're communicating."

"How?"

He took one hand off the wheel, brought it back down with a smack. "I don't know. Radio waves of the dead?" He uncricked his neck. "The point is, it's planned, orchestrated. We're not just running into random bands while outmanoeuvring Milo. Groups in different places are acting in consort. They're connected."

Polly's elbow thudded against her car door as she twisted round. "Connected how?"

"Think of it like an open com-link in their heads. Or a... a kind of swarm mentality." He pictured a mound of earth heaving with a colony of ants at battle stations and his voice dropped. "Basically, as soon as one knows, they all do."

She'd tied her hair into a ponytail and it twitched left and right. "So it just takes one to read the latest draft and then he or she can broadcast it to all the others?"

"Yeah, or one out in the field relay things the other way. So we need to decide what we're going to do."

Her arm flopped sideways. "Well, don't ask me." She tapped the glass with a fingernail. "Ask them."

"I'm serious, they're closing down our options. They don't want us to leave."

"Kettled by the dead?"

"Yeah."

Her ponytail jerked. "Oh, God."

His grip on the wheel tightened. "We need to find another way out."

She sat up. "How? How can we outwit them when, before too long, they know what we're going to do?"

"Lateral thinking." He resisted the forward pull on his head as he braked to avoid a dead couple lying in the road.

The pair bit each other's ankles, and not just bit but ripped, chewed and swallowed.

His and Polly's heads tilted back, and the brake and accelerator creaked like organ pedals as he transferred his foot from one to the other.

She stared out of her window. "What if we hid somewhere?"

He shook his head. "We can't stay in any place too long. Wherever we go, they'll track us down."

She turned his way. "What about the bank vault? We could lock ourselves in."

He met her gaze for a moment. "And then what?"

"Well, we can't kill them all. We haven't even got any ammunition. And they're just going to keep coming and coming."

"Which is why our only hope is to get far enough away."

She flung her hands apart. "How? We're trapped. You said so yourself. There's no way out."

He opened his mouth to speak, shut it.

At the next roundabout, he wrenched the wheel to the right. Polly fell against her door. The tires squealed. He kept on going, round and round.

She held on. "What are you doing?" she cried.

"Thinking."

"No, you're not. You're driving round in circles like a madman."

"I'm keeping them guessing."

She pushed herself off the door. "So they can't know what we're going to do because we haven't decided yet?"

"Exactly." He caught her eye for a moment. "As soon as we make a decision, a new draft gets written, remember? If we can keep them guessing, they can never make that call."

"But we can't take too long."

He sighed. "You're right." He glanced up each passing exit for signs of the dead. "We've got to decide now, and it's got to be the right choice. Something left-field."

She thumped her door. "Oh, why can't they just get back in their airships and leave us alone?"

Suddenly, in his memory, he had a clear line of sight from the cable car to London City Airport.

"That's it. That's our way out." Flooring the accelerator pedal, he turned the wheel the other way and they peeled off up an exit.

Polly rolled in her seat. "What is?"

"The airship they left behind."

She turned sharply towards him. "One of theirs?" she cried.

He took his cap off, threw it in the back and gripped the steering wheel. "You saw our gravestones, with today's date on. It's our only way of getting far enough away from here."

She stared out of the window, folded her arms.

The road ahead shimmered like a mirage. He kept the accelerator depressed. The Tarmac darkened and whatever it was didn't disperse. As they got closer, it took on a solid aspect. He hit the brake. Polly pitched forward. The hearse juddered to a halt. She rebounded.

Water lapped at the road.

Polly peered out. "We at the Thames already?"

He cleared his throat. "Yes and no. We haven't arrived at it… It's come to meet us."

The waterline ran from a Coral on one side to a Boots on the other. With the latter's sliding door open, the same restless surface extended seamlessly inside. A red post box waded up to its black base. Gallons poured down the steps of a tube station. His mind flew on ahead like a drone. The water deepened all the way. If it was flooded here, it would be flooded at the airport. How could they even get there?

"Oh, Greg…" Polly sighed like a burst bicycle tire, with a hiss. "What have you done?"

CHAPTER 23

STOWAWAYS

"It worked," he said after a long pause, more to himself than to her.

"Uh, yeah. A little too well." She whacked his arm. "You were supposed to sabotage their chances of catching us, not ours of escaping."

He looked round. "I didn't know we'd be coming back."

Polly breathed in as if sighing in reverse. "There's no way we can get out of here now."

She sniffed, with finality.

"Actually..." He held himself rigid so as not to disrupt the gestation of a thought. "There might be a way..."

"Just when I think your choice of transport can't get any worse, somehow you excel yourself." Seated at his side, Polly clung on. "So this is your brilliant idea? Really? Fleeing London by bus?"

He swung the 30-foot-long vehicle round the corner and headed up a street similar to the one they'd stopped on in the hearse. "Yes, but it's not just a bus, is it?"

Instead of pulling up before reaching the canalized end of the street, this time he kept on going. They ploughed through water as in a log ride until all four wheels left the ground.

Correcting for a slew to the side, he laughed as they bobbed and swayed. "It's a Duck bus."

The engine of the World War II amphibious truck growled as he piloted them through the submerged streets. Their wake slapped walls and windows on both sides. Secondary glugs and chocks echoed from behind façades and deep within buildings.

Each one had him turning his head in case of an assault.

Yet the dead hung in the water. Only their eyes moved, in time with the craft.

Running up and down the aisle clutching a paddle as if it was a bat and lunging between seats to peer over the side, Polly checked that none attempted to climb aboard.

But the dead all drifted the same way as unseen currents carried them along.

Where did the Thames begin? Where did it end? Greg didn't know anymore.

Then the underwater faces fell away. It worked. He'd got rid of the dead.

He and Polly didn't just reach a crossroads, the gap between this side and the next widened to a gulf. The river had turned into a sea with a strait between an archipelago of buildings to north and south. Previously too long, the bus now struck him as out of scale the other way. It rolled, pitched, as he performed a ninety-degree turn.

The wind baffled his ears.

A seagull sheared across the bow to flap level with his shoulder. It chattered. Another one farther back, and off to the other side, answered.

As soon as Greg glanced at the first, it got whipped aloft as if on a string.

Made it. Spluttering water, he grabbed the metal ladder up to the gondola.

He'd climbed the mooring mast, released the line and swum back to the airship before it drifted off. Now he got a foot on the ladder and climbed as out of a swimming pool, just with river-heavy clothes shrink-wrapping his body.

Something grabbed his ankle. He tried to shake it off. It ratcheted tighter.

The airship blotting out the sky darkened the water. He peered downwards. *It can't be...* The surface smashed and reformed over a blue-tinged pate close to his submerged shins. *Oh, shit, it is.* How could he think a flood would ever stop them? *They don't need to breathe.*

Another hand closed around his ankle. A set of teeth sank

into the flesh between them, fortunately through his jeans, yet even so, a shock of pain shot up his leg. His breathing snagged on itself. *This it?* His eyes sought out Polly above. *So close!*

"Go," he mouthed.

She leaned out of the cabin door towards him with the paddle in her hand and reached out with it, handle first. Only when he grasped it did he understand. He held on with his other hand, lifted the ex-human clamped to his ankle, and whacked it, hard.

It released its jaws and snarled, hissed.

Jerking his leg inwards and upwards, he swung the paddle. A crack and the head rolled, the hands' grip relaxed. The spindly body fell backwards in an explosion of water. The dark, featureless surface quickly reformed.

Greg scurried up the ladder to the gondola, where metal struts had regularly-spaced holes in them like oversized Meccano. With water dripping off him, he stood swaying. "Thanks." His heart banged in his chest. "I..."

Polly pointed out of the window, where City Airport looked like the Thames. The whole flat expanse of the plane they rested on looked like the Thames. They drifted backwards, sideways. The wind turned the airship. Extrapolating from their present rate of drift and turn, they'd collide with the terminal's gates, if not the terminal building itself.

"Right." Used to never having enough time to say what needed to be said, not that he would have known how to express it if he had, he ran up to the front of the cabin, looked around for a seat. There wasn't one. He remained standing on the bridge of the airship with a puddle forming around him.

The wheel in front was like a modernist version of the wheel of a galleon: spokes protruded as handles but metal and with holes in. Another stood at right angles to that. The first had a brass compass beyond it. The latter had a panel of instruments behind it. He recognized a rudimentary altimeter and that was pretty much it for now. Facing the panel, on a post within reach, he spotted two gear levers either side of a large dial labelled Idle, Slow, Half, Cruise, under Ahead, and Idle, Full, under Astern. At present they were on Stop, in the middle.

"Greg... Greg..." Polly tapped him on the shoulder.

He tore himself away from the controls. "What?"

"Um, look..."

He turned to see another patch of darkened water with nothing above it—moving. Elbows and crowns fretted the surface. *A shoal of dead.* A shiver ran through him. Galvanized, he pushed the right-hand gear lever. The engines that side immediately buzzed, and the buzzing only increased as he pushed through Slow to Half. He spun the front wheel to the left and their turn towards the buildings slowed without ever quite stopping until now they turned the other way. As he straightened up, he pushed the other throttle level with the first, then pushed both to Cruise. The terminal receded. Picking up speed, they skimmed across the water, right through the middle of the dead. Yet they didn't take off.

He looked around for some kind of pitch control. Spotting a series of toggles to the side that read Release Ballast, he pulled a succession of them. Behind the cabin, several bodies of water dropped from the keel. He grabbed the side wheel and rotated it anticlockwise.

The airship's floats unsucked themselves from the flood.

The titanic craft rose, nose first.

"Greg," cried Polly.

As the dirigible came away from the water, dead came with it, suspended from mooring lines. One by one they fell, splashing into water, a higher and higher drop each time. Yet a few clung on. A woman in a bedraggled black dress who'd climbed arm over arm dangled close to the gondola. She swung backwards and forwards, backwards and forwards, getting nearer and nearer.

She smacked into the window and, with the squeak of skin on glass, slid out of sight.

By now, only one remained. At the nose of the airship, the stringy man hung from the main mooring line. Although his body faced outwards, his head bent back, and he glared at them.

As if with a tendency to only sway one way, the rope wavered towards them. Greg's ankle throbbed, and his veins drew as the man's eyes bore into his.

Backwards-headed like some kind of human insect, the

stick-man crawled up the rope.

"There's a hatch at the nose," said Greg.

"What?" shouted Polly, over the roar of the engines.

Greg pointed at the man, then upwards. "Hatch!"

"Oh, God. If only we still had a gun. And some bullets."

Greg ignored what was probably a dig at him and took it at face value instead. "We couldn't use it up here." He gestured above them. "I don't know if this thing's full of hydrogen or helium or what."

Lifting his feet and placing them either side of the rope, the man hauled himself closer and closer to the access point.

Passing one another high above the river this side of the O2 Arena, ahead hung the gondolas of the Emirates Air Line.

Levelling out not much higher, Greg steered towards the centre.

No longer toy size, the towers, wires and pods rapidly expanded.

The man made it to the last quarter of the rope.

The cable car approached full scale.

What? Greg stared at the rope-climber. *Was that...?* Did a member of the dead just run a blue tongue around non-existent lips?

Greg dipped the nose.

The cable car neared quicker and quicker.

With a concentrated knottedness in his stomach, perhaps from crossing old routes, Greg steered for the dip in the top wire. Then the front rope caught on the nearest cable and the dead man shot upwards. Where the rope bent, he got swept off it, right in front of them.

Pods bounced to either side.

Greg punched the air—"Yes!"

Polly cheered.

He laughed, smiled at her, laughed again.

She smiled, looked down.

He turned back to the front, with a start. "Jesus Christ!"

The towers of Canary Wharf loomed ahead.

He released more ballast and spun the second wheel to put the airship into another climb. Polly held on. He leaned forwards. Something like a spirit level blipped. The creaking and groaning of the hull communicated itself to the cabin via an open hatchway. They soared but fast enough? On and on went the towers, up and up, with no sign of the top, just storey after storey, each one closer than the last. A man in a suit at a window raised his pale eyes in time with their ascent even as he sank as if in a lift.

Finally, sky, clouds, filled the sloping windshield.

Greg levelled out and, hinged on them, the horizon came back up.

The pointy tower of One Canada Square passed to the side.

Below, the Isle of Dogs merged with Lewisham, which merged with Tower Hamlets, which merged with Southwark, which merged with the City. All had been subsumed into one vast stretch of pewter punctuated, in patches, by buildings.

Occasionally running a hand through his drying hair, Greg stood steaming in his clothes as he followed the course of the river.

The Shard came up on their right. With its windows, decks, empty again, it stuck up above them with its familiar unfinished quality in the upper reaches before sliding by.

He leaned out over the slanting side windows and checked behind them. Except for a giant bomb-shaped shadow at water level, no airship followed them.

His eyes lingered on the Veniced streets, the islanded landmarks. The river ran on both sides of the London Eye. It surrounded the Houses of Parliament.

He thought of all the dead still going through the motions of their lives, underwater, and—somewhere down there—the piece of office equipment at the heart of it all.

He turned to Polly. "We're giving up access to the printer, permanently."

She shrugged. "There's no way we can get to it." A wince. "Plus, I'm not sure I want to know what it says anymore."

"Yeah, true." He patted her shoulder. "We did the right thing."

She tilted her head. "We didn't have any choice."

He nodded. "Two one-way tickets out of here…"

"Yeah." She straightened up, stretched. "Two singles."

Greg turned away.

His heart bounced around his chest as he swung back.

At a comfortably close and clear magnification, England Google Earthed below.

Above the green of the landscape, a white sheet of high cloud obscured the sun.

Keeping the helm steady, Greg maintained their present course between the one and the other.

The main compass had a button on it like the snooze button on an alarm clock. It read Automatic Pilot. He preferred hands-on.

Polly came and stood at his side, only half a step back.

He glanced round at her, twice, twisting from the waist both times.

Apart from a few unpleasant damp patches in intimate places, he'd largely dried off.

She stared straight ahead. "Where are we?"

He peered down.

"Er…" Their height had a flattening effect on the landscape, which rendered it more a patchwork of fields with the occasional town or village than a navigable map. "No idea."

They sailed over huge tracts of land with no human dead, no wildlife, just the corpses of cattle and what could have been horses.

"Oh, my God," she said. "They've eaten everything."

Reaching out, he clutched her hand. "Pretty much." Her arm hung slackly. Failing to grasp back, her hand curled up in his. "But in a way, you know, that's good."

She jerked round, pulling her hand away in the process. "What? Why good?"

He let his arm drop. "Well, remember that couple we saw from the hearse, biting each other's ankles?"

"Yeah."

"They were eating each other."

She pulled a face. "Ew."

He shook his head. "No, Polly, it means they're so desperate for food that they're turning on their own kind. I mean, you've seen them. They're still decaying." Her head veered this way and that until their eyes met. "I'm starting to think the dead might have an expiration date."

She blinked. "So we just need to try and outlive them?"

He smiled. "Exactly. Then, you never know, there might actually be an end to this nightmare."

Her head listed from one side to the other. "What about our own death date?"

His smile slackened, gave out. He couldn't dismiss what they'd read in the cemetery as just another draft. It was written in stone. Gravestone. He tipped his head, scratched an eyebrow. "Well, we've escaped that now, haven't we?"

He looked up.

She looked at him.

Turning as she turned, his eyes alighted on a grey patch below, slowly shifting, changing shape.

She leaned out next to him and her voice rose. "What the hell's that?"

Yet even side on, he could tell from her face that she knew exactly what it was. A whole army of dead on the move.

He and Polly were still staring down when a door creaked above them.

The breath he'd been taking caught in his throat. Her eyes widened as if about to pop.

He touched the top of her arm and this time she didn't try and dislodge his hand.

Another door, farther back, clicked shut.

Heart pounding like a drum solo, he gripped the ball of her shoulder. *Why didn't I check?* "There's some up there."

CHAPTER 24

DEATH CLONES

He lowered his voice. "We need to go up."

Polly had turned away to listen. She whirled back. "What?"

"Well, we can't leave them wandering around up there." Having raised a hand, he let it drop.

He peered ahead, out to where clouds hugged the earth at one extreme, filled the sky at the other, and paused with his finger on the autopilot button.

It clicked, lit up, as he pressed it.

The dirigible dipped and rose as he strode across the floor 600 feet above the ground.

Hurly-burly air currents?

Falling against the partition at the back, he stuck his head through the opening. Charts and maps covered the desks along with a compass, a stopwatch and a pair of headphones plugged into a radio set. He lifted the headphones, put them to his ear.

Whispering voices leaked out.

Throwing down the cans, he climbed the ladder. "Let's get this over with."

He emerged out onto a narrow walkway. V-shaped struts to either side met beneath it. A forest of metal and wires filled the space above.

Polly's boots rang out on the rungs.

"Ssh." He peered down, straightened up as she joined him.

Holding on to girders with each seasick lurch, they headed back along the keel, past a series of drums, under giant gasbags.

They came to a ramp with strips of aluminum set into it at intervals. A door stood ajar at the top. It swung gently. *False alarm*? What about the other door, farther away, higher up?

The size of the treads left little room for anything other than tiptoeing up.

Noticing grease on one of his hands, he rubbed it on his jeans. "Come on."

The door opened onto a windowless corridor.

Getting used to shifting his weight from one foot to the other to ease out each pitch and roll, he stepped along it until they came to a transverse corridor with, beyond that, a staircase heading up.

They climbed the stairs.

Coming in to view, the entrances to two corridors, one to the left and another to the right. This was definitely the correct level for the second, sharper sound, only which room?

Picking a corridor at random, he opened and closed door after door. Each disclosed the same view of a sink, a fold-down desk and a bunkbed with a giant Meccano ladder leaning against it. Berth after berth. Identical.

He froze with his hand on a door handle because in the bottom bunk of the next one he tried a form lay heaped. The corpse, male, turned slowly. Bones started from its hanging-open shirt as if its body had started consuming itself. It unclasped bluish hands, lifted a face drained of blood.

Greg lurched backwards. It wasn't the smell, though that tarred his throat. However many times he looked, he came to the same crazy conclusion. If from the other side of the gulf, the one that separates us all from ourselves and everyone we've ever known and loved, he recognized the man.

Himself, post-death.

He shook to the muffled crumps of his heart and put his hand to it as if at any moment it would give out and consign him to the other body. *This shouldn't be happening.* He dragged his eyes away. *This shouldn't—* "Polly?" *Where's Polly?* "Polly!"

She clattered round the corner in her boots, charged up the corridor.

"There you are," he said.

"Run."

"What?"

She thudded past him. "Run!"

One set of footsteps drew closer to the corner, another to the doorway behind him.

Jumping out of the way of his other self's clutches, he set off after her. "Who is it? Who did you see?"

"You don't want to know." She flung her head round. "One of them."

She clunked down a flight of stairs.

He caught up with her at the bottom, grabbed hold of her arm. "Polly, Polly, we're going the wrong way." They'd come from the other direction. This way led deeper into the airship. He pointed over his shoulder.

As far as they could, given the different layout, they retraced their steps on the deck below the one they'd been on.

A sliding door led to a room with a doorway at the far end and another half way along. Scraps of paper littered the floor. He picked up a handful and each one had a number on it. Why couldn't they hear any footsteps behind them?

He let the pieces of paper flutter down and smacked his forehead with the flat of his hand. "Oh, God."

"What?" she said. "What is it?"

He clenched both hands. "We need to get to the gondola."

She leaned in. "That's where we are going, isn't it?"

"Yes, but we've got to get there before they do."

Her eyes widened. "What?"

"They'll turn us around, take us back."

Her gaze slid from one side to the other.

He shook his clenched hands. "The cemetery!"

Her gaze jerked.

Just as they were about to pass the side door, his doppelganger from beyond the grave burst through it.

"Run," he cried, sprinting back the way they'd come.

When, at the sliding door, he paused and looked round, she wasn't there—and neither was the other him. *Damn, damn, damn…* She must have used the far exit.

Turning and heading back up the airship through the next

door along, the other side from his double, he cupped his hands around his mouth to try and project his voice without shouting: "Polly... Polly?" A long, empty pause. "Polly!"

Oh, hell.

The heavens clap-clapped, the side of the flying ship lit up and the booms reverberated back and forth and all around. A distant alarm hectored. From the cockpit? Sparks shot across his mind. *God Almighty.* He sprinted past windows that leaned outwards. The landscape scrolled the other way. "Polly!"

He'd just passed the last doorway of the room they'd been in when he heard a creak.

He sprang back against the partition.

Holding his breath, he peeped round the corner at the landing.

No-one there.

Exhaling and leaning against the panel, he jumped because someone stood next to him.

He quickly absorbed the jolt because, although his peripheral vision blurred the precise features, the outline at his elbow and the stature of it flooded him with the warmth of familiarity, which was why he didn't immediately swing round but instead leaned closer to whisper, "Where did you get to?"

He turned, raised his eyes to her face, and leapt backwards. "Oh, Jesus Christ!"

Thunder dinned in his ears and strobing light recast the hollows in Polly's grey, clay-like cheeks. Her hair encroached on her face in long, lank straggles. Her lashes jiggled them as her eyes swivelled independently of one another.

She twitched, leered.

His ears rang. His heart jackhammered.

With nails extended, she reached out and gripped his neck. The nails dug into its soft flesh.

He turned the other way to try and wrench himself free and she turned with him, gripping harder. Unable to breathe, burning up and feeling as if his eyeballs were about to explode, he delivered a chop to the inside of her elbow joint. Setting off running, he weaved this way and that, through the doorway the original Polly had used, through the doorway his dead self had used, to arrive back at the landing.

Long chestnut hair disappeared through the door at the end of the short corridor at the foot of the flight of stairs.

Oh, shit. He flew down them. He had to reach the controls before dead Polly did.

He barged through the door at the end of the corridor, thudded, bouncing down the bendy ramp and made it past a jutting tank just in time to see her climb down the hole in the keel. The huge gasbags that hung above him passed in and out of sight as he sprinted up the gangway. The whole floating structure creaked and groaned. Taut wires sung to themselves.

Footsteps thunked behind him and he looked over his shoulder to see his other self. *Oh, give me a break...*

Reaching the hole, he slid down the outside of the ladder. The alarm set the membranes of his ears fluttering. He hit the bottom, wrenched a canister from its bracket, spun round and raised it over the chestnut head.

The face turned with blooming, living skin.

"Polly!" he cried, stopping just in time.

"Greg! What the hell?"

He put the canister down. "I thought you were... her."

She threw her head back. "Charming..." A sidelong look. "For what it's worth, I mistook you for your Madame Tussauds' waxwork too."

Footsteps clanked closer.

Greg scurried up the ladder, closed the hatch, turned the wheel to secure it and jumped back down.

One set of footsteps stopped above them. Another set approached.

Greg dashed up to the bridge. "You saw them?"

She came and stood next to him. "Saw them? Yours tried to kill me!" She showed him the fingernail indentations in her wrist. "Then you try and finish the job."

He turned off the autopilot, which silenced the alarm, rotated the pitch wheel and peered out.

He couldn't see a thing for thick black cloud.

"What are you doing?" said Polly.

"If there's one thing you shouldn't do in an airship..." He

had to pause for another crash of thunder as the cloud lit up from within. He thought of all the gas, all the fuel. "…it's fly into a thunderstorm."

The canister rolled to the front. He stepped out of the way of it and it lodged itself between two posts.

He kept an eye on the altimeter. 515, 505, 495… How low did this cloud go?

The second set of footsteps stopped above, and the hatch clanged under an onslaught of blows.

Polly pressed her palms to her ears. "That's doing my head in."

"Don't worry, it should hold."

She took her hands away from her ears. "Should?" Her arms dropped. "What… What is this? What's going on? What are they?"

"They're us, as we will be when…"

"I know that for Christ's sake but why are they here *already*? We're not dead." A breath. "Are we?"

His gaze shot from the blank window to her and back. "What? No." He gripped the front wheel. "This is their world now. They're not the ones who shouldn't be in it, we are." He swallowed. "We weren't supposed to survive the apocalypse, remember? They must have stayed aboard the last remaining airship ready to be deployed as soon as we…"

She threw her hands up. "Oh, and of course you had to go and choose it. And wake them up." Neon forked and squirrelled through the clouds. Thunder rolled above and around and below. Metal bang-bang-banged. "So now we're trapped up here with dead homicidal effigies of us." She tossed her hair, snorted. "Absolutely brilliant, Gregory. Probably your best plan yet!"

He slapped the helm. The wheel spun, and the airship yawed to starboard. They leaned to port. "Well, how could I possibly predict that? Plus whatever we do, they come up with an opposing plan, don't they?"

Her laughter hack-hack-hacked away at him.

"So you keep telling me," she said.

He grabbed the wheel. A shudder ran through the craft and they both had to step wider. "But, yeah, you're right. They want to kill us to replace us and complete the transition."

She left off laughing.

He looked up. The banging had stopped. When?

Footsteps receded, back the way they'd come.

She whispered, "Where are they going?"

"I don't know," he whispered.

In direct contravention of gravity, his stomach tugged upwards. With what, queasiness?

He checked the altimeter, the big needle of which spun anti-clockwise. "Oh, shit."

"What? What is it?"

"We're sinking way too fast. Either we're stuck in a downdraught or..."

"Or...? Or what?"

He checked the indicators for gas pressure and, in cell after cell, the levels dropped. Twisting round, he stared at the underbelly of the fuselage. They wouldn't, would they? *The dead have nothing to lose.* He cleared his throat. "They're rupturing the gasbags."

The windshield flashed. He ducked as his eardrum convulsed to what could just have easily been a detonation.

He straightened up. "In a thunderstorm."

The nose dipped, and they lurched forwards.

His stomach lifted inside him like a helium balloon. The rest of him threatened to follow.

Throwing himself on the pitch wheel, he turned it the other way.

"Hang on," he shouted. "We're going down."

He glanced at the indicators. Although their death twins had nearly reached the end of the airship, they'd missed a few cells.

"Don't worry," he called out. "Getting low will help us make the most of what we've got." *Better to crash-land than crash.*

They sank as if on a cable-car wire.

He stared out of the windshield, where every now and then a clear, cavernous pocket opened up only to shoot in the opposite direction.

The clouds fled apart. Fat drops drummed against the skin

of the ship. More a series of different textures than colours in the rain-blurred, night-dark day, canted land filled the windshield.

A hill stuck up in line with them.

He grabbed the front wheel and flung it to the right. It clacked and squeaked as it went round. More hills revolved around them. *Where can we land?* Where can we land?

With his other hand, he rotated the pitch wheel back still farther. They flared out but carried on coming down.

Through sheets of rain, they cleared a small hill. Losing height all the while, he swung the wheel to starboard to avoid a higher one.

They sank over the woods that clothed its base. *Come on, come on, come on.*

Finally, a field of crops.

He gripped the wheel tighter. *Perfect.*

"Look out, pylons!" cried Polly.

"What?" *Oh, shit.* He hadn't spotted the skeletal towers in the rain.

He pushed the throttle levers forward. Their rate of descent slowed. Their passage over the wires accelerated.

Oh, God. What about the rest of the airship?

He craned round.

The belly cleared. The fuselage would be narrowing.

What about the tail?

The thought hung suspended.

The fins cleared the wires with just feet to spare.

Suddenly all around them rather than below, the ground came up quicker and quicker. They'd never make it over a line of trees.

He reduced the power.

"Jump," he said.

She looked out of the window, back at him. "What?"

"Jump!" he bellowed.

They weren't too high, and she'd land on crops.

She turned, scuttled over to the door, shouldered it open and leaned out.

"No, wait." *I'm doing it.* The controls responded to him. They came down steadily. Heading into wind, they maintained their position in relation to the ground.

Metal scraped behind them and he swung round.

On narrow walkways between the fuselage and the middle pods, one on one side, the other on the other, their death clones drove metal rods into the engines. Sparks fountained. *Jesus.*

The propellers came to rest.

The airship started to lose ground, drift.

"Now!" he screamed.

Polly leapt.

The gondola scurried backwards over the tops of the crop.

He applied more power and leaned against the window. Eyes searching, he held his breath in sheer concentration.

Polly's head and shoulders surfaced above the waving wheat.

He exhaled.

She pointed, shouted.

Hand on the glass, he mouthed, "What?"

Then he remembered: the pylons they'd come in over.

More chronic scraping.

Another pair of engines puttered out.

He increased the power, yet it failed to even slow the rate of retreat. The nose rose.

Something, whether the canister or something else, crashed against the rear partition.

The tilting floor helped him on his way. He skidded back down the cabin, dived out through the open door.

The ground thudded against his side. Wind frisked him. Wheat thrashed him. Raindrops pelted his hands and face.

"Greg, Greg," called Polly.

He tottered to his feet, blinking in the rain, just in time to see the airship, still tipping upwards, hit a pylon.

Their doppelgangers clung on and rolled around on the stubby walkways to either side.

A shower of sparks from the pylon's wires and an explosion ripped the air, shooting flames and a column of smoke up to the clouds.

Within seconds the conflagration engulfed the entire ship, flaying it of its skin. He saw them clearly, their dead selves, ignite and burn like candles. He watched their blackened bodies drop and the structure buckle and warp and collapse on top of them.

Polly turned his way.

Rain streaked between them as he pushed towards her through the swaying wheat.

Panting, he clapped his hands on her shoulders. "Love, love, are you okay?"

Even upwind, a lick of heat swept over him, and the scorched tang of the wreckage coated the insides of his nose and throat.

"Yes." She smacked her lips, drew them back, as she glanced at the flames feasting on the pile of mangled metal. "Are you?"

Her hair plastered her head. He could feel her shaking.

Yanking her towards him, he clasped her tightly.

Her arms hung down by her sides. Raising them from the elbow, she patted his back.

"God, that was close," he said, as they disengaged.

"I know."

The rain abated.

He peered around. "Where are we?"

Her voice brightened. "Oh, it's okay."

He looked at her. "It is?"

"Yes, don't you remember? This is very near where my parents live…" Her chin dipped. "Lived."

"Wh—?" His clothes clung to him. The wind gusted. He shivered all the way down to his shoes.

She lifted her chin, turned to the side. "Look. We're just the other side of the hill."

He spun around, taking in in one sweep the precise configuration of the hill, the pylons, the wood, the little lane snaking off to the side. Is…? *Where's…?* He just made out the top of it… Their old Vauxhall.

"Holy fuck!" His heart gripped his throat. "Polly, listen, we need to get away from here."

Her head shook, vertically, laterally. "What? Why?"

Still staring at her, he jabbed an arm in the direction of the hill. "This is where it ends, remember?"

Her eyes darted this way and that. "Oh, God."

He grabbed her hand. "Polly, we need to get out of here, now."

Chapter 25

The War Against Death

The rain had stopped. The wind had died down. Stretching away in all directions, yellow seed heads drooped.

He and Polly were pushing towards the road when she grasped his arm. They halted.

Figures approached from that edge of the field. They hadn't been there a minute ago, had they?

"Damn." He dabbed his wet eyebrows with his sleeve. "They must have heard the explosion."

He turned to the side. Heads rose from the crop.

He glanced over his shoulder. The dead stood up there too.

He spun around. *Outflanked by the dead...* "They were waiting for us." *Bastards in hell.* "It's all been planned."

They ran in the direction that had the fewest figures. Hanging stalks tugged at their flying feet. Decaying faces lurched towards them. Bony arms reached out. Hands clicked.

He and Polly dodged the dead as the land tilted under them, the crop gave way to grass and the gradient only increased. Stooping over bent knees, pushing off hard and bounding from fold to fold with black-faced sheep baaing and scurrying out of the way, they powered up the hillside. Greg clutched his heart, out of synch with the rest of him, like the heart of one labouring under a doom. Even when the incline started to flatten out, they kept on going and, arms up, backs arched, only staggered to a standstill when they ran out of hill.

Greg pitched forwards, gripped his knees and panted and wheezed after the near-vertical sprint. His body had warmed the dampness deep in his clothes. Now the drying wind caused that dampness to flare up and chill his skin.

He glanced over his shoulder, reared up, around.

Stepping back over to the edge, he peered down.

Still on the slope, dead fell upon the sheep. They threw them around like pillows, bit into them and ripped hunks of flesh from their bodies. They plunged their arms into the wounds, yanked out livers and kidneys and hearts and pushed them straight in their mouths. *To build their strength up.* A cacophony of bleating. Each second a half babylike, half elderly, all too human voice ceased.

Greg staggered, tripped over a tussock. "Oh, shit. Oh, fuck."

His gaze swept the panorama that had opened up, out. Singly or in small bands, more and more dead arrived from every direction.

In the distance, hundreds blackened the horizon—one of the armies they'd seen on the way. *Wave upon wave of death.*

Off to the side, beyond the black girders and hoops that stuck up where the pylon had stood, a fire raged in the wood.

He dashed over to the head of the rear escarpment.

Out on the flat, in the fields, individual dead shuffled towards the hill.

Peeping through tatters of cloud, the sun sank towards the flamed horizon. Sunset.

He glanced behind him at the legion on the hills in the distance.

The bleating had stopped. Bones crunched. "Oh, Jesus." *We're next.*

He grabbed Polly's hand and, letting gravity do all the work, just taking long leaps to try and keep up, they ran full pelt down the slope.

His footfalls thumped the earth through the long, wet grass.

Short, sharp, angular breaths coming and going, he and Polly pounded up a field bordered on three sides by a wood that, on the fourth side, stretched all the way back to the hill. Dead rounded the corner behind them.

He couldn't see the sky's fiery furnace anymore for the trees.

A fuzziness had crept into the light. The sun could have dipped below the horizon already.

A stone barn stood at the top of the field, in the right-hand corner. A pair of dead stepped out from behind it. One male, one female, both had white hair. He and Polly could dodge them easily. *A barn...* A tightness gripped his throat. When a hand scuttled across the grass, his whole body stiffened and jerked at the memory such that it pivoted him round, altered his course as he ran.

He peered over his shoulder to check that Polly turned the same way.

The heads of the dead couple bobbed beyond her. He glimpsed their faces. *Oh, you've got to be...*

Panting, he stuck an arm out. "Poll."

Her eyes flicked his way. "What?"

He snatched breaths like a swimmer. "Your parents..."

Her head canted. "What about them?"

He gasped, swallowed, licked dry lips.

Her eyes widened. "What, they're alive?"

"Well, I wouldn't go that far..."

Following his line of sight, she stopped as if she'd run, slam, into a wall. "Oh, my God!" She clapped a hand to her mouth.

Huffing and sniffing and wiping clear mucus from his nose with his sleeve, he halted. "Don't look." Dead swarmed across the field on one side, her mother and father dragged themselves towards her on the other. Greg held a hand out. "Polly, we have to go."

"They've come back for me."

His neck jolted. "What? No!"

She took a step towards her parents, away from him. "Mummy... Daddy..." Her voice had a breathless, girlish quality.

Greg darted after her. "No, Polly, it's not them." He stopped where she had stood, right behind her. "Or if it was, it's not now."

Death-faced, Polly's parents' eyes swivelled. Their mouths opened.

She lifted a foot, inclined towards them.

"No, Polly." Greg gripped her shoulder. "They're just a

proxy, remember? He's the one animating them."

Her mum and dad bared their teeth.

Bumping into him as she leaned back, she looked round with creased forehead. "Greg, they don't look right."

Greg's gaze rebounded back and forth.

The mob closed in on them.

Her parents reached out for them.

His voice tore out of him: "Polly, run!"

Scratched by the branches that had clawed at them in their scramble through the wood and taking huge plunging gulps of air, they emerged out onto Bedgley's Chantry Lane. In the thinning light, he recognized the cottages, the tiny red post box in the wall.

Leaves rustled behind them, not that far back.

Twigs snapped, now here, now there.

Again, closer.

He puffed, wheezed. "Too many of them." Having run bent, twisting this way, that, through the wood, he stretched his back. "We need to find somewhere we can hide out."

Polly clutched her waist.

Doubled over, she pointed off to the side, down the close to her parents' place.

A bungalow? Picturing the badly repaired broken window pane, he shook his head. "No, somewhere..."

Turning towards the church, his gaze travelled up the tower. "Come on, quick."

They sprinted the rest of the lane.

The lychgate squeaked as he opened it. Branches hung over the path. Untenanted graves yawned.

Notices in the porch fluttered as they flew past. Pausing only to get the heavy door open, they clattered over tessellated flooring in the dim coloured light shed by the stained-glass windows. Skidding round the font, they ran towards the back of the church.

What was that tapping? They stopped.

A skeleton stepped out from behind a pillar.

It clickety-clicked towards them.

Greg grabbed a brass candleholder, turned it upside down and shook it.

A thud and the candle rolled under a pew.

The skeleton lunged.

Greg whacked it with the candlestick and it broke up into its constituent parts. Bones rattled against the floor.

He barged open a door in the wall and, closing it behind them, wedged the candlestick between it and the first step. In near darkness, they jogged round and up a stone stairway.

That opened out into a low-ceilinged chamber level with the roof-loft. Rosy light not unlike the light of the stained-glass windows, just unicolour, poked in through adjacent slits in one of the walls. The corners it didn't reach harboured folds of darkness. A ladder fixed to the nearest wall led up through an opening in the ceiling.

Grabbing hold of it, his feet left the floorboards. His head arrived in the belfry. He kept on going and, stepping off the ladder at the top, turned and took Polly's hand as her head surfaced.

The two slatted lancet arches in each wall let in enough light to illuminate a set of four huge bells. A plank straddling the joinery housing the bells offered the only way over. They wobbled across it in turn to the other side and climbed three wooden steps onto a ledge.

Reaching up, they slid back the hatchway cover.

He gripped two perpendicular edges of the opening, walked up the wall and hooked his elbows over the top. His legs dangled. His heels kicked. Getting his arms under him and pushing off, he shuffled along like a sealion until his centre of gravity rested over the lip, rolled and lifted one leg out, then the other.

Scrabbling back and bracing himself over the hole, he extended a hand to Polly, but she was already on the way up. Crouching on slate tiles surrounded by four castle-turret-like walls, they peeked out of adjacent embrasures.

The sight that greeted him sucked all the air out of him. A cortège of dead shambled up the lane.

They know.

Sure enough, the dead filed through the lychgate as if for Sunday morning service, yet spilled out onto the grass to stand among the crosses, tombs and gravestones.

Polly rested her chin on the dip in the wall. "Greg, I don't think..." Her head jogged up and down as she spoke.

"Yes?" he whispered.

She turned around, slumped against the wall. "I don't think you quite thought this through."

Did she mean they'd escaped the cemetery only to end up trapped in the middle of a churchyard? Or did she mean they'd spent all this time running from the dead merely to wind up surrounded and facing almost certain death themselves above the very church they'd arranged to get married in?

He didn't ask.

The dead kept on coming, more and more of them, groups and stragglers swelling the numbers. Where were they all coming from? How many did it take? When the door below came down, there wouldn't be enough of them to go round.

He pushed the hatch's lid back over the hole with his foot, slid his buttocks over to sit on it. A jolt as it slotted into place beneath him.

The trees... Could they jump to a branch?

They didn't have enough room to make a run-up, and then they'd have the wall to get over. No, even given their level of desperation, the distance combined with the drop made the odds too risky.

He drew his knees up, wrapped his arms around them. "I have to be honest. I don't see any way out of this." Polly nodded, with grim, compressed lips. "You can't win against the dead. Statistically."

She put a hand up. "Greg..."

"What?"

"Just—" Her hand gave a little flourish before dropping. "Never mind."

He glanced at the bloody glow over the tops of the trees out to the west.

His fingers dug into his wrist. "I was wrong last time. That wasn't the final sunset. This is." He let go of his wrist to point at what they could see of it. "The date on the gravestones confirms it. The apocalypse has finally caught up with us."

She opened her mouth, closed it.

He hugged his knees, tighter. "It's like, whichever way you go, there's only ever really one direction, isn't there? One destiny. Going out of your way to avoid it just means you run smack into it."

"It's okay, I get it." She turned away, looked down. "It was always going to end down here no matter what."

He sighed. "I guess that's the thing about fighting death. You can win battles, never... never the war." A tightness in the chest bubbled upwards, burst out of him. "I'm sor..." Choking on a sob, he couldn't speak for a moment. "I-I'm sorry, Polly." He wiped away the tears that slid out of his eyes. "I feel like I've caused all... all this." He gestured at the universe.

She folded her arms. "What do you mean?"

He rested his chin against his knees. "I don't know. I just feel like, way back when, I turned left when I should have turned right."

She shrugged. "I think everyone feels like that, Greg." A long sigh. "I wasn't the one for you. That's all there is to it."

He lifted his chin. "No." He shook his head. "No!" Were the dead listening? "You're wrong."

Polly quirked an eyebrow. "You don't have to say that just because..."

She didn't need to finish.

He turned from smoke rising above the wood to the sunset's last blush. The clouds that side were being smelted down to make something else, something darker, like lead.

The imminence of death made his heart thump. He didn't have time to tell her how he'd been on his way home to try and put things right the very day that all of this started and how he'd regretted it since that first morning they'd fallen out. He needed to get straight to the point. "I found this." From the small pocket of his jeans, he took out a ring, her engagement ring, the one that she'd flung away. "Look, I've still got mine on." He flashed his ring finger in the sun's dying embers. "I never took it off." He held her ring up between the thumb and forefinger of his other hand and she stared at it as if in a daze. "Please, Polly..."

Her gaze settled on him.

He jumped up, half way, onto his knees. Then one knee. "Will you marry me?"

She blinked in the reddish light, tilted her head to one side and back in a quarter roll. "Isn't it a bit too late for that?"

He stood up. He could see all the tattered heads below. "No. If we're going to die, I want to at least die as your husband. To be your husband, even if it's only for five minutes." He watched the swerves of her mind in her eyes. A glance at the multitude below. He focused on her and she focused on him. "If I'm not with you..." Staring into her speaking eyes. "...it's like I'm dead already." He took a breath, smiled. "I know we drive each other mad but..." He couldn't disguise the choky things going on inside him. "...my life had no meaning until we got together. I..." His heart pounded as if bigger than his body. "I love you."

Her eyes turned filmy. She nodded. "That's all I wanted to know." A pause as she smiled. "You idiot."

A smile gripped his face. A warm fuzziness swept down from his head and, radiating outwards, upwards from his abdomen to meet in the middle. Was an inability to lie counting in his favour for once?

Dropping the ring in his pocket, he rushed up to her, pulled her to her feet.

As if to avoid looking over the low wall, she sagged against his chest.

While one sun went down, another came up on the other side. At least, a gathering glow pulsed deep in the woods.

He turned back to her. "Love lets one stick two fingers up at death." Taking hold of both her hands, he took a step backwards. "I guess all lives are finite. We can live our little life up here." He locked eyes with her so that she didn't look down. "As long as they give us."

"What are you doing?" she said.

Smack, smack, smack went his heart as he continued staring into her eyes. "I promise, before these witnesses..." Half human, half animal groans from below. "...to love you, honour you and always tell the truth, no matter how much it drives you crazy."

A smile wrinkled her nose. "And I promise to love, honor and disobey you."

He threw his head back and laughed.

Letting go of her right hand, he retrieved the ring from his pocket and slid it onto the fourth finger of her left hand.

He planted his lips on hers. Her lips parted, and he encountered the longed-for anemone mouth.

They unclasped and, swaying near to the parapet, the warmth in his stomach turned to a drawing, a tightening.

Polly shook her hands in front of her face as if trying to cool herself down. "Till death do us part?"

A mountain would have been easier to swallow than the lump lodged in his throat.

"Till death do us part," he croaked.

A smattering of stars made little difference. The fire of the sun had gone out. Although another fire had taken its place to the east, night closed in around them.

He shivered.

Polly leaned out over the wall. "Why aren't they coming up?"

He peered over the edge beside her. "It's like they're waiting for something."

"What for?" She turned towards him.

He sighed. "I don't know."

Block by overlapping block, soft colour made inroads into the graveyard and fell upon the heads of the dead, the stones, the crosses, the trees.

Oh, hell. "They've turned the lights on."

"Greg..."

He rushed to one side, the other, peered down. "They're in the church."

"Greg..."

With one foot on the parapet, he bent low over the wall. "Yeah?"

"There's something I didn't tell you."

He straightened up, swivelled round. "What?"

"I'm..." Fingers interlocking across her diaphragm, she

moved her hands downwards. "Pregnant."

He rushed up to her, grabbed her arms, let out a wild yelp of joy. "That's..." The arrival of more dead below pushed the words off the back of his mind. *Oh, no—not now.* His right forearm twitched as if tugged by an invisible string—the kind of movement he normally experienced upon falling asleep and that collapsed dream worlds. "Polly, we need a plan." He placed a hand on her belly. "Our unborn child's depending on us." Turning and bending, he gripped the back of his neck. "Not to mention the entire human race."

She snuffed. "No pressure, then."

"There must be an answer. There must be." Pacing up and down with very little space, he twisted, turned, every few steps. "Must be. Must." His mind roved like a searchlight through the darkness. He could see the space where the answer should be, almost the shape of it, just not the answer itself.

Standing off to one side, she rocked back on one hip. "Don't mind me."

He threw an arm out, brought his forefinger back up to his lips. "Ssh."

The heels of her boots shuffled and knocked together. "Careful. There's still time to get divorced, you know." She glanced down at the surge of heads. "Just."

He stopped, turned to face her. "Wait. There's always been a hand at our back, nudging us in a particular direction, correcting for any deviations." He pointed over his shoulder. "We've been so busy running from them that we forgot about him."

"Him?"

"The one who's doing this to us. The one who brought them back." He clenched and unclenched his hands. "He's been jerking us around from the very start."

Her head slid to one side. "So our free will was only an illusion?"

"Or built into the plan. We've only caught glimpses of that plan, but it's always been there."

She stuck an arm out. "Hey, if he can bring them back, he can bring us back."

"You want to come back like that?" A shudder passed

through him and he hugged himself to keep the next one at bay. "Besides, our replacements got incinerated."

Her arm flopped to her side. "Well, does that mean we can't die, or can't come back?"

He bent over, clutched his brow. "I don't know." He reared up. "We need to think laterally, do something different. Which he'll then have to make adjustments for..." He slapped his thigh. "That's it! We encode our wishes in our speech and actions and behave like they've already been granted." He stared at her. She stared back. "We *believe*."

"Believe? Believe in what?"

"In death's oldest adversary..."

She held her hands out. "Which is?"

He smiled. "Love."

He couldn't quite make out her face in the gloom, but her head inclined towards him. "How?"

"We can exploit the little bit of leverage we've always had, just reverse the polarity."

Her hanging hair shook. "Reverse what polarity?"

"Remember how we made each draft redundant by straying from the script at a critical juncture?" He made out a nod. "Well, now we act like what we want to happen is going to happen. We assume we're going to survive. And if we're firm enough in that belief, absolutely unshakeable, he has to incorporate it." Greg waited for some kind of response, got none. "Trust me. This is the ultimate way to wrong-foot him. He can't get rid of us if we only believe. It wouldn't all fit together. He has to accommodate that, in some way, even if he doesn't want to."

She turned a hand over. "Well, what can we do to wrong-foot him up here?"

Bonfire smells drifted over the trees.

The moans of the dead rose from below.

"Go down."

CHAPTER 26

LORD OF THE DEAD

Greg started when a hand clapped him on the shoulder at the foot of the steps. His hair brushed the ceiling. He nearly knocked his head.

He peered round, up at Polly.

She bent towards him. "You sure about this?"

He smiled. "Of course I'm sure. That's what makes it work."

He stooped, removed the candlestick.

Straightening up, he turned the handle. The door creaked as he opened it. A stench worse than all the gone-off offal in all the end-of-the-world supermarkets pushed him back. He almost shut the door on it. *No, we have to.* He opened the door wider, turned to Polly. "Think nice smells. Er, freshly mown grass..."

"Peppermint..."

The dead stared at them, a hundred or more with immobile countenances like bad face transplants. They stood in between the pews, all round the edges and all up the aisle. David, the vicar, lolled in the transept. He had dark stains down the front of his surplice. What was going on? Some kind of black mass?

Greg leaned towards Polly without turning his head. "Let's get out of here."

"Satsumas..."

Shoulder to shoulder, they headed up the aisle. The dead turned side on to give them room to pass.

"No going back now," he whispered.

"The first coffee of the day..."

"Your head after you've washed your hair..."

The organ started up. *What the devil—* He jumped. Going by the jolt he received, so did Polly.

Spotting her parents in the congregation, he half expected "Here Comes the Bride". Instead something requiem-like blared out of the vast array of pipes.

He grabbed her hand and they turned and scuttled towards the big door.

Outside, more exhalations of hell, just with fresh air blowing in between.

There was nothing unusual about the dead filling the churchyard, only now they crammed it vertically rather than horizontally. As if lining up to throw confetti, they left a space just big enough for two to pass through. He and Polly raced up it with heads lowered and hands over their noses.

They made it through the lychgate.

"You were right," said Polly. "This is actually working."

The dead filled the lane. Yet here too they parted. Those at the outside stepped up onto the verge so that those in the middle could leave an opening stretching back and back.

Beyond the church grounds, the darkness had a different texture: here the smoothness of Tarmac, there the layeredness of trees. Through the wood, yellowy light flickered and jumped.

The last few rows of dead parted. Greg grinned. *We've done it.* He could see empty lane beyond.

He raised his gaze a notch. Through drifting smoke, he made out dragging feet, stiff legs, a thrusting workout from the hips, corresponding arms following through with elbows up and out, repeated over and over. It was the army of dead he'd seen from the hill.

He and Polly stood in no-man's-land with back-from-the-grave deceased behind and in front, a tall hedge to one side and burning woods to the other. The new arrivals steadily closed the gap.

The one nearest looked up.

"Ha!" Greg coughed a laugh, and his breathing got tangled up in it.

"What? What is it?" said Polly.

Greg waited for his lungs to re-inflate. "Is that...?" He shook his head as the one at the front stopped and held up a staff. "It is. It's fucking Milo." He patted Polly's arm. "Well, glad to see he's finally put his managerial skills to good use."

The rest halted.

What was that bluish halo around Milo?

Settling, the nimbus resolved itself into what it was.

Greg dug Polly in the ribs. "Lord..." he whispered, trying to contain a bubble of laughter and feeling as if he were about to burst. "Lord of the flies!"

Polly snuffed.

Milo raised his staff higher.

"Is that... Is that a coat stand?" Polly sniggered into her hand. "Looks like he's gone and crowned himself king of the dead."

King of the dead... Greg blenched. *Oh, God.* The dead hadn't parted for him and Polly. They'd parted for their leader. He was the one they'd all been waiting for. Milo, the one member of the dead for whom all this was personal.

Greg's head jerked as a flutter started up in his neck. *No, no, no, don't start thinking now. Not now, not now.*

"Er, Polly," he said, voice shaking.

Her head swung back and forth between them and him. "Yes?"

He sniffed, and he had a hitch in his throat. "I'm sorry but I think we might need to..."

CHAPTER 27

JUDGEMENT DAY 2: SETTLING ACCOUNTS

Milo slammed his staff down with a grunt.

"Run!" shouted Greg.

They bounded into the wood as the massed ranks of the dead, on both sides, surged towards them.

He peeked over his shoulder.

Unliving poured off the lane after them.

"Oh, God," said Polly at his side, though whether as prayer or imprecation he couldn't tell.

He looked at her sprinting just a few feet away, sometimes slightly ahead, sometimes slightly behind, sometimes veering the near side of a tree, sometimes the far side. Like him, she ducked to avoid hanging branches, leapt to avoid protruding roots. With each glance, his soul dripped molten drops of love.

Maybe if it hadn't been for Milo arriving, the plan would have worked. Or would his arch-rival have tracked them down no matter what?

Who knew, now?

A wavering, fitful glow illuminated the wood. Smoke hung like cobwebs in the spaces between shadows. It curled back on itself, the light changed or new mini-vistas opened up and suddenly it was hammocks slung between the trees. Tendrils of wood smoke cut into his eyes, found his nostrils, lanced his brain. He and Polly coughed. The dead didn't.

A rustling like leaves. A cracking like branches. Light danced. A wall of it reared up in front of them, right across their path. Slicing diagonally through the wood, it had already annexed most of it and claimed more and more all the time. Smoke billowed, churned. His eyes streamed. The roaring flames warmed his forehead. Shadows quailed in the face of them. The two of them inhaled, exhaled, smoke. Drawing ever closer, the fire's hot breath blasted his forehead, cheeks and hands, forcing him back, and Polly with him.

Leaning forwards as if using the momentum of a deferred fall to quicken their pace, dead loped through the wood behind them.

He and Polly lined up with gaps between trees. Fire flared from below, frilled trunks and dripped from above.

Coughing, hacking, they hung back.

A thousand feet padded closer.

He and Polly flung each other a look. Throwing their arms up over their heads, they made a dash for it through ragged holes in raging, undulating light. Blinding heat flashed across his arms, neck, back, legs. Their feet barely touched the burning brush as they flew through hell.

They emerged out the other side in what could have been another planet. Blackened petrified foliage crackled underfoot. They dodged charred boles and stumps and the remains of cooked wildlife. Patches of smoke wafted like ghosts from the odd pocket of fire. Bluey grey in the fading light, the ossified wood turned to dust whenever he knocked into it.

Greg peered round. One by one, ragged silhouettes popped through the back of the receding crest of flames.

Oh, Christ.

His skin, or patches of it, particularly on the underside of his arms, throbbed as if to let him know that all was not right with it, yet given their current predicament, running from dead through a crumbling carbon world, in as understated a manner as possible.

Why was one ankle hotter than the rest of him?

He glanced down. Flames flapped around the hem of his trouser leg. *Oh, shit.*

He slowed, hopped, shook his leg. Dead gained on him.

He sprinted to catch up with Polly. Fire and smoke trailed after him.

Polly turned her head, tripped and, arms out in front of her, ploughed through grey powder.

She lifted her head, spat, spluttered.

As soon as he stopped, flames rose up his leg.

He dived to the ground beside her and rolled around in soft ash.

Feet kicked towards them. *What?* A hand grabbed him. *No!* Then another. *Not like this!* And another and another and another. He couldn't move for the stick-thin and dried out bodies pressing in upon them. Maybe it was just the woody, bonfire miasma and cloaking ash but these dead didn't even smell. Teeth bared, jaws clicking, two leaned towards his arm. He yanked another's arm in front of them and their mouths bore down on that instead. It was like instinct. Once they had their teeth into something, they didn't let go. The stand-in's arm tensed and shook as they chomped through it. Greg tried to push all three out of the way. The press of bodies meant they fell on top of him. He tried to crawl out from under them, but others pinned him down.

Through shuffling legs, he stared at Polly.

She rolled onto her back as what had once been a young woman bent over her, clawed at her. She kicked the twiggy legs out from under her desiccated assailant but more and more dead arrived all the time. Several held her down while a man circled her. His waxy features looked as if they'd melted, slid down his face and then reset. As if in a warped fairground mirror, Greg recognized him.

Milo.

Greg redoubled his efforts to wriggle free but bony hands gripped his limbs. Bodies lay across him. Mouths snapped all around him. One bit his shoulder. Teeth clamped down on bone, tendons and ligaments and wouldn't let go. He screamed. Another bit into his side, easily removing a chunk of flesh and chewing it with bloodied dripping jaws. He watched half masticated morsels of his skin and arteries roll around the black hollow of its mouth. The resulting lump disappeared down its throat as it swallowed before bending for more. Like a hundred operations all going on at the same time, gradually opening him up, more joined in, gnawing, chewing and swallowing. Warm soupy blood flowed from fist-sized wounds. Air circulated around vital parts of him that had never been exposed before. One of the dead ate through his cheek. Its dry tongue poked through. As bits of him disappeared, one pain cancelled out another and then another cancelled out that. Soon there wouldn't be anything left.

Straining to catch glimpses of Polly through the milling figures, he watched Milo push his hand into her stomach.

"No!" he yelled.

Milo plucked out a fetus, held it up, leaned back, dangled it over his face and lowered it into his open mouth. He looked over, and was that the curl of a smile? *For Nicola?* No doubt savoring the taste of revenge, he smacked his lips, and swallowed.

Raising her head, Polly projectile-vomited over him.

Dripping with sick, Milo made a chopping motion with his arm and the rest fell upon her.

"Polly!" screamed Greg.

He caught two last, separate, glimpses of her. She banged her head on a rock. The longest of pauses. She lay completely still.

The world turned to ash in his fingers.

The pulsing in the region of his ankle stopped only in so far as it became continuous. It cancelled out all the other pains put together. Over the curved backs of the feeding dead, flames rose from that quarter of his body. *My leg.*

Flesh. Just flesh…

Right before he didn't feel anything at all, something wrenched inside him. *I told her we'd be alright.*

PART 3

CHAPTER 28

THE HAND OF GOD

A long sniff re-inflated collapsed lungs.
Greg opened his eyes and looked around.

Polly gasped, coughed at his side.

"It worked!" cried Greg. He shook her by the shoulder. "Polly, it worked! We made him write another draft!"

She stared at her hands. "We died, Greg." She turned them over. "We did."

They lay on the floor in some kind of large windowless anteroom with neither pictures nor furniture.

He patted his shoulders, his neck, his chest, his abdomen. No mouth-sized cavities. No wet, or dried, blood.

He sat up, brought his foot up, reached for it, patted it, all over. Whole, with skin intact. Not black and burnt to a crisp.

Polly sat upright, blinked, murmured.

He squeezed her shoulder. "I told you he'd let us live. He had to." Greg laughed. "We made him."

"How?" Her voice croaked as if she were learning how to use it again.

He grinned. "The immortality of love."

"But…" She put a hand to her belly, stared down at it.

"Maybe he could only act to change things in retrospect. Because of that built-in delay." Greg got up.

She beat him to it. "Where are we?"

He stared at the white walls, ceiling and floor, all brightly lit but with no visible source of illumination. "Er, hotel maybe?"

"Or hospital."

They pushed through a double set of doors and stopped at the head of a long corridor.

Like the rectangular hall, the corridor had white walls, a white floor, a white ceiling and, as if composed of light, no shadows. Greg struggled to make out the joins.

Unlike the blank hall, the corridor featured single doors to either side, alternating at intervals, and a dark opening at the far end.

They set off up it.

"It's very quiet," she said. "You don't..." She blinked, chuckled, coughed into her hand. "You don't think this is heaven, do you?"

"Let's find out."

They'd passed several doors. He stopped and gripped a handle.

"Sure we should?" she said.

"What's the worst that could happen?" He laughed, turned the handle.

The door swung open and he went with it because, having followed through with a step, his foot sank and didn't touch the floor. There wasn't one. Just blackness. The room was dark, or non-existent. Light from the corridor stopped at the entrance. Even as he leaned one way, he bent the other. The lintel smacked him in the temple. Polly grabbed his collar, choking him. He remained lodged there for a moment, swaying as the door swayed.

Collecting himself, he reeled back, away. If the door hadn't been slightly smaller than his height, more like the door of a cabin, he would have fallen, who knew how far.

"Christ," he said.

His breathing seemed to be under the impression that he'd just completed a 10-mile hike.

Polly leaned against him. "Maybe we're in hell."

The next door didn't open outwards, it opened inwards, to reveal a brick wall that filled the frame.

"Or limbo," she said.

"I don't know about that but..." He patted the solid, rough brickwork. "Given we just died, logically it has to be some kind of adjunct to space, or spur of time."

She hiccupped. "Unless we're still dead."

They continued up the corridor.

Walking faster, he got increasingly out in front and was about to wait up, look round, when he banged his head. "Bloody hell." He rubbed furiously at the spot just above his hairline. "What is it with this place?"

He stepped back, looked around. Either the floor inclined upwards or the ceiling sloped downwards.

He put his hands out. Now they spanned the corridor. He could touch both walls at the same time. *"What the..."*

Stooping, he forged on. The ceiling pressed in on him from above, the floor from beneath, the walls from either side. He couldn't stretch his arms out anymore. The corridor pushed them together, forced his head down. Soon it had him on his knees. He shuffled along on them.

"Greg, it's not..."

"It's alright. Just a little..." He crawled towards his goal. Yet the door at the end remained as elusive as ever. He flattened onto his belly to keep on pressing forwards.

Finally he couldn't budge. His shoulders wouldn't fit through.

He stuck an arm up the angular tube the corridor had become, reached as far as he could. His fingers brushed the doorway at the end. *What the...* His mind flipped over. It wasn't a doorway at all. It was the size of a mouse's hole. The dimensions of the corridor according to perspective had turned out to be actual.

The nearest door was more like one in a doll's house. He turned the nodule of the handle and the door opened with a tiny squeak. He tried to peer inside but couldn't see properly.

He wriggled in reverse and the doors increased in size.

When he was back on his knees, he paused beside one just big enough to fit through.

Upon opening it, he saw that, judging by the quality of the light and the breaths of air, it let out onto some kind of outdoor area, about six feet below. With his head up against the ceiling and neck bent, he could see the base of a wall and part of a stone floor with a bit more room to move.

They could probably get down, yet could they get back up again?

Standing, and unstooping as the ceiling let him, he hurried up to Polly.

As he passed her, she pivoted, and her arms shot upwards and outwards. "Where are you going?"

"Doors." He pointed to the earlier, bigger ones.

She clonked after him.

The first door wouldn't budge. He kicked it. It sounded wall-solid.

He opened the next, on the other side, and what hit him wasn't so much the sight of money, heaps of notes and coins, but the smell of it. Something either overlaid it or leaked out of it, turning it all into one big foul gloop. A cloud of flies hung over the putrefying piles. The stench, pitched somewhere between week-old rubbish and untreated sewage, incited movements, revolutions, uprisings, in his stomach.

A fly zipped towards him.

Slamming the door cut it off mid-buzz.

Recrossing the corridor, in the next room a black CCTV camera stuck up from a gleaming white pedestal as if part of an art installation, only with the security camera at the centre of it. The electronic eye whirred as it moved, tracking them.

Who was watching? Where from?

Retreating, Greg shut the door.

The room after that also had a pedestal at the centre, this time with a white printer-cum-fax machine on top.

"Oh!" Polly rushed towards it, reached out to touch it.

Her hand passed through it.

It reformed around her arm like a liquid solid.

She leapt back, forefinger waggling. "That isn't... That's not..." Backing up to the X-ray-bright wall, she turned and pressed her hands against it. "What is this place?"

He shrugged. "We were in our world. Now I guess we're in his."

"I'd say I was dreaming if you weren't here too."

"Exactly. We can't both be dreaming." He scratched the inside of his wrist by running it up and down his chin stubble. "Unless..."

"What?"

He squeezed his temples. "Maybe it's not our dream."

Polly put her fingers up to an ear stud. "What?" She turned it, round and round. "Whose? Milo's?"

Greg wrenched his jaw open so quickly that it clicked. "No, not the puppets, the puppet master." He swung an arm in the direction of the printer. "Him. I mean, what was the point of plotting against us only to put us in here? Has he finished toying with us, torturing us, gone straight to forgetting us?"

He ran out of the room and back up the corridor. This time he was sure he registered the floor rising, in his breathing if nothing else, and maybe it was just his brain filling in the gaps, but he thought he saw the ceiling sinking, the walls closing in. He definitely noticed the doors decreasing in size.

"Where are you going?" called Polly.

"We're getting out of here."

Bending, crouching, finally kneeling, he made it to the partially open door.

He dropped back onto one haunch, stuck his feet out through the hole and shuffled forwards on his side. Like crawling down through someone's nostril, he squeezed through the gap, straightened up and, letting go as Polly approached, popped out. Having landed in a squatting position on a balcony, he steadied himself with splayed fingers, reared up, stepped forwards and leaned out over the edge of the parapet.

"Ohhh, shit."

"What? What is it?" Polly's face veered from side to side at the opening.

"You may as well come down." He swallowed. "There's no other way out."

She stuck her feet through the gap, then clunked to the floor.

Taking her hand as she straightened up, he turned back towards the view.

Sloping down to the sea, a town lay spread out before them, while, to either side, though more to one than the other, the bay curved round like an amphitheatre. Each row of higgledy-piggledy houses in the pastel shades of childhood sat set back from, yet as if on top of, the last. The sun coming up over the smaller of the two headlands tinted even bare stone and brick with its rosy glow. Over a small patch of green down towards the water's edge, crows gyred one way, seagulls the other, up and down, in and out, black and white, cawing and crying. A long, elaborately wrought, brightly painted pier started in the shallows and waded out to sea.

"Picture perfect," said Polly.

He remembered walking hand in hand on the pier with her. "Yeah, it was."

She looked round at him with her head on one side and he dipped his chin, sucked the inside of his cheek, because that was Draft 1, a whole other life. *Counterfeit memories?*

His mind flitted to the copier up the corridor. *Facsimile worlds?*

"Are you alright?" she said.

He wrenched his head up and down. "I think so."

She slapped the top of the wall. "We'll never get down there, will we?"

The balcony, which had no visible means of support, projected out from the side of an inland cliff that stretched as far above them as it dropped below.

He hooked a thumb over his shoulder. "I could give you a leg-up back inside."

The portions of her hair that were free to swung from side to side. "What's the point? There's God knows how many doors and no exits. This is as close as we can get to the outside world."

He breathed in, sighed out. "Looks like it."

She turned away.

Turning back, she touched his arm. "We could try shouting for help."

Apart from white lines scrolling across the sea that built and then terminated where they reached the shore, the endless flapping of the birds, the vertical swipes of breeze, nothing—at least from this elevation—moved.

He looked at her. "Who to?"

She held a hand out. "Well, if there's any dead, I doubt they can get to us up here." Flipping the hand over, she held the other out. "And if there's any living, maybe they can get us down."

"Alright."

"Help!" she shouted. "Help! Help!"

"Help! Help!" he joined in.

The echo of their shouts overlapped silence.

"No living," he said.

"No dead either."

"True." He balled a hand. "God, it all looks so dinky. You almost feel you could reach out and..." Opening his hand, he stretched it out in the direction of a red Mini Countryman parked in an end-on street outside a pub called The Fisherman. One of his fingernails struck something metallic.

Polly rocked back. "How... How did you do that?"

Greg peered over the edge of the balcony looking for metal protrusions. He checked the line of sight for wires crossing it within arm's reach.

None that he could see.

"I don't know. I just..." He put his hand out as if over the Mini, lowered it and, pinching forefinger and thumb locked apart as if obstructed by something, raised it. He held up a toy-sized Mini. *What*—? The pub now had a space outside it. *No, no, no no no no no no no.* Polly let out a long gasp beside him. He lifted the car to eye level between them, gripped the front wheels with the forefinger and thumb of his other hand and shunted them from side to side. He prodded the tiny air-filled tires, pricked his finger on the stubby roof mast, fiddled with and readjusted the minute wing mirrors.

He stuck his arm out like a crane, lowered his hand over the pier, slower and slower until the car came to rest.

He took his hand away.

The Mini balanced crossways on the pier.

"Bloody hell," said Polly.

Withdrawing his hand, he knocked the cupola off one of the more ornate buildings. It clattered to the leafy cobbled square in front of it, toppling two ancient trees and crushing several stalls in the process. *Oops.*

"It's a model." Her face contorted. "Is it?"

"No." The sky, the birds... The sea...

He leaned out and, amid an uprush of air, stuck a finger in the bay.

It glistened as he withdrew it.

Giving it a lick, he tasted salt.

"It's real, only the scale and perspective's all, sort of, literalized."

Surveying the town, he spotted a multi-storey carpark with an open flat upper deck. *Perfect.* Leaning into an uprush of air, he plucked it out of the ground.

"What are you doing?"

"Increasing the odds in our favour." Cars rattled around the decks. A couple fell out. He deposited the box-like building just in front of the balcony.

"Odds?" She peered down. "Are you sure you know what you're doing?"

He lifted a leg over the parapet. "I'll be fine."

"You absolutely sure?"

He swung his other leg over and sat leaning over the dizzying, alternately out-of-focus, in-focus drop. "Er, yes."

"Okay, be careful." She hung over the parapet at his side. "Yep, you're in line. Looking good. Just keep your feet together, you don't want to scrunch that hotel."

A gust ripped upwards. *How come so strong?*

He clutched the back of the wall.

He'd have turned around and lowered himself without necessarily committing himself to letting go but the top of the wall sloped to either side and would have been difficult to grip from beneath, so it was all or nothing. "I hope I'm right." The drop was two feet, or 200.

"Of course you are." She patted him on the back.

"Whoa!" Air blasted him from beneath and, for a second, he thought he was going. *Whew.* Just thwarted air currents. "Watch it."

"You'll be fine."

"Really?" It was his fingers that needed convincing. They didn't seem to want to give up their tenuous purchase.

"Yeah, of course."

"O-kay." He clung on.

"Just release your grip."

He jumped.

PART 4

CHAPTER 29

THE LONG GAME

Amid quadraphonic birdsong, the dull percussion of rain subsided. The last drops slipped from freshly-laundered clouds and slapped the ground.

Greg stuck a hand out of the bus shelter. "It's passing."

He and Polly resumed their way along Updown Road, the wider middle part of it, hand in hand.

Gardens spilled out of their modest plots. Grass sprouted in the street, thick tufts of it. Moss carpeted driveways. Bulked-up hedges two stories high screened property from property. Pavements buckled. Massive roots shouldered their way up, in the middle of the road. Small trees inhabited places they shouldn't. Two closed off a side street. One jutted out of a first-floor window. Yet wetness conferred dullness, rendering the street muted and humdrum.

Greg took Polly's hand.

Gliding in from the side in her trainer skates, Dottie dashed in front of them and hopped and skipped, zigged and zagged. Whenever it looked like she was going to fall behind, her tiny, flashing, trainers broke into a trot and her Smiggles rucksack shook on her back.

The sun came out and the world went from matte to gloss. Light-refracting drops of water ornamented the tips of twigs and fronds, turning them into radiant pendants, until they dripped. A swatch of whiteness shone on the damp Tarmac in front of him, yet moved as he moved—always three, four steps ahead.

Dottie slid right over it.

Swerving to a halt, she stared off to the side. "Look, Daddy, cities have fields too."

Glancing at the two posts that stuck up out of the tall grass with another, longer post along the top, he glimpsed the world as she saw it, matter-of-factly.

The road ahead rippled with squirrels. Dottie ran through the middle of them, yelping.

Polly chuckled.

"Ah, here we are," said Greg. "Through here."

"Dottie," called Polly.

Stars-in-the-hedgerow clematis had spread up into the trees.

He stretched the gap in the chain-link fence while, placing her hands over her protuberant belly, Polly ducked and sidled through. Her hair hung all the way down her back, like Eve's. Whooping, Dottie darted after her.

Greg's backpack swung as he shimmied through.

He caught up with them on the other side of the trees. Dottie pushed through high grass as if swimming through it. He picked a course between saplings that had sprung up as tall as him. As if in stop-go animation, birds bending the flimsy boughs jerked this way, that, before flicking off. A pair of dragonflies buzzed Polly like incandescent mini-helicopters. In clearings, plump rabbits lolloped and flopped.

Dottie bent over a tangle of undergrowth. She reared up holding a small round dimpled ball. "Daddy, what's this?"

"Remnants of an earlier civilization."

Polly glanced at him. He lowered his head.

Dottie ran round the back of a copse. "Hey, Mummy, Daddy, there's a sandpit."

"Yes, there will be," he said.

"Can we stay?"

"Not when we're so close," said Polly.

Trainers caked in sand, Dottie came running back and bounded on up a grassy mound. He and Polly followed on behind.

Half way up, Polly clutched her swollen belly.

"You alright?" He put his arm round her. "Want to stop?"

"No, just give me a minute." Stretching her back distended her tummy even more.

"Look! Look!" Feet higher than their heads and jabbing an arm at the sky, Dottie jumped up and down.

As he and Polly climbed the slope, the fresh breath of the breeze hit them side on.

The arc of a rainbow rose to greet them.

They stopped level with Dottie.

"Is it me or has that got an extra colour?" he said.

Dottie took a deep breath. "Onetwothreefourfive-six, seven, eight!"

Shaking his head, he whistled a gasp.

Polly crouched at Dottie's side. "And there's our old place, look, see?"

He spotted it, too, over the tops of the out-of-control grass and low, shaded-in, wood.

Amid the gentle steady sideways pressure of the breeze, the shower withdrew, the sun continued to burn a hole in the sky and everything glistened on this most immaculate of mornings as nature's hydraulics reconfigured the city millimetre by millimetre. Above, behind it all, coming from left and right, front and back, from all across London and beyond, that ear-ringing birdsong.

"We're home." He could feel Polly's gaze on the side of his face, warm, like sunshine, and his heart swelled until his body could barely contain it. "We're not vestiges of a former civilization. We're the beginnings of a new one. A human race raised on love."

A kiss exploded in his ear.

The next day, the three of them tramped up the stairs in wellies purloined for the outing and pushed through into his old office.

More polystyrene ceiling tiles lay on the floor than covered the ceiling. Sections of lagged duct hung down. Thick dust furred desks. A table lay on its back with its legs in the air—proof that he hadn't imagined the fight with the dead. Even now, thinking about their cold hands upon him, the black caves of their mouths opening and the animal sounds that issued from deep within their throats, the shudder of a chill entered, and exited, him like a ghost.

Dottie picked up a stapler from Rob's cobwebbed desk and clicked it, repeatedly, as she wandered around.

Greg dashed over to the printer, retrieved the manuscript from the tray and blew the dust off it. *What?* The same draft as before, this time it had more heft. The fax machine must have finished printing while he and Polly hid from Milo and Nicola.

He slapped the manuscript face up on the lid of the dead printer and turned the bulk of it over.

Flapping erupted from the other side of the room. He and Polly jumped.

A pigeon butted the ceiling. It swooped and rose, with Dottie bounding after it.

Greg lowered his gaze and tingled beneath the envelope of his skin as he skim-read how he and Polly crashed in the airship, hid at the top of the church tower, found themselves surrounded, attempted to play their tormentor at his own game, tripped and got eaten, slipped straight back into the sleeves of their bodies and jumped from a great small height. How they'd waded out to sea until they couldn't touch the bottom and then turned and swum for shore to get everything back to scale had been omitted. Likewise their years in the seaside town. The account, or prophecy, picked up again with their return to London and concluded with their visit to the oracle of the printer. "It's all exactly as it happened, right up to now."

"He wrote it since?" said Polly.

Greg double-checked the front. "No, no, this is still Draft 4, just more of it."

Polly's forehead puckered. "So he must have known what we'd do all that time ago?"

"Down to every rout, rebellion and reversal." Greg leaned against the printer with his elbows resting on it and breathed in and in and in, only to sigh out all the longer and deeper with his hands cradling his head. *He'd even do us out of our free will?*

He raised his head as Dottie jumped down from the upturned metal bin she'd stood on to open a window, clapped her hands and ran towards the pigeon.

It fluttered the other way.

Greg banged the base of the printer with his oversized wellington as he stood up straight and felt the lower half of his face twist around the words, "It's the first time I've got to see the ending properly."

The pigeon circled the room.

Dottie ran after it.

With a gentle whistle of wings, the grey bird sheared off out of the window.

"Yay!" cried Dottie.

Polly turned away, swung back. "So he wanted us to make it all along?"

What? Floors gave way in Greg's mind, crashing onto floors that crashed onto floors. *He was on our side*? "It's possible, I guess." *Just*.

Laughing through her nose, Polly waggled a forefinger in the direction of the manuscript. "So how far into the future does it go?"

"Er, it doesn't." Greg held up the last page. "It comes up to date and that's it." *Freedom*?

Her head tilted. "You mean it ends now?" He nodded. "Well, what's the last line?"

"It says, 'And then he looked at her and smiled.'"

ABOUT THE AUTHOR

Mark Kirkbride lives in England. He is the author of *The Plot Against Heaven, Game Changers of the Apocalypse* and *Satan's Fan Club. Game Changers of the Apocalypse* was a semi-finalist in the Kindle Book Awards. His stories have appeared in *Under the Bed, Sci Phi Journal, Disclaimer Magazine, Flash Fiction Magazine, Titanic Terastructures* and *So It Goes: The Literary Journal of the Kurt Vonnegut Memorial Library.*

https://markkirkbride.com/

Curious about other Crossroad Press books?
Stop by our site:
http://store.crossroadpress.com
We offer quality writing
in digital, audio, and print formats.